USA TODAY BESTSELLING AUTHOR

JANIE CROUCH

Cover by Deranged Doctor Design.

A Calamity Jane Publishing Book

ANGEL: LINEAR TACTICAL

To the person out there in the middle of writing her first book:
It may take you a year,
A decade,
A lifetime…
But write it.

We need your story.

Chapter 1

Most people would call Jordan Reiss a fool for standing out in her front yard in the middle of a storm.

Actually, *fool* would probably be the nicest thing anyone in Oak Creek, Wyoming, had called her in nearly a decade. Why waste their energy on a word as benign as *fool* when they had much more creative options to describe someone from the Reiss family? *Thief. Liar. Con artist.*

Murderer.

And those choices were only if the name-callers wanted to stick with the truth.

She'd actually been found guilty of vehicular homicide, so it wasn't *premeditated* murder.

But no matter what it was called, it wasn't ever going to bring back the mother and toddler she'd killed when she'd fallen asleep behind the wheel.

If *fool* was the worst thing someone in this town called her, she would take it. It was her choice to stand in the rain, a choice she hadn't had for the past six years.

Life inside the Wyoming Women's Center hadn't been too traumatic overall. Not like something out of an MArated TV show. She hadn't had to buy protection with cigarettes or become somebody's bitch.

But all Jordan's choices had been taken away from her there. Since three months before her eighteenth birthday, she'd been told when to get up, when to go to bed, when to eat, when to go to the bathroom, and definitely when she was or was not allowed outside.

For six years of her life, other people had made choices for her.

But not today. And not for the seventy-seven days since she'd been out.

There wasn't anything special about today except for the fact that she was *choosing* to stand in the rain like an idiot. She was letting the rain wash over her. Maybe, if she was lucky, it would wash away a little of the past.

She lowered her head and held out her arms, breathing in the smell of the wet earth. This land had always brought her strength. Jordan's mother's family had lived here in Teton County for five generations. Each daughter had had only one daughter, and the house had been passed down to her.

She wished any of her family were still alive for her to talk to now, to lean on and borrow support. But she only had one family member left, one she had no interest in talking to, even if anyone—particularly law enforcement—knew where her father was.

He'd lit out eight years ago, taking everything of any value with him, including most of the town's retirement funds. He'd left a lot of people in dire straits.

No, she didn't want to talk to him.

Suddenly, standing outside in the rain took more energy than she had available. So instead, she just lay down on the grass.

"I miss you, Mama." Rain dripped into her mouth as

she whispered the words, but she didn't care. She just wanted to lie here, to revel in the fact that she was allowed to lie here if she wanted.

How would her mother feel if she could see Jordan now? Alone, pretty much the enemy of the entire town, an ex-con. Not the dream any mother had for her little girl.

Jordan should leave this place. The people of Oak Creek hated her, and with good reason. Combine her sins with the sins of her father, and it wasn't hard to understand why most of them would contribute to a run-Jordan-out-of-town Kickstarter.

But where would she go? She couldn't leave the state of Wyoming for at least another year and a half because of her parole limitations.

Not to mention the only reason she had a roof over her head at all was because this one was paid for free and clear, since it had never been in her father's name.

Plus, she had a job. She'd never thought she'd be able to find one in Oak Creek, but the owner of the new bakery had agreed to give her a chance. Probably because the owner, Violet Collingwood, had just moved to Oak Creek and wasn't well versed in the town's tradition of hating the Reiss family.

Or maybe it was because Violet had recently lived through a rather traumatic abduction and wasn't making completely logical decisions.

Either way, Jordan would take the job and be grateful for it. She would show up every day and never give Violet a moment's reason to regret hiring her. Every cent she made would go toward *The Plan.*

As the rain began to pick up into a true storm, she decided to move to the steps on her porch so she could watch. She loved storms. Wyoming was wild, fierce, unpredictable. She'd dreamed about being all those things as she was growing up.

Now, she would settle for just being free.

She watched the storm as it raged, distantly worried that the wind might blow down a couple of trees in the acres of forestland that surrounded her property. As long as a tree didn't blow into the house, it wouldn't really matter. The forest could certainly afford to lose a couple. And at the very least, the violent storm would wash away the animal feces that had *somehow* ended up coating the walls of her house yesterday.

What better way to communicate that you thought someone was a piece of shit than by taking some and smearing it everywhere?

What Oak Creek's residents lacked in imagination they certainly made up for in tenacity. Once or twice a week since she'd gotten out, without fail, she'd come home to a fouled house.

But no matter what they did to make things uncomfortable for her, she couldn't leave. Not just because she didn't have any other options, but because this was *home*. She'd been away for six years, and she never wanted to be away again.

She had a job. That was the most important thing, and it would enable her to stay in this house. On this land.

Maybe the job required her to stay hidden in the back kitchen so as not to rub her presence in anyone's face. She didn't care. She didn't mind hard work, and she didn't even mind staying out of sight.

She'd long since stopped hoping the people here would ever accept her again. But she could sit on her porch and be happy. That was more than enough.

The storm eventually began to ease, and she stiffened as a car came barreling up her long driveway. More often than not, a car at that speed meant nothing but trouble. Especially a car she didn't recognize.

When she did finally recognize the driver, she didn't relax.

Gabriel Collingwood, her new boss's brother.

The rest of the storm dissipated, and the sun peeked through the clouds just as he parked in front of her house. He stepped out of the car; rays of light shone down on him, making him look like the archangel he shared a name with.

"Seriously?" Jordan whispered up to God.

She wasn't sure if she was talking about the light haloing those wide shoulders in his dark blue T-shirt, biceps stretching the sleeves, or the fact that he was here when they had just met—and fought—a few hours ago.

"Lost, Collingwood?" she asked, not getting up.

He leaned back against the car with the ease of a man comfortable with his own body. He knew his own strength.

Undoubtedly, he knew his own good looks too. Dark hair cut military short, a rugged face with a slightly crooked nose, and lips full enough that they would look feminine on any other man.

On Gabriel they just looked kissable.

And, whoa, that was not where her thoughts needed to be.

"What are you doing with my sister?" those lips asked now.

She forced her gaze away from his mouth. "You mean besides working for her?"

He studied her, green eyes taking in everything but giving away nothing. "Violet is a good, kind person. I don't know how much she's told you, but she's been through a lot—"

"Violet told me about her kidnapping. And like I said

back at the bakery, she knows what she's doing and what she wants. She's smart and capable of making her own decisions."

His granite jaw got tighter, if that was even possible. It already looked like it had been chiseled out of stone. "And as *I* mentioned at the bakery, I've known my sister a lot longer than you have."

Jordan looked up at him and tapped a finger against her lips. "Was that before or after you called me a *tart*?"

She had to give him credit. He at least had the good grace to look sheepish. As sheepish as someone six foot three and two-hundred-plus pounds of pure muscle could look.

"I love Violet." Jordan started to cut him off again, but he held a hand up to stop her. "And I'm fully aware that she's not only an adult, but a brilliant one. She wants this bakery, and although I don't understand it, I'm not going to begrudge her the joy it obviously brings her."

"Good." They'd almost come to blows over this a few hours ago. She was glad he was at least seeing reason.

He crossed his arms over that massive chest. "But I'm also aware that my sister went through a life-altering trauma just a few weeks ago. Whether she wants to admit it or not, that makes her emotionally vulnerable right now. So, I'll ask you again, what are you doing with my sister?"

Jordan forced herself not to wince. She shouldn't be surprised he was suspicious of her. Instead, she stretched her own long legs out in front of her on the steps, crossing them at the ankle, leaning her weight back on her palms. She batted her eyes up at him.

"Well sir, I can assure you that my intentions are strictly honorable. I want to date Violet, but as soon as she will have me, I will make an honest woman out of her. We'll get married and hopefully within a few years make beautiful babies together."

He was trying his damnedest to swallow a smile. "You're a smart ass."

Evidently only around him. She'd never talked like this to anyone else. Granted, she rarely talked to anyone else at all. Definitely not long enough to release any snark.

She shook her head. "I'm not doing anything with your sister except showing up for a job I'm very grateful to have. As you so quickly pointed out to her, past happenings have not exactly endeared me to this town."

As he pushed off the car and took a few steps toward her, Jordan leapt to her feet. It was one thing to face that hulking strength sitting down when he was ten feet away, quite another to do it when he was this close.

And why did her traitorous body get a little heated at him moving closer? This man held nothing but contempt for her. That, she was used to. But she'd never been turned on by someone despite it.

He stopped a couple of feet from her. "If you take advantage of my sister, you'll answer to me."

Her hands flew to her hips of their own accord, her eyes narrowing. "Like I said, she gave me a job I was pretty desperate for. I have no intention of stealing pastry cream bags or whatever it is you're worried about. I'll somehow resist the temptation."

Another smile pulled at the corner of his mouth—like he had the perfect comeback but wasn't allowing himself to say it—before he tightened his lips and erased it.

Fierce and serious once again.

"You'll excuse me if I find the wisdom of Violet hiring you a little questionable."

She swallowed hard and looked away. The words were nothing short of the truth. Hiring her was pretty unorthodox for any business owner, much less someone whose life had been through an upheaval like Violet's.

He was just echoing what everyone else thought about Jordan. She'd long since accepted that as standard, so why did the opinion of a man she'd known less than a day hurt?

"What I did can never be fixed. Believe me, I'm well aware of that." Her voice was soft. She could never talk about what she'd done without choking up. "But it's never going to happen again, and it won't ever affect Violet."

He gave a short nod. "Actually, I was referring to your father and what happened with him."

"I'm sorry if my father stole any money from your family." The words came out of her mouth before she could stop them. She'd been saying them so long they were automatic. But Gabe and Violet weren't even from Oak Creek; her father couldn't have stolen from them.

There actually seemed to be compassion in those green eyes. "That's SOP for you, isn't it?"

"SOP?"

"Standard operating procedure. For you to apologize for what your dad did."

She shrugged. "For all the good it does. It won't get anybody's money back, but somebody should say sorry." Michael Reiss certainly hadn't.

Gabriel took a step closer, putting them within arm's reach. Jordan didn't know exactly what she was expecting, but him reaching out and tucking a wet strand of hair behind her ear wasn't it. "How old are you?"

"Twenty-three."

"You look even younger with your hair all wet and no makeup on."

She shrugged. "I'm not really much of a makeup kind of girl."

He took another step forward, so close she could almost breathe in his scent.

And evidently, he could breathe in hers. "You smell like rain." His voice was gruff, but his fingers were tender as they trailed behind her ear before his hand dropped to his side.

"I was standing in the rain." She should move away, crack some joke, do something to break this tension between them. But she didn't want to.

God, how long had it been since she'd been close to someone like this? How long since anyone had touched her out of more than necessity?

Most people never gave a second thought to all the casual touches in their lives. A hug, a nudge of the shoulder. Besides guards patting her down in prison or guys groping her at the bar she'd worked at when she'd first gotten out, no one had really touched her in years.

She'd learned to live without it, and she certainly didn't need it.

Yet when he took a half step closer, she didn't move away.

He was staring at her lips, his fingers once again reaching up to play with a wet tendril of her long, brown hair. She was standing on the first step, and he was down on the ground, so they were almost eye to eye.

She wanted the touch of *this man*. When he trailed his fingers across her cheek, she couldn't help but lean into it. Even though she shouldn't.

"Were you standing in the rain on purpose?" he murmured.

"Yeah." She didn't recognize the husky pitch of her voice. "A fool in the rain—just like the Zeppelin song. Idiotic, right?"

But he wasn't looking at her like he thought she was

idiotic. He was looking at her like he was envisioning her standing in the grass, face tilted toward the crying sky, before he'd arrived.

And that he liked the thought of it.

He inched forward, giving her plenty of time to back away. Too much time—her brain screamed at her that this was a bad idea.

She didn't care.

The kiss wasn't hesitant. His lips were full, but they were also firm and commanding. His hands threaded into her hair and tilted her head to the angle he wanted. His lips nibbled at hers, his tongue licking at the seam between her lips.

"Open," he murmured against her. "Open for me, Rainfall. I've got to taste you."

She did.

If she thought she'd been kissed before, it was nothing compared to what he did once he had full access to her mouth.

His lips plundered hers, stealing her breath, stealing her thoughts. All she could do was feel.

She had no idea a kiss could be like this. Her hands fell to his wide shoulders, clutching him to her. She wanted to stay here and kiss him forever. She wanted him to take her inside or, hell, take her right here on the steps and do something about this ache he'd started in her body.

She wanted *him*.

But he was pulling back. She took a little comfort that he was at least breathing as hard as she was.

"We can't do this," he said, his green eyes pinning her.

But then his lips fell against hers again.

The second kiss wasn't any less devastating than the first. This time, her lips parted for his without his command.

One of those strong arms wrapped around her hips and lifted her, backing her up until she was wedged against the post at the corner of the porch stairs. His hands slid under her thighs and she wrapped her legs around his hips automatically. They both groaned as their bodies came together.

It was overwhelming but in the best way possible. Her fingers threaded through the brown hair cut short against his scalp. This time she angled his head so she could get better access to *him*.

When his tongue worked its way deep into her mouth, she did what came naturally, sucking on it.

The groan that fell from his throat was the sexiest thing she'd ever heard.

But a moment later, he stepped back again. He reached down and unhooked her legs from his waist and set them down on the ground. She stood there, staring, as he put distance between them.

"That's not what I came here for. We need to talk." The mouth that had just been kissing hers was now bracketed with tension.

"Oh." Yeah, starting something with her boss's brother couldn't possibly be a good idea. Not that she would've let that stop her thirty seconds ago. A nuclear war might not have stopped her thirty seconds ago.

"How much?"

The question hung between them for a long second. When Jordan realized what he was asking, she stumbled back a step on the stairs and would've fallen if he hadn't reached out to assist her. She snatched herself away from him. "H-how much for sex?"

He'd made that remark about her being like a tart earlier today at the bakery, but she hadn't thought he really took her for a prostitute. He ran a hand through his hair. "No. I'm sorry. That came out wrong."

Thank God.

"How much will it cost for you to stay away from Violet and the bakery?"

Her arms wrapped around her middle. "I don't understand."

He tilted his head to the side, studying her. "How much do I need to pay you for you to quit your job? To find another one that's not connected to my sister?"

She stared at him. She almost wished he *had* been asking how much it would cost to have sex with her. At least that would mean he was trying to get closer rather than pushing her away.

"A thousand dollars? Five thousand?" he continued.

She wasn't going to quit her job. Not because of the money—five thousand dollars would go a long way toward establishing *The Plan*—but because she loved her job. She enjoyed being around Violet and Charlie and some of the other women who actually talked to her as if she wasn't a leper.

It made her feel like she had friends, even if it was just an illusion.

She tamped down all the desire that had been flooding her system a minute ago. "No. I'm not quitting my job. Now get off my property before I call the sheriff. Believe it or not, the police come even when an ex-con calls."

She didn't know if that was true, but it probably was. Hopefully, she wouldn't have to find out.

Without looking at him or saying another word, she walked inside and shut the door, locking it behind her.

Chapter 2

Before his parents had died and he'd had to leave the military to come take care of his teenage sister, Gabe had been a Navy SEAL. He'd survived twenty-four weeks of BUD/S training, including hell week, watching man after man ring the bell and quit.

Because he was a big guy, naturally gifted in strength, his instructors had tried to use that against him.

The bigger they are, the harder they fall was an adage for a reason, and Navy SEAL instructors knew how to use it to force many of the more muscular men to quit. Because too many of those men thought strength alone was enough to become a SEAL.

It wasn't.

Gabe had survived hell week and had gone on to become a successful warrior because he was *smart*, not just because he was strong.

After leaving the military, he'd built one of the most successful technology companies in the country. Again, because he was smart. Shrewd. He knew not only how to think, but also what to say to be successful. He'd sat across the boardroom table from some of the most brilliant minds in the country and had out-strategized them.

So it was difficult for him to fathom that he couldn't keep his shit together around one twenty-three-year-old woman who liked to stand in the rain.

Could he have handled that situation any worse?

First, he'd shown up at her house uninvited and unwelcome, then he'd proceeded to come on to her like some high school jock who couldn't keep it in his pants. Finally, he'd insinuated that she was a prostitute for the second time in one day.

All that, *plus* he hadn't even accomplished what he'd gone to her house to do: keep Jordan Reiss away from his sister so she couldn't do Violet any harm.

Although it was difficult to consider the wet waif he'd kissed on that porch a danger to anyone.

Except maybe to his sanity.

Those lips. For the ten days since he'd seen her, he'd gone to bed hard and woken up harder, thinking about the kisses they'd shared.

He pushed her file around on his desk with one finger. He didn't need to open it to study the photo clipped to the inside. He already knew what he'd see.

A mug shot.

Even in the small photo, teenage Jordan's pinched features didn't hide the endless gray of her eyes. The color should've been cold and hard, but instead her eyes were pools deep enough to drown in. Her lips were pursed, her cheeks hollow, her forehead wrinkled. Someone on the edge of breaking.

Gabe knew pretty much everything there was to know about the incident leading to Jordan's incarceration. She'd fallen asleep behind the wheel a couple months before her eighteenth birthday. She'd sped through a red light just as

Becky Mackay was taking her son to preschool. Jordan had T-boned their car; killing them both instantly.

Nothing short of a tragedy.

Before that, Jordan had just graduated high school. A straight-A student, she'd never been in trouble with the law.

Gabe was no lawyer, but it didn't take one to see that she'd been sentenced pretty harshly for her crimes, given her age. The sentence had been more appropriate for a repeat-offending drunk driver than an honor-roll kid exhausted from working two jobs who had made a bad judgment call.

"You studying Jordan Reiss's file again?"

Kendrick Foster stood at his office door. Kendrick had been working for Gabe as a security consultant since Violet's kidnapping last month, although he'd known the younger man long before that.

Gabe leaned back in his chair, motioning for Kendrick to come in. Gabe could've pretended he was looking at any of the dozen things that needed his attention, including the possible weakness in some of their accounting programming that could lead to theft. But he didn't. He and Kendrick had known each other too long.

"Just trying to figure out why she got such a harsh sentence, especially considering she was a minor. Did Zac Mackay go on a rampage demanding justice for his wife and kid?"

Gabe knew Zac personally. He was co-owner of Linear Tactical, a survival, self-defense, and weapons training facility in Oak Creek. Zac and some of his army friends had started it a few years ago.

Gabe had nothing but respect for Mackay and the Linear guys. They'd even worked a couple of missions together before Gabe left the SEALs.

Going for the blood of a seventeen-year-old girl didn't sound like something Zac would do, but hell, losing a wife and kid like that could make anyone react unpredictably.

"No." Kendrick shook his head. "Mackay basically left town and was back to his special forces team almost immediately after the funeral. Didn't wait around for the trial at all. As a matter of fact, it looks like Mackay actually argued pretty hard for Jordan's parole three months ago."

"Then why six years for someone with no priors and who was basically a good kid? That's pretty harsh, right?"

Kendrick ran a hand over his bald, dark head. "I guess the judge decided to make an example of her since she had petitioned the state for emancipation at sixteen. He used that against her in sentencing. Said since she'd asked to be treated as an adult, she'd be sentenced like one. And I'm sure that he didn't like that her father had gotten away with a lot of Oak Creek's money."

Gabe's lips pursed. Sentencing her that harshly hadn't been illegal, but it hadn't been impartial either.

Gabe pushed the file away. What had happened to Jordan wasn't his problem. Violet's well-being was his problem.

"Anything to report about Violet or the bakery?" There shouldn't be much. Stellman, the man behind Violet's abduction, had been arrested a few days ago.

Kendrick shrugged. "With Stellman out of the picture, you're basically paying me a lot of money to hang out with the fine citizens of Oak Creek and eat your sister's delicious concoctions. But hey, rich and fat is a good way to go out."

Gabe laughed. Kendrick was in his late twenties, half African-American, half Asian. The man wasn't as big as Gabe, but he was blisteringly quick and damned smart, both academically, as evidenced by his degree from Princeton, and on the street. Sparring with him kept Gabe on his toes. And there was no way Kendrick Foster was going to allow himself to get fat, no matter how many pastries he ate.

"It's probably time to take you off watching Violet full-time since she's not in any more danger. You haven't seen anything suspicious?"

"No. But what you're really asking is if I've seen Jordan Reiss doing anything suspicious, right?"

Gabe gritted his teeth. "I want to know my sister is safe. She's been through enough. I want all possible threats circumvented—whether from forces outside the bakery or within."

Kendrick studied Gabe for a long second. "No threats from outside the bakery. Nobody has been watching or following Violet at any time. Unless you count Aiden Teague."

Gabe all but growled. Teague had been instrumental in getting Violet away from the traffickers who'd held her, but that didn't mean he liked the man hanging around her now. He was ten years older than Violet, for Christ's sake.

He ignored the voice in his head that told him he was eleven years older than Jordan. Shit.

"Teague isn't a threat," Gabe finally said, rubbing a hand over his eyes. "I'll handle him—and by that I mean kick his ass—if it's needed. Tell me about Jordan."

Because hell if he didn't want to know everything there was to know about the woman, partly to keep his sister safe, but also for reasons he damn well wasn't going to discuss with Kendrick.

Although the look in his friend's dark eyes told Gabe he wasn't fooling the younger man.

"I don't know what to tell you, boss. Jordan is a good employee. She shows up on time, rarely comes out of the back kitchen, and has never even so much as glanced in the direction of the cash register. Violet seems to really like her."

That didn't mean she was trustworthy.

Not that his body seemed to mind whether Jordan was trustworthy or not. It just wanted her.

"And your follow-up on Jordan? Any indication that she's been in contact with her father since she got out of prison?"

"No. According to all records and my source inside law enforcement, Michael Reiss hasn't been in contact with his daughter since he left town with the money eight years ago."

"Mother?"

"Died when Jordan was ten."

Gabe tapped his fingers on the file. "And the dad didn't try to make any contact with her while she was incarcerated? I assume they'd be looking for that sort of thing."

Kendrick studied his tablet. "No. He never showed up."

"Are you sure? Couldn't he have come in under disguise, using a different name or identity? He would've had the funds to make that happen."

"He didn't."

Gabe raised a brow. "How do you know?"

"Because nobody came to visit her the entire time she was incarcerated. Not a single person."

"*Nobody*? Shit. She was just a kid."

Kendrick nodded. "Yeah, pretty much my thoughts exactly."

"Okay, so her mom died when she was ten, her dad robbed the town blind when she was sixteen, she went to jail when she was a hair shy of eighteen, and got out three months ago." Gabe ran his fingers over his eyes. Jesus.

"Anything else happen to her I should know about? Unfortunate Medusa encounter?"

Kendrick grimaced. "Her life does read sort of like a Greek tragedy. And it hasn't gotten a ton better for her since she got out of prison. Oak Creek is polarized about her. People either like her or *really* hate her. All the Linear guys and their girlfriends—ironically, some of the people who have the most legitimate reason to dislike her—are pretty chummy and protective of her. But some of the other townspeople . . ." His breath whistled out through his teeth.

Gabe's eyes narrowed. "Bad?"

Kendrick shrugged and cocked his head to the side. "Look, I understand the appeal of Oak Creek, I really do. Last week I saw three teenagers rush to help an old lady carry her groceries out to her car. Crime rate is low, sense of community is high. But not when it comes to Jordan Reiss. Except for the Linear people, there's some sort of mob-mentality shit going on."

Gabe rubbed the back of his neck. "People hurt her?" Goddammit, he could not stand the thought of that. It was one thing for the town not to like her living there. That was understandable. It was quite another to physically harm a woman living alone and isolated like she was.

"Not that I've seen. They're just determined to cast her as the villain in their little play."

"Does she fight back? Tell them to go to hell?" The feisty waif who'd gone toe to toe with him wouldn't stand for that.

Kendrick just shrugged. "Jordan has been working at Fancy Pants for two weeks now, so I've seen her a lot. But besides your sister and Charlotte Devereux a couple of times, I've never seen her talk to anyone else. That's got to be lonely at best. Maybe downright scary if any of the townspeople decide to do some of the shit they talk about."

Gabe stood up. "I'm taking the rest of the day off. I'm pulling you from watching Violet. You're right, she doesn't need constant protection anymore now that we've caught Stellman. Focus on this accounting leak. See if you can come up with anything."

Kendrick crossed his arms over his chest and leaned back in his chair. "It's going to be nearly dark by the time you make it up to Oak Creek. You know that, right?"

"What makes you think I'm going to Oak Creek?"

"I've known you for a lot of years, brother. Never seen you this interested in a woman."

Gabe didn't respond. He couldn't remember the last time he'd been this interested in a woman either. Especially one he had every reason in the world to stay away from. Gabe had never been drawn to trouble. He had always been willing to step up and do his duty, whether that be protecting his country or leaving the military career he loved to help raise his sister.

Trouble in any form—even a slender brunette with huge gray eyes—had never been something he'd migrated toward.

Until now.

Chapter 3

The early October sun hovered just above the treetops as Jordan made her way up her driveway. The shorter days meant frigid weather wasn't far behind.

Wyoming winters were not for the weak. But Jordan had always loved them.

Her weary body sunk into the seat of her old pickup truck as she made her way toward her house. It had been a long day. She loved working with Violet at Fancy Pants, but the work in the kitchen definitely wasn't easy. It required constant movement and attention to detail. Violet paid her well, much better than she would've ever dreamed a job in Oak Creek would pay, but the hours required arriving long before dawn and often working twelve- to fourteen-hour days. Such was the reality of a new and busy business.

But that was okay, because it wasn't like she had much of a social life. Plus, all the money she could spare was going toward *The Plan*.

She'd made some headway with it when she'd purchased a new computer system a few days ago.

She was an ex-con with a gift for coding and developing computer security systems. The irony of that wasn't lost on her, nor would it be to anyone who she might look to for employment right before they slammed the door in her face. So she was going to build her own company.

She'd had six years to work out the details. Now, she just had to make all the pieces fit together. It would change everything about her life if she could pull it off.

But it was a long shot.

She pulled the truck to a rumbling stop beside her porch.

"Good girl." She patted the steering wheel. The truck was on its last leg. Hell, it was almost as old as she was. She prayed it would keep running, because finding someone in Oak Creek willing to work on her vehicle would be tricky. Maybe Baby, Finn Bollinger's brother. He'd always been relatively nice to her, even in high school, when everyone else had completely shunned her after her father left. But then again, helping her might negatively affect business at his garage, so maybe not.

She got out and was only a few steps from her truck when she saw the broken window at the side of the house.

"Goddammit." Again? As if throwing shit at her house every week wasn't enough, someone had to come and break another window? They'd stopped for a while when Charlotte had lived here as her roommate. But since Charlie had moved into Finn's house, Jordan had evidently become fair game again.

Her stomach dropped when she realized what room had been vandalized—the one she had set up with her new computer system.

If whatever they had thrown had hit her desk . . . She couldn't see the damage from here. She rushed toward her front door.

And heard the snickering before she even rounded the corner of her porch.

Allan Godlewski was sitting on her rocking chair, studying his nails as if he didn't have a care in the world.

"Hey, Jordan," he said without looking up.

She'd dealt with Allan before. He didn't live in Oak Creek but was friends with a couple of the guys in town. Last time she'd seen Allan, he'd been hanging around Adam DiMuzio, even though Adam was still in high school, and Allan was closer to her age.

She was pretty sure both Adam and Allan were the driving force behind Project Crap On Jordan's House. They'd also "accidentally" bumped into her a couple of times and made her drop the grocery bags she'd been carrying, as well as regularly letting the air out of her tires.

Her father had stolen a lot of money from the DiMuzios, she could understand Adam's behavior. His family had almost lost New Brothers, their pizza restaurant in town—and the place where Jordan had worked a few hours a week on weekends in high school. She'd never forget the look in Mr. DiMuzio's eyes when he fired her after everyone had realized her father had run with the money and was never coming back.

But she'd hadn't met Allan until recently. She had no idea why he was harassing her.

"Get off my property before I call the cops and have you arrested."

He looked up, his face the very picture of innocence in the waning sunlight. "Arrest me for what? Checking on a neighbor when I saw that a large rock had been thrown through a window?"

"First of all, we are not neighbors. You don't even live in Oak Creek. Second of all, how exactly do you know it was a large rock that went through the window unless you're the one who threw it?"

His eyes narrowed as he ran a hand through his brownish-blond hair that either had way too much styling product in it or was just greasy. Either way, it was disgusting.

He stood up. "Well, that little slip would just be your word against mine, wouldn't it? I wonder who the cops would believe."

"It's been a long day. You've had your fun. Just go." Where was his car parked? She lived far enough outside of town to be surrounded by forest and wilderness, so he must have parked somewhere else and walked through the trees to get here. The fact that he didn't want any traces of his vehicle on her land did not reassure her. She stayed where she was on the bottom step.

He crossed his arms over his chest. "I didn't come here to start a fight. Things are about to change in this town, Jordan."

"Change how?" She grimaced as he leaned on the column and spit chewing tobacco over the side of her railing.

"Never mind that. I'm here to talk about my offer."

"And what offer is that?"

He smiled and sauntered a couple steps toward her. "The one where you and me hook up, and I take care of you, baby."

She fought the urge to laugh. She knew firsthand that Allan didn't like to be laughed at. Last time she'd made that mistake, he'd grabbed her arm so hard that she'd had bruises for days afterward.

He gave her what was supposed to be a charming smile. But when he stepped closer, she stepped back.

"Come on, Jordan, don't be that way." He ran his

fingers through that greasy hair again. "I've been on the inside. I know how hard it is. I mean, maybe girly prison is different, but I know you have fires that need to be put out. I'm the man to scratch them."

Explaining a mixed metaphor to him would probably be a lost cause. "As tempting as that offer may be, I'm going to have to pass. My fires and itches are just fine as they are."

All traces of Allan's attempted charm flew from his face. "You know, you're pretty uppity for someone everybody hates. Adam says his dad talks all the time about how your family nearly ruined his life. If you get with me, maybe I can talk them into letting bygones be bygones, you know? A sort of payment plan."

She rolled her eyes. "Again, going to have to pass. I'm not great with payment plans."

He took another step closer, sneering. "I can't even figure out why you even stick around here if you're not trying to get a little action."

She wasn't surprised Allan didn't understand. Nobody understood her need to come back here.

But nobody had been around all those years she and her mom had walked through the woods together, when her mother had told her stories about the people—the *women*—in her family who had forged a life out of this harsh, beautiful territory, surviving when nobody had thought they would.

She was going to survive too. She didn't need the people of Oak Creek to like her or forgive her, not that they were ever going to.

"I'm not interested in action. I just want to be left alone." She prayed he'd listen to her. She continued to move back as he moved forward. She was almost to her truck.

"I think you're just playing a little hard to get. But that's okay, Allan doesn't mind helping you get over your shyness." Now, he spit the entire wad of chewing tobacco on the ground and smiled at her.

Most of her life, Jordan had loved how isolated her house was. Even when she'd lived here alone when she was in high school, she'd never minded it.

But right now, she wished she lived in the middle of town where someone could hear her if she screamed.

She held an arm out in front of her.

"Allan." She looked him directly in the eye. "This is not a game. I'm not flirting or playing hard to get. I don't want this. You need to leave. If you don't, what you're trying to do will be attempted rape."

She hoped the words would be enough to jar him from his present course of action, to make him think about what he was actually doing.

Not that she had plans to stand by and let him attack her. She knew better than that, and she knew how to defend herself. But it would be much better all around if Allan just left of his own accord.

For a moment she thought it might work. He was processing what she was saying, the fact that he would be attacking her. But she saw the exact moment when he shrugged off her words.

He shook his head slowly, a sneer falling over his lips. "No, I don't think so. That's just what girls like you say to make yourselves feel better about what you want to do."

He was on her before he'd even finished the sentence, catching her off guard with unexpected speed. His face rammed up against hers, his rancid breath hot against her cheek as she turned her head away. He used his weight to back her against the hood of the truck. She kept her face turned away even when he reached up and tried to yank her chin forward with his hand.

She did not want this asshole to kiss her. It was ridiculous, but she still had last week's kiss from Gabriel imprinted on her lips, and she didn't want someone else's there in its place. This sort of violence from men had been all she'd ever known. Except with Gabriel.

The thought gave her a renewed burst of energy. Allan was so busy trying to get his lips on hers that he wasn't paying attention to any other parts of her body.

He was definitely paying attention a second later when she used all her strength to shove him back and crash her knee straight into his groin. The squeal that escaped him should've been oh, so satisfying, along with the picture of him backing away in agony and clutching his privates, but she had to use the time to her advantage. She turned to the driver-side door of her truck, snatched it open, and dove inside. She'd learned over the last couple of months to keep weapons close, and she had a hunter's knife stashed under the passenger seat.

She'd just reached under and grabbed it when Allan's fist in her hair dragged her back out. He spun her around, slamming the door—barely missing her fingers—and threw her back up against the truck again.

"You bitch." Allan's face was mottled in rage.

He brought his arm up like he was going to backhand her, but Jordan quickly slipped the knife against the delicate area of his body she'd already damaged.

"You hit me, and I can't be responsible for my hand jerking and further damaging your family lineage." She pressed the tip of the blade against his thighs so he would understand exactly what she was talking about. "I'll even be nice enough to call an ambulance for you when you're lying on the ground, holding what's left of your balls and squealing like a pig."

This time, she was able to enjoy it as the color drained from his face. In the distance she heard a vehicle pulling up her driveway and prayed it wasn't one of Allan's buddies. Nobody else had ever made such an overtly violent move against her, but there was no way she would be able to hold two—or more—of them off with a knife. She needed to get to her house.

Allan backed away, but she wasn't sure why. Because he was afraid of being caught in the act by whoever was coming up the drive? Or because he was biding his time until his buddies arrived?

His beady eyes narrowed. "You're going to regret this."

She pushed away from the truck, knife firmly in hand, and bolted up her porch steps, keeping an eye on him over her shoulder to make sure he didn't follow her. She was prepared to spin the knife on Allan again as she dug her keys out of her pocket, but he didn't follow her.

She didn't pause, just got the door open and ran inside, grabbing the shotgun she kept by her refrigerator.

It was loaded with birdshot, so it probably wouldn't kill anybody, but it would get the job done. She grabbed some extra shells from the counter in case she needed them for Allan's buddies.

But when she turned around and walked back outside, shotgun ready for action at her side, it wasn't Allan's friends who had shown up.

It was Gabriel.

And he had Allan by his shirt collar.

"Look, man," Allan whined, ridiculously scrawny compared to Gabe's massive strength, "I was just coming to see my friend Jordan."

"Then why did it look to me like Jordan was holding a

knife on you, then running for her life?" Gabriel's green eyes met hers before continuing. "Here's Jordan now. And with a gun. Seems to me like she probably wouldn't be meeting her *friends* with a gun in her hand."

Allan had the idiocy to try to get tough with Gabe. "Maybe that gun is for you, man. You're not from around here. You don't know the situation."

Gabriel's fist tightened in Allan's shirt. "If the *situation* you're referring to is that you think it's open season on this woman for any reason, then you and I are going to have a long chat. I'll bring my friends from Linear Tactical along. I may not be from around here, but they are, and I'm certain they feel the same about Jordan's safety."

Allan's voice dropped lower. "It's not like that, man. Everybody hates her. Nobody cares what happens to her."

Jordan's heart lurched in her chest as Gabriel's eyes narrowed, and he let go of Allan. Oh God, did he believe Allan?

Not that Allan wasn't telling the truth. There weren't very many people who cared what happened to her.

Gabriel leaned closer to him and whispered something she couldn't hear. Allan nodded frantically, then took off running into the forest. Gabriel watched him go until it was obvious he wouldn't be coming back, then turned back to her. They stared at each other for long moments, those eyes of his that never missed anything studying her intently.

Violet had told her that he used to be a Navy SEAL. Jordan had done a little research on that, then almost wish she hadn't. The training SEALs went through was pretty damn impressive, as well as the sorts of missions they were part of. The Linear guys had all been part of the Army's Green Berets. SEALs were the Navy's equivalent.

Gabriel hadn't moved toward her. He was still standing

right where he had been with his arms held close to his hips, palms facing her. A pose of nonaggression.

She wasn't deceived into thinking the pose meant he *wasn't* aggressive, just that he was keeping it restrained for her sake.

Or maybe the pose was because of the shotgun she had pointed at him from her waist. Not the most accurate way to shoot, but again, it would certainly get the job done at this range.

"Are you all right?" he asked. "Did that asshole hurt you?"

"What did you say to him?" She should lower the gun but couldn't force herself to do it.

He shrugged. "Just a little talk about how no means no, and how the guys and I would be happy to help him understand that more clearly if he was having difficulty comprehending it."

"Really?"

"I don't care if you kick puppies out onto the highway. It's never okay for a man not to accept it when a woman says no."

She believed him, believed that he had fought for this country to protect those very basic freedoms. Even for someone like her.

She lowered the gun. "For the record, I only kick puppies out onto dirt roads, not highways."

He gave her a half smile and took a step closer as if to judge whether she was going to point the gun at him again.

She couldn't quite decide that either.

"Thanks for your help with the riffraff, even though I could've handled him myself." But more important was the question she could find no logical answer to. "Why are you here, Collingwood?"

Chapter 4

Jordan still held that shotgun in her hands—obviously comfortable with it—as Gabe stood looking at her on her porch.

Why *was* he here?

The truth, that he hadn't been able to get her off his mind since the last time he saw her, and that he'd driven the hour and a half from Idaho Falls with no real plan in mind, would just have her pointing the gun in his direction again.

"I came to see Violet. But evidently she and Teague have plans for the weekend."

That was partially true. Gabe always wanted to see his sister, but in this case, Violet had just been an excuse to check on Jordan. And given what he'd just driven up on, he was damn glad he had.

Jordan placed the shotgun down against the column. The same column that had been fueling his fantasies for the past ten days.

She looked a little shaky as she sat down in the rocking chair. He walked toward her, keeping his steps slow and easy. She'd been spooked enough already. Those big gray eyes studied him warily.

"Who was that guy?" he asked.

She didn't have to tell him, Gabe was going to find out either way, but understanding the nature of their relationship would at least help him understand how to move forward. Was he an ex-boyfriend?

Hell, *current* boyfriend? Some relationships were volatile like that.

"Allan Godlewski" was all she said.

"Friend of yours?"

She laughed, but the sound held no humor. "No. He's just one of the— Shit."

She jumped to her feet and ran toward the door.

Gabe was on her heels in a second, fighting the urge to pull her behind him in case there was any danger as she rushed inside. But hell, it was her house. She ran to a small bedroom, the same one with the broken window he'd noticed when he'd pulled up.

A large rock lay on the floor in the middle of the room. Jordan pretty much ignored it and rushed over to the desk in the corner, where a computer and monitor sat unharmed.

"Thank God." The words came out on a huff of breath. "The computer is probably the most expensive thing I own. I doubt Allan knew it was in here, but I was afraid he had gotten lucky."

"That asshole broke your window?"

She shrugged. "I'm sure he'll deny it if anyone else asks, but yeah, he pretty much admitted it to me." She walked over and picked up the rock before he could stop her.

"You probably shouldn't touch it. It might have fingerprints."

She snorted. "I'm pretty sure that won't matter. I reported it last time. But, you know, sometimes nature is crazy in Wyoming. At least that's what the deputy they sent to investigate the last time told me."

He flattened his lips, crossing his arms. "Did you ever think about moving somewhere else?"

"No."

She didn't have any more to say about that, just brushed by him so she could exit the room to the rest of her small house. It was nice, clean, with a floor plan that had the kitchen and living room open to each other. Her furnishings were a little sparse, but she had the basics: couch, television, small kitchen table in the eating nook.

She got a broom from beside the fridge, took it back into the computer room, and began silently sweeping up the glass. Gabe held the dustpan for her, then dumped the pieces in the trash can outside.

She studied the broken window with a sigh. "I've got some plywood out back. I'll just cover the sill until I can replace it. I can do it later."

"Do you have someone you can call to help?"

She gave a long exhale and a little shrug. "I'll be able to get it myself."

He shook his head. There was no way in hell. "I'll help."

She looked like she was going to argue but stopped. Instead, she led him out the back door to a small shed that contained some wood. Using a handsaw rather adeptly, she cut the size plywood she needed, then he carried it over to the window.

"Does this happen often?" He held the wood in place while Jordan nailed it.

"There's only been one other time a window has been broken."

Which didn't mean she wasn't regularly harassed, just that there wasn't physical evidence of it.

They finished in silence. The end result wasn't pretty, but it would at least keep out the elements until she got it repaired professionally.

How and when she was going to get that done, and whether she could afford it, were none of his business, he reminded himself.

"Thank you," she said softly as they walked back around to the front porch. "At the very least, you've got good timing."

He sat down on the porch steps. "Are you sure it's safe out here by yourself? It's one thing for law enforcement to ignore vandalism, but things looked a little precarious between you and Godlewski when I got here."

She let out an exhausted sigh and sat down next to him on the steps. "Allan is never a prince, but he was in rare form tonight. I can handle him. He and his buddies generally keep it to petty and mildly annoying stuff. I ignore it."

"But what if petty and mildly annoying grow into violent?"

Because there had definitely been violence on Godlewski's face. Although, damn it, that should not be an issue in a place like Oak Creek.

"It won't. Like I said, I can handle Allan, and I think he's the only one who would step over the line in that way. The people of Oak Creek may not like me, but they've never tried to hurt me." She picked at a small string on the hem of her pants. "Plus, it doesn't matter. This is my home. I'm not leaving. I've been away long enough."

He nodded. "And you obviously know how to handle yourself." He gestured to the shotgun still leaning against the column. "Would you have really shot him?"

She gave him a small smile. "It's birdshot."

He laughed. "Would've still gotten the job done."

"That's what I thought, too."

"Are you even allowed to have that thing? I thought ex-felons couldn't own a gun unless they specifically got those rights reinstated."

She laid her head on her knees, wrapping her arms around her thighs, looking at him sideways. The pose reminded him how young she really was. "It was my mom's. Nobody knows it's here except you and Allan. Are you going to turn me in?"

He smiled. "No. Just want to make sure you're not going to use it on me."

"That depends. You planning on busting up one of my windows?" She lifted an eyebrow and grinned.

That smile. It changed her whole appearance. Those big, solemn eyes tended to dominate her features, but he realized that was because she didn't normally smile. When she did, it balanced out her face and changed her whole countenance.

And hell if he didn't want to put that look on her face all the time.

Jesus. What was wrong with him? There were a lot of reasons he needed to stay away from Jordan Reiss—she was too young, she was his sister's employee, she had trouble all but leaking out of her pores when he had enough trouble of his own—and he was sitting here thinking about ways to *make her smile*?

No.

He was here because he'd wanted to make sure she was safe. That was the decent thing to do. And to make sure none of the trouble surrounding Jordan rubbed off on his sister.

He didn't say anything for so long that the smile slipped off her face. He ignored the pain at seeing it go.

He stood up, crossing his arms over his chest. He needed to get this back on a business footing. "You shouldn't be out here by yourself. It's not safe." His words came out rougher than he meant them and stupider than anything he'd ever heard himself say.

Evidently, she agreed. She was on her feet almost before he finished the sentence. "Um, in case you missed it, it's the twenty-first century. I can live wherever I damn well please."

He raised an eyebrow. "For you, as long as it's within the state of Wyoming."

Throwing her parole back in her face was a douche move, and he knew it. He watched as ice blanketed those gray eyes. "We never did establish why you're actually here, did we, Collingwood?"

"I was just swinging by to see if you'd changed your mind about my offer." Nothing could be further from the truth, but if he was going to be an asshole, he might as well go all the way. "Five thousand dollars could buy you quite a few window replacements. Looks like you're going to need them."

She shook her head. "Wow, my evening has come full circle. Let me say to you the same thing I said to Allan when he also mentioned an *offer*: get the hell off my property. Unless you're planning on trying some of those same moves he did."

Gabe was on his feet and in Jordan's personal space in less than a second.

"That's not my style, Rainfall." He leaned in closer, knowing it was the last thing he should be doing, but he couldn't stop himself. To her credit she didn't shy away. "If you don't want me around, you just say no, and I'll always back off."

But damned if it wouldn't be the hardest thing he'd

ever done if she said it right now. She gnawed her bottom lip with her teeth.

He wanted to take that lip and nibble on it himself.

"Tell me no, Jordan." Because if she didn't tell him no right now, they were going to have another make-out session here on the porch.

He gave her two seconds, and that was all the control he had.

He had every intention of crushing her to him, of ravishing her mouth the way he had last time, of letting the fire blazing between them burn them both to ash.

But the second his lips touched hers, everything changed. They gentled of their own accord, teasing and finessing rather than devouring.

She sighed and relaxed into him, her hands feathering up his arms to his shoulders. His hands moved to her waist, holding her gently.

This woman needed gentleness.

He kissed her like that—closed mouth, innocent kisses—until their lips were sore. He kept expecting—*hoping*—she would take the lead and deepen the kiss or press up against him in invitation like last time. But she didn't. So he didn't either.

And he was surprised to find he was more than okay with it.

Finally, he stepped back, hands still on her waist, just staring at her in the darkness that now surrounded them. In the distance, thunder rumbled.

He ran a finger down her cheek. "There's going to be another storm. You going to stand in the rain again?"

That smile. "No, not tonight. It's been a long and crazy day."

Thank God. Because if she'd said yes, every good intention he had would've flown out the window.

The smell of rain on her skin, in her hair, had already permanently marked his senses. The urge to lead her out to the grass right now, strip her naked, and ride her in the fury of the storm about to hit was almost more than he could resist.

It would happen. But not tonight.

Tonight, he would respect that maybe she needed a little space to make the choices that were right for her. He would respect that, like she'd said, it had been a long and crazy day.

He still didn't know exactly why he had come here. But whatever it was he'd needed, he'd gotten already.

He stepped back.

"Are you leaving?" she whispered.

"For now. For tonight. It's what's best."

"Okay. I still don't know why you came by in the first place."

He gave a one-shouldered shrug. "To be honest, neither do I. But I'm glad I did."

She nodded. "Me too."

"Go inside and lock your door, Rainfall. I'll see you soon."

She did what he asked, and he waited until he heard the lock slide into place before moving. He couldn't help but feel like he was making a mistake.

He just didn't know if it was because he was leaving, or because he knew he would be back.

Chapter 5

Thank God it was Thursday. Okay, maybe that wouldn't catch on like its Friday counterpart, but Violet had decided that Fancy Pants would only be open until midafternoons on Thursdays. That meant Jordan was getting home by five o'clock rather than early evenings like the other nights that she worked.

She was looking forward to getting some work done on the computer.

And not thinking about Gabriel Collingwood at all.

It had been a week and a half since she'd seen him, since he'd kissed her—*again*—on her front porch. Those kisses had been totally different from the first ones. So much more tender. She'd found herself comparing the two make-out sessions over and over as she lay in bed each night, her body aching in ways she'd never really felt before.

She only knew Gabriel was both the cause and the solution for the ache.

But she hadn't seen him at all since the night he'd kissed her so softly and left.

Violet had mentioned that there had been some computer security issues at Collingwood Technology, so maybe that was keeping Gabriel away. Or the fact that Idaho Falls was an hour and a half from here.

Or maybe he'd somehow picked up on the fact that he made up ninety-five percent of her sexual experience.

By the time she'd been old enough to date, she'd been a social pariah thanks to her father's actions. Nobody had been interested in dating her. And then she'd been in prison for the past six years.

Didn't take Sherlock to figure all that out. So maybe Gabriel had decided that staying away from her was a good idea.

She felt a little stupid for buying the short, flirty skirt she'd picked up in Reddington City. She didn't have many —*any*—girly clothes, so she'd driven into the city to get some in case he asked her out on a date.

It was cute. A soft blue with little purple flowers. A loose, flowing cut that showed off her legs. She might never get to wear it on a date, but she was still glad she'd bought it. It made her feel good. Confident, even.

She slipped on her cute skirt before she left the bakery, walking down the main street toward where she'd parked her truck this morning. She needed to stop by and get some groceries since she didn't have anything to cook at her house, but she hated to go all the way to the next town over to buy them. She could just grab some fast food at the gas station outside of town. They tended not to harass her too much. The grocery store here wasn't an option.

"Jordan!"

She stiffened at the yell before she realized it was Violet with her boyfriend, Aiden, waving at her from across the street. Violet was motioning for her to come over.

They were standing in front of New Brothers Pizza, Mr. DiMuzio's place.

"Hey, guys." She crossed the street, forcing a smile.

Violet immediately linked arms with her. "You look so cute in your skirt! We're just about to grab some pizza. Come eat with us."

Violet was too new and too kind to even see Jordan's predicament. It never occurred to her that people would treat others unkindly, because she wouldn't treat people unkindly. But there was no way Jordan could go into New Brothers. She pulled away as Violet stepped closer to the restaurant door.

"You know, I don't even like this place."

Violet laughed. "What are you talking about? You order food twice a week from here and have it delivered at the bakery. Adam DiMuzio and I are on a first name basis since I always seem to be the one out front to pay him when he delivers."

It was true. Jordan gave money to Violet to pay for her orders and stayed in the back; that way they wouldn't know the food was for Jordan and refuse delivery.

The last time she'd gone in, Mr. DiMuzio had cursed her in front of the entire staff and told her never to come back. But that had been six years ago. Maybe things had changed.

"Come eat with us," Aiden said, eyes full of compassion, much more aware of what was going on than Violet. "You can sit surrounded by all of us. Finn and Charlie are in there. Peyton. The kids."

They would protect her. Buffer her. There was safety in numbers. Mr. DiMuzio wouldn't want to throw them all out. Jordan felt tears sting her eyes. God, she would love to just go have a normal meal at a restaurant in her cute skirt.

Violet was saying something to Aiden, but Jordan wasn't listening. Could she do this?

Yes. She would try. Maybe it could be a first step in a new direction. New skirt. New Jordan. She smiled at Violet and they took another step toward the door.

But when Aiden opened it, Mr. DiMuzio was standing just inside—obviously someone had gotten him from the back—with his arms crossed over his chest.

The stance was clear. Jordan would not be eating at his restaurant without a fight. He might cave and let her in but not without a scene.

Aiden shot her a look of encouragement, but Jordan couldn't do this to Violet. She freed her arm from Violet's and backed away from the door.

"You know what? I just remember I have something that I've got to do right now." She forced a smile. "But rain check, okay?"

Violet looked like she was going to argue, but Aiden understood. He ushered the other woman inside as Jordan backed away, careful not to make eye contact with Mr. DiMuzio through the door.

She tucked her head down and made a beeline toward her truck. She would not cry about this. What was there to cry about? Five minutes ago, she'd been fine with the thought of going home and making some progress on the computer. Nothing had changed. She was still doing that.

She was just going to do it with a little piece of her heart cracked. She should be used to it by now.

She made it to her truck and climbed inside. When she cranked the key and the engine wouldn't turn over, she let out a sigh.

"Come on baby. Not now." She couldn't get stuck in Oak Creek right now, not without falling apart.

She rested her head against the steering wheel and tried it again. Nothing.

Now the tears were really threatening to fall. She closed her eyes, willing herself to keep it together.

She let out a little shriek when someone tapped on her window. All she could see was a massive chest, but she recognized it right away.

Gabriel.

She rolled down her window with the hand crank. He bent down and leaned his elbows against her door.

"Problems?" He smiled at her. Not a smirk. Not a slick grin barely veiling innuendo or violence. But a real honest-to-God smile that softened his warrior features and lit up his green eyes.

Jordan burst into tears.

Damn it, what was wrong with her? She'd been through much worse than this without crying.

"Hey. Hey." She could hear the concern in his voice even after she covered her face. "Most women don't start crying until I've been around them at least a couple of hours." His fingers trailed up and down her arm.

"My truck won't start," she finally managed to get out.

He leaned back and made a special show of studying the vehicle. "If you cry every time this POS won't start, you must spend half your life in tears."

She laughed. She couldn't help it, even though it came out as an unattractive little hiccup. "You should be more respectful to the elderly."

"Why? Nothing this old could possibly hear me."

She laughed again, this time her tears drying.

He trailed a finger down her cheek. "You okay, Rainfall? You don't strike me as the type to cry because your truck won't turn over."

His kindness was almost her undoing once again. She

sucked in a deep breath and let it out slowly. "What are you doing here in Oak Creek again, Collingwood? Besides trolling for people whose cars won't start and smothering them with kindness."

Now he laughed. "I actually had some business over at Linear Tactical. Thought I would stop by and see Violet, but Fancy Pants was already closed."

"We close early on Thursdays now. But if you're looking for your sister, she's gone to dinner at New Brothers Pizza down the block."

"Nah, I got myself a sandwich at the sub shop when I couldn't find her. It's a nice day, and we've got another couple hours of sunlight. I'll make you a deal since you're from around here and, I assume, know the area pretty well. You show me where there's a nice place to enjoy a Wyoming sunset, and I'll split my delicious sandwich and the six pack of beer I'm about to pick up."

She wanted to, God how she wanted to, but it wasn't a good idea. What had just happened at New Brothers served as a blunt reminder that she was never going to be accepted around here. Dating someone would just make it awkward for *two* people rather than just her.

"Gabriel . . ."

His smile didn't falter. "I can see you're not convinced, and I appreciate a woman with a good head for a deal. How about I throw in getting your truck to start? I'll even apologize for calling her old if that's what it will take." He ran his fingers tenderly along the edge of the steering wheel.

Resisting serious, Navy SEAL Gabriel was hard.

Resisting playful, smiling Gabriel was damn near impossible.

"C'mon, Rainfall. Show me what makes this town worth it, what made my sister pack up and move here and has made you stay when anyone else would run for the hills. Show me one of *your* places."

"You've got to get the truck started first." That alone could take the rest of the evening.

Gabriel held the door open for her, and she slid out, allowing him to ease his much larger body inside.

She watched his fingers gently caress the steer wheel. What would they feel like caressing her? Goose bumps broke out all over.

One of his hands moved down to the stick shift, and his foot shifted to the clutch. He grabbed the key and turned it, popping the clutch out as he did so.

Damned thing started without so much as a stutter.

"Traitor," she murmured.

Gabriel stuck his elbow out the window. "So, where we headed, Rainfall?"

Chapter 6

There were lots of beautiful places around Oak Creek—the quarry to the north, the cove on the west side of town, some other isolated places. But taking Gabriel somewhere they might be surrounded by teenagers making out in their cars was definitely not an option.

Taking him where they might run into anybody at *all* didn't seem like a good plan. It was one thing to be shunned while she was alone, quite another to be shunned while with him.

That really only left her with one place if he wanted to catch a pretty sunset.

"Are you bringing me out in these woods to kill me?" He was a few steps behind her, carrying the sandwich and beers he'd picked up at the gas station on the way to her house. They'd parked there because it was the closest place to where they were going.

She smiled at him over her shoulder. "Actually, my plan is to lead you out here, then run away so you can never find your way back."

"I was a SEAL, you know. Believe it or not, that didn't only involve water. I'm pretty efficacious on land too."

"Did you do your initial training at San Clemente Island?"

"Yes, for some of BUD/S. You've heard of it?" He caught up so he was next to her.

She definitely wasn't bringing up that she'd researched the Navy SEALs after Violet had mentioned he used to be one. But she could redirect him with a different truth.

"I did a little research of the military back in high school. Thought that was the route I would go. Not a Navy SEAL, of course."

"Really, you wanted to go into the military? Why? Which branch?"

"The Army, for the usual reasons, I guess. Didn't have a clear grasp of what I wanted to study and no way to pay for college even if I did. And I wanted to travel, see the world. And because . . ."

Shit. This conversation had its own pitfalls. She would've been better off telling him she'd researched SEALs because she thought they were hot.

"Because what?"

"Never mind." She shook her head and walked faster.

He just lengthened his own stride. "No, tell me. What made you want to join the army rather than one of the other branches?"

She shrugged. "Because Zac Mackay and Finn Bollinger went into the army. All of us younger kids looked up to them so much; they were basically the town heroes."

And then while Zac was away serving his country, she'd gone and killed his wife and kid.

She hadn't even realized she'd wrapped her arms around her middle until she felt his fingers trailing over her arms.

"Hey." He stopped walking and gripped her arm, stopping her too. "I know there are no magic words that make all of this better. What happened was a tragedy. But not just for the Mackay family, Rainfall. For you, too."

She just shrugged. What could she say?

"I don't know a lot about you, but I know that you would never have done that on purpose. It was an accident."

She stared at the ground. "Labeling it an accident doesn't bring Becky or little Micah back."

His fingers traced gentle circles on her arm. "No, it doesn't. But you served your time for what happened. Probably more than you should have. At some point, you've got to forgive yourself. It's always going to be part of you, but it doesn't have to be the *defining* part of you."

"The group therapist I was required to see while I was in jail basically said the same thing." But the words had sounded so different coming from her. "But she didn't . . ." she trailed off.

"She didn't what?"

Jordan shrugged again. He was still rubbing those light circles on her arm, both distracting and comforting. "I don't know. I just never felt like she knew what she was talking about. Like it was just something from a book or a class she'd taken."

"I'm not sure someone who's never taken a life can truly understand. Sympathize, yes. But not empathize."

She looked up into his face, finding nothing but compassion centered in strength.

"Have you taken a life?"

He nodded. "Yes. More than one."

"But it was different. You were supposed to. You were on missions, and they were your enemies."

He trailed a finger slowly down her cheek. "Not always,

Rainfall. We tried our damnedest to make sure innocent people didn't get hurt, but that's not how the real world works. Shit happens. The bad guys get away, and normal people just living their normal lives get caught in the crossfire. I may not have done time for it, but I know what it's like to live with the knowledge that my judgment call caused the death of someone innocent. Calling it an accident, or in the military's case *friendly fire*, doesn't make those people any less dead."

She reached up and grasped the wrist of his hand that was now cupping her cheek. There were demons in his green eyes, and for the first time, someone truly understood the pain that ate at her heart every day.

She was about to reassure him, but he continued speaking before she could. "You want to tell me that it's not my fault. Same." He tapped her on the forehead with a finger. "Intent does matter. You never intended to hurt Micah or Becky Mackay. And you're right, you'll have to carry it forever. Nobody can carry it for you. But don't let it define you, Rainfall. Zac would be the first person to tell you that. You're so much more than a single mistake."

She closed her eyes, just soaking in his words.

Maybe. *Maybe.*

He kissed her forehead. "Now, are we going to get to this secret spot anytime soon or am I going to die of hunger?"

She grinned up at him as they started walking again. The fact that he'd taken hold of her hand and hadn't let go was not lost on her. "Good thing you decided to be a Navy SEAL. You obviously never could have hacked it in the army with your delicate disposition."

With those words, she took off running as he laughed behind her.

"Oh, you are in so much trouble now."

She ran for a few more seconds, then stopped when she got to where she'd been leading them. He rushed up behind her, whatever he been about to say lost as he looked around.

This was one of her favorite places on Earth. The path that had been surrounded by trees all the way from her house opened up to a tiny meadow that looked down on a creek. Her parents had built a picnic table out here before Mom had died.

"Wow. Look at this place," Gabriel whispered, setting the sandwich and beer on the table.

Jordan smiled, looking around. "This was one of my mother's favorite places."

"And your dad's? It's okay to talk about him too, you know. What he did was wrong, but that doesn't mean you don't have other memories of him."

She gave a one-shouldered shrug. "Dad was never one for the outdoors."

"Has he ever tried to get in touch with you?"

She walked over to the picnic table and began unwrapping the sandwich, mostly just to give herself something to do. "No. Never."

Honestly, she wasn't sure if she wanted him to at this point. She didn't want to be responsible for the burden of knowing where he was. But on the other hand, he was the only family she had left.

Gabriel opened two beers and handed one to her. "Thank you for sharing this beautiful place with me." He held his beer up in a salute, and they both drank.

As they ate, the conversation turned much lighter. He kept her entertained with funny stories from his navy days and how he'd travelled all over the world.

"Where was your favorite place? I would love to travel

someday. And no need to make any cracks about how I can't leave the state of Wyoming."

He winced. "That was such a shitty thing to say. I'm sorry."

"Eh. It won't always be true. So where were some of your favorite places?"

They finished the sandwich, stuffing their trash back into the bag as he told her about places he'd been. Spain. Germany. England. Italy. They climbed up to sit on top of the picnic table, looking down at the creek.

"I loved Morocco. Marrakesh's Jemaa el-Fnaa market at night is a sight to behold. Santorini, Greece, with the ridiculously blue waters of the Mediterranean? I still dream about that."

Jordan shifted her weight, lying back on her elbows on top of the table, closing her eyes. "I can just picture it. I don't know if I'll ever make it to the Mediterranean, but I'll settle for just the Pacific Ocean. I want to go to the Santa Monica Pier."

He chuckled, but she didn't open her eyes. "That place is a tourist trap, you know."

She made a sour face, sticking her tongue out at him. "I don't care. I want to be a tourist."

When he spoke again his voice was much closer to her ear. "If you keep doing stuff to draw my attention to your lips, I'm afraid I'm going to have to kiss you again."

She opened one eye and looked over at him. "You mean like stick my tongue out at you?"

"Yeah, and all that other stuff you do."

"What other stuff?" She hadn't been deliberately trying to get his attention, although she had to admit it didn't upset her that she had.

"Really obvious stuff." His voice got deeper, and she

could feel the heat of his breath on her ear. "Like talking and breathing."

"I'll try to keep my hussy instincts in check."

Now his lips were nuzzling at the side of her neck. "Please, not on my account."

She couldn't hold back the little gasp that escaped her as his nuzzling became nibbling.

"Gabriel." His name came out as an entreaty. She didn't even know what she was asking for. More? Less?

His hand threaded through her hair, tilting her head; giving him better access to her throat. "I love that you say my full name."

"It's an angel's name."

He bit gently at the spot where her neck met her shoulders. She couldn't hold back her shudder as sensation flooded her system. "I'm no angel, Rainfall."

Maybe not. But at least he didn't treat her like she was a demon.

His lips and teeth continued their nibbling onslaught along her neck. Her fingers threaded into his soft brown hair, pulling him closer. When his hand slipped under her blouse at the waist, she didn't even think about stopping him.

Or the moan that fell from her lips as his hand worked its way up to cup her breast, thumb flicking across one hardened nipple, before moving her bra to the side.

God, she'd had no idea her body could feel this way—like electrical currents were pulsing just under her skin.

His lips made their way up her neck until they were against hers, nibbling, nudging them open.

As soon as she did, his tongue thrust deep into her mouth, and she jerked against him. They were half sprawled on the table, and all she could think about was that she wanted him closer. Her leg shifted, moving to hook around his thighs, pulling him toward her. With a groan, he gave way to her silent demand, leaning more of his weight on top of her, pushing her back onto the table.

When his mouth found hers again, the knot of need inside grew until it was a tangled mess threatening to consume her. Her body ached deliciously as his mouth dominated hers. And his hands—those very talented hands—had her gasping, then moaning as he toyed with her breasts, alternating between soft touches and nips of pain. She scratched her nails along his chest and loved the heartfelt groan that escaped his lips.

She wanted him. Wanted to touch his naked skin. Wanted him to touch hers.

When the hand on her breast slid down over her belly, then lower, down her hip, over her skirt until it was resting on her naked thigh, electricity bolted through her system again.

"I think I forgot to mention how much I like this skirt. I've never seen you in one before," he said against her mouth.

"It's new."

His tongue licked along her lower lip as his fingers inched their way up her leg. She opened her eyes to find him watching her face as his hand reached the juncture of her thighs, cupping her through her underwear. Rubbing along her slit.

If she hadn't been tangled up with him, she would've flown off the table. She couldn't stop her gasping moan.

"God, that sound is so sexy."

His lips were back on hers the next second. She was going to say something but was distracted as his tongue slipped deeper.

Thrusting deep into her mouth. No matter her lack of

experience, there was no mistaking the actions his tongue was mimicking.

She needed to tell him she'd never done anything like this before. That she wasn't on birth control. That she had no idea what she was doing.

But God, she didn't want him to stop. Didn't want him to pull away as she told him, cutting off this heat between them.

Even worse, she didn't want him looking at her with pity because she was a twenty-three-year-old virgin. Not just a virgin, but someone with hardly any experience *at all.*

But it wasn't like he wasn't going to find out anyway.

"Gabriel . . ." She finally got the word out as his lips moved away from her mouth to kiss down her jaw again.

He groaned, the sound deep. "I know, Rainfall. We can't do this here. Believe it or not, I hadn't planned on this happening. So unless that six pack comes with a condom . . ."

She smiled even though the thought of stopping made her want to cry. "That would probably be a really good idea, wouldn't it?"

His eyes zoomed in on her teeth gnawing at her bottom lip. She shifted her hips restlessly, the need inside her almost a physical pain. His fingers trailing up and down her upper thigh were not helping.

"You okay, Rainfall?"

"Yeah. I don't know what's wrong with me." She smiled at him although it was pained.

"No?" Those green eyes studied her. "I think I do."

"What?"

She swallowed a protest as he slid his torso off hers. When she started to sit up, he put his hand on the middle of her chest and pushed her back down until she was lying flat on the table.

"What are you doing?"

"You stay right there." He sat up, moving his hand from her chest, fingers trailing over her nipples as he did so. He stood and gently repositioned her so her body was fully on the table, and her legs were resting on the bench.

"I'm still feeling a little hungry." His voice was deep, gritty, as he slid his fingers up the outside of her thighs, bringing her skirt up with them until it pooled at her hips.

Her breath sawed in and out of her chest. She could feel him looking at her *there*. "I-I don't think we have anything else to eat."

"Oh, I think I've found something."

Streaks of heat spiraled through her as Gabriel's fingers skimmed up her legs to her hips, gripping her underwear and pulling them gently down her legs.

Instinct had her trying to press her legs together, but he kissed her knees.

"Open for me, Rainfall. I've got to taste you."

Just what he'd said when he'd kissed her that first night on her porch. She'd opened for him then, and she opened for him now.

His lips worked their way up her thighs as he opened her legs wide and sat on the bench between them.

She should be embarrassed, laid out like she was on a picnic table. But his tortured "so damn gorgeous" reassured her. She relaxed, opening her eyes to look up at the darkening Wyoming sky, giving herself over to him.

"That's right, Rainfall. You just feel."

He slid a gentle hand under first one knee, then the other, hooking her legs over his wide shoulders. Before she could find anything else to be worried about, his lips were on her core. She nearly shot off the table—would have if he hadn't snaked one of his arms under her legs to pin her down with his big hand spread out on her navel—as he licked her from top to bottom.

"Oh my God, Gabriel!" Her scream was a whisper, no less intense because of the lack of volume, as his tongue kept a steady pressure against her.

When his fingers joined the onslaught, she couldn't breathe for the pleasure. Her back arched off the table as one rough finger moved inside her, thrusting in and out gently at first, then pumping harder as his thumb and tongue took turns teasing her clit.

He knew just what she needed, working her expertly until that knot of need grew and tightened unbearably.

And then finally burst.

Jordan's toes curled and her fingernails grabbed at the table beneath her as her body exploded. Gabriel continued to lap at her, stroking her as the orgasm tore through her body, until she finally lay exhausted and boneless, her legs limp around his shoulders.

She'd had no idea it could be like that. That *anything* could be like that.

When she finally had enough strength to lift her head, she glanced down at Gabriel, still trailing his fingers up and down her leg, dark head resting against her inner thigh.

He smiled up at her. "I'm never going to think of a picnic the same way again."

Chapter 7

Her blush at his words might be the sweetest thing Gabe had ever seen, but the words were nothing short of the truth. Her sprawled out on the picnic table in her sassy little skirt, face flushed from an orgasm, would play front and center in his dreams for a long time.

The temptation to make her come again just so he could hear those breathy little cries was almost more than he could resist.

He would've laughed a little at how dazed she looked if he wasn't afraid of overwhelming her. Because she very much looked like she was having a hard time comprehending what had just happened.

Hell, he was having a hard time comprehending what had just happened. But he planned on it happening again soon.

The taste of her, the smell of her, was damn near addicting.

Of course, none of the reasons he shouldn't be with her had changed. She was still too young, still worked for his sister, and still wore trouble like it was her coat of arms.

But as he sat up on the table and pulled her into his lap—her body still shuddering every once in a while—he knew he didn't care about any of those things.

She didn't say anything at all as he continued to hold her. That was fine. The fact that she was burrowed so deeply in his arms was enough for him.

It was only as it was truly getting dark that she finally began to move away.

She didn't look at him as she grabbed the trash bag. "I guess we need to head back before it gets too dark. I think I can find my way with no light, but it's been a long time since I've tried.

He stopped her hands from their frantic gathering and tilted a finger under her chin so he could see her face in the dimming light. She immediately flushed and looked away. "You okay?"

She looked everywhere but in his eyes. "Yeah." She laughed, but it was obviously stilted. "Why wouldn't I be okay?"

"You seem a little embarrassed."

"I just never knew it could be like that. And I guess I am a little embarrassed by my overexuberance. Plus, it couldn't have been much fun for you, since, you know . . ."

He picked her up by the waist and set her on the table. "First of all, if I have my head between your legs and you're not exuberant enough to scare away nearby animals, then I'm doing something very wrong."

That at least got a smile out of her.

"Second of all, driving you crazy might be my new favorite pastime. So don't go thinking I feel cheated, because I certainly don't."

"But—"

He tapped a finger on her lips. "No buts." He helped

her down off the table, and they began walking back toward her house. "We've got time."

"You mean like time later tonight?"

At least she sounded enthusiastic at the thought. But that wasn't what he wanted. He had an early morning meeting tomorrow about the systems breach inside Collingwood Technology. He couldn't miss that.

He didn't want to have sex with her and then need to leave immediately. When they slept together for first time, he wanted to be able to sleep next to her afterward. Hold her. Wake her up the next morning and hear those breathy little cries again. He didn't want it to be rushed.

He wanted to take her out on a date, take his time, show Jordan that she was worth taking time for.

The rest he would have to figure out as he went along. So he didn't answer her question about tonight.

She was quiet for most of the trek back to her house, and he realized he didn't know if that was usual or not for her. Was she normally chatty and quiet meant bad news, or the opposite? He basically knew nothing about this woman except for the fact that he wanted her with a ferocity that ate at him.

When they got to her house, he stopped at his car. She was on the front porch steps by the time she realized he wasn't right behind her anymore.

She turned to look at him. "Are you going to buy condoms? I'm sorry I don't have any here." She shifted uncomfortably. "And there's some . . . stuff we should probably talk about before we have sex."

"Why don't we save the talk for another night."

She flushed so deeply in the porch light, he was actually a little concerned for her. "No. We definitely need to have it before things go any further between us."

That didn't sound promising.

But it was one of the things they could talk about when they went out on their date. Although seeing her standing on the steps where he'd kissed her so many times was playing hell on his plan to take things slow.

He stepped away from the car and walked over so he could put his hands on her hips. She was three steps up, making her hips almost chest height.

"I want you to come in," she whispered. She grabbed his wrists and tried to take a step back, pulling him with her, but he wouldn't budge. "I want to say this and get it over with and then for you to have *your* turn. Or for both of us to have a turn together. Whatever."

He sighed. "Not tonight."

"Why not? Let's just get it over with."

He dropped his hands, eyebrows furrowing. "Just *get it over with*?"

She flushed more. "I meant the conversation. Not the sex part."

Gabe ran a hand through his hair. This wasn't going the way he'd wanted it to go. "Look, I have an early meeting tomorrow, and I don't want to have to leave your house in the middle of the night to make it back to Idaho Falls on time. So a raincheck on both the conversation and the sex, okay?"

"Oh. Okay." She didn't sound very sure of herself.

Probably because he was being a dumbass and handling this all wrong by not making it clear he would like nothing more than to go inside and have sex with her in every position and on every surface in the house.

He ran a hand through his hair. "I'm not saying good night because I don't want you. I do. But before we jump into bed, I want to take you out on a date first. How about that place Violet went tonight? New Brothers Pizza? Why don't we go there on Saturday? You can even wear your pretty skirt again if you want to. I promise to behave." At least for a little while.

He didn't know exactly what he was expecting, but all the color draining from her face and taking two steps backward wasn't it.

"No," she said, voice barely audible in the night air. "I don't want to."

"Another night then. Sunday?"

"No."

He ran a hand over the back of his neck and told himself to be patient. "I know you like their food. I saw a couple of carryout boxes from there in your kitchen last time I was here."

"I don't want to go." Her voice was so soft he almost couldn't hear her.

"Fine. There's like, what, five other restaurants in Oak Creek? If you don't want pizza, then just pick one."

If anything, she got even paler. She was gnawing on that bottom lip again and actually wringing her hands.

Did she not want to go out with him? Was that what was happening right now?

"Jordan, what's going on?"

"I can't go out with you."

"Can't or won't?"

She shook her head. "It's just not a good idea."

Was she seriously saying she wouldn't go out with him?

"My mouth between your legs seemed like a good idea thirty minutes ago. But you don't want to be seen in town with me?"

Now she crossed her arms over her chest. "Don't be crass, Collingwood. And it's not like that. It's not you. I just can't go out with you. Leave it at that."

"Why?"

Those slender shoulders stiffened. "It doesn't matter

why. I just don't want to, and for the first time in my adult life, I get to choose what I want to do. Now do you want to come inside, or should we stand out here yelling like kids?"

Anger lit through him, and he took a step away. He'd wanted to do things differently with her, show her she was worth treating with respect, and she'd just thrown that back in his face.

"What are you, Jordan? One of those women who only want to be with a guy if he treats her like crap? Maybe I should call Allan Godlewski and let him know you *are* actually available."

Her entire body froze. Hands that had been crossed over her chest in temper now gripped arms as if to hold in the hurt.

Fuck.

Fuck. Fuck. Fuck.

Why had he said that? Jesus. Jordan had every right to say no to going out with someone for whatever reason she wanted. He knew she had walls, had issues, had concerns.

"Jordan, I'm sorry—"

"Thanks for the picnic, Collingwood."

He was up the steps in two seconds, his hands gently closing around her arms. He didn't want to leave things like this. "Rainfall . . ." She flinched, but he continued. "I shouldn't have said that. I lost my temper—"

"No." Those gray eyes stared at him coldly in the light from the lone porch bulb.

"No, what?"

"Last time you were here you told me that if I didn't want you around, I could just say the word 'no' and you would back off. Was that the truth, Gabe?"

He mourned the loss of Gabriel from her lips. "Yes, it was the truth. But—"

"Then no."

He dropped his hands from her shoulders. He was a man of his word, even when he was an asshole.

She took a step back from him. “Don’t come back.”

She turned and walked inside the house. The door locked with a resounding click behind her.

Chapter 8

Jordan punched the security code that allowed her to enter the kitchen of Fancy Pants without setting off the alarm. Tears she refused to shed burned her eyes as she closed the door behind her.

It was the middle of the night, just after two a.m., hours earlier than she would normally show up for work. She shouldn't be here at all, but she didn't have anywhere else to go. And she couldn't stay at her house.

It was time to leave Oak Creek.

She leaned back against one of the counters, then covered her face with her hands and slid down it.

There was nothing left for her here. For the past two months, since the night she and Gabriel had fought so bitterly, she'd put every second she wasn't working at the bakery into *The Plan*. And it had been working. She'd spent hours at her computer, figuring out the details and developing the security systems she was going to build.

She'd thrown herself into it, using the skills and knowledge she'd gained from the web security and design classes she'd taken while in prison. She'd been limited to what she could actually do there—inmates weren't given tremendous access to the internet—but she'd been able to learn the basics of coding and had worked out in her mind, and in her notebook, the systems she would build. Doing it that way took a lot of time and trial and error, but time was something she'd had plenty of. By the time she'd been paroled, she'd had complete systems developed in her head.

All she'd needed to do was work them out on actual computer systems. She'd been making steady progress on the computer she'd bought. Once again, she'd had plenty of time, doing whatever it took to keep her mind off Gabriel.

He had apologized. He left that night when she'd asked but had returned a couple hours later to say once again that he was sorry. She'd opened the door to him and told him she accepted his apology.

But then shut the door in his face once more.

It had been the hardest thing she'd ever done, leaving him standing there when everything in her just wanted to pull him inside, into her life.

But she couldn't do that. He'd meant his apology sincerely. That wasn't the issue. But she couldn't date him, couldn't put him in the middle of this battle between her and the rest of Oak Creek.

Not because she didn't think he would fight for her, but because she knew he *would*. It was his nature. The Navy SEAL warrior in him.

Then flowers had shown up the next day, a beautiful bouquet of stargazer lilies. She'd never had anyone send her flowers. She'd stared at them for hours. But it didn't change the situation.

Nothing was going to change the situation.

So she'd ignored him, and by the time the last flower

had died, Gabriel had stopped trying to contact her to apologize.

And she had felt like the biggest bitch on the planet.

She'd done the only thing she could do to stay sane—work on her programming. It was going to take months, years probably, before she was able to build and grow it to the scale she needed it to be, but that wouldn't stop her from working on it every day until it was successful.

And once it was, it would be enough to get her what she wanted. *Needed.*

Six hundred twenty-two thousand dollars. *The Plan.*

Then maybe, oh God *maybe*, she could try to have a real relationship with Gabriel.

But who was she kidding? There was no way Gabriel was still going to be around, even if by some miracle he would ever be interested in her again after how she'd treated him. Maybe she was destined to only have the Allan Godlewskis in this world.

But she had to do this. *The Plan* was the only way she'd ever be able to truly be a part of this community again.

Or it had been.

She wrapped her arms around her knees, curling herself into a ball. Now it looked like even that option was gone.

Allan Godlewski and a bunch of his buddies had been back at her house tonight. Gabriel's warning had kept them away for a while, but evidently copious amounts of alcohol and time's ability to fade all things had provided them with enough courage to forget any warnings.

She'd been awoken by loud yells and laughter. A few minutes later, rocks had flown in not one window, but nearly every window she had in her house.

She's been trapped in her bed by a couple of rocks flying through her bedroom window, scattering glass all over her floor. By the time she had gotten to a pair of shoes, gotten dressed—because she definitely wasn't facing anybody in her nightshirt and pajama pants—and gotten to the shotgun by the front door, they'd been gone.

It had taken a while for her galloping pulse to settle. Honestly, at that moment, she'd just been glad that they had left, that the little mob hadn't decided to take any moves from the Allan playbook and offer to *scratch* her itches. They'd just run off into the woods. No permanent harm done.

Until she'd gone into her computer room.

Ironically, of all the rooms they'd targeted, this one had been the least vandalized. But one randomly thrown rock had hit her desk and destroyed the computer and, moreover, everything she'd poured her heart and soul into for the past two months.

All her work was gone.

The computer she needed to continue the work—or now, start over again—was gone.

She was basically right back to where she had started the day she'd been paroled. Alone and with nothing.

It was winter now, and although it had been mild so far, it was too cold to stay in a house with most of the windows broken. Jordan didn't want to waste money on a hotel, even if one in town would let her stay, so she'd come here to the bakery.

But this was just a stopgap. Something that would get her through today.

She couldn't fight the inevitable any longer. She would have to leave Oak Creek.

Starting over somewhere else would be hard with her record and now having to pay rent somewhere else. But what were her other options? She couldn't afford to get her house back to a livable standard. Wood over the windows wouldn't work all winter; it would be too cold to live there.

Plus, what was to stop them from coming back and doing it again? Or worse?

Jordan stayed on the ground for a long time before finally forcing herself to get up. She might as well do something rather than feel sorry for herself. Sitting on the floor wasn't accomplishing anything. She'd been wanting to reorganize the storage room to utilize the space more effectively.

Maybe it could be a sort of parting gift to Violet. Jordan and her boss had been almost on opposite paths over the past two months. Violet had been working—training like a beast—to become fierce. A warrior. Being kidnapped and held by human traffickers had left a scar on her psyche, but Violet refused to ever be anyone's victim again. She was fighting, growing stronger.

Jordan felt like she was drowning, growing weaker. And tonight had just sealed it.

She would miss Violet when she left. She wouldn't miss nearly biting off her tongue every day so she wouldn't ask how Gabriel was doing. But she would miss this place when she left.

She squared her shoulders, put on her headphones, and cranked up Jimi Hendrix, charging into the storage room to get started.

She hadn't been at it very long when she opened the storage room door to drag out some bags of flour and salt that needed to be used soon—and shrieked. Violet stood there in some sort of Jiu-Jitsu fighting stance.

She snatched her headphones out of her ears. "What are you doing here?"

Violet relaxed her stance. "I happen to own this business and live on the premises. What are *you* doing here?"

Shit. It had to look suspicious that she was in the bakery kitchen in the middle of the night. "I'm not stealing anything."

Violet rolled her eyes. "Jordan. It never crossed my mind that you would be stealing something."

She shrugged, then ran a hand over her eyes. "I just couldn't sleep, and my house . . ." She didn't want to drag Violet into this mess by explaining it all. "I just couldn't be there alone right now."

"Ugh. I don't want to be alone either."

"Why don't you call Aiden? He's got to be up for a booty call even if it's the middle of the night." And Jordan was only slightly massively jealous that her friend had someone like that she could call.

Violet leaned against the counter near the sink. "Unfortunately, my boyfriend thinks he knows what's best for me and that is for us to be apart for a while."

Jordan leaned on the counter next to her. "I don't have very good luck with guys, so I'm probably not the one to give you advice."

Violet nodded and slipped an arm around her shoulder. The friendly gesture felt nice. Nobody had hugged her since Gabriel. She could feel the tears welling up again.

"I had an idea for a *gougère* pastry the other night," Violet said. "Want to try to make it now? We'll both be exhausted tomorrow together."

"Anything is better than facing my house alone." But God, she was still going to have to figure out what to do about it. Maybe the light of day tomorrow would help it seem less overwhelming. She hoped so.

She turned to Violet. "Let's do it."

Chapter 9

Jordan sampled their latest effort—was it variation three or four? After an hour of measuring, mixing, and tasting, they all blurred together—and none of them were quite right. Probably working on it in the middle of the night wasn't the best idea. They'd finally left the new recipe behind and gone into the large walk-in cooler to get the supplies they needed for the day's regular offerings when heat and a terrible noise exploded in the kitchen behind them.

"What the hell?" Violet screamed as they both ran back out of the cooler.

The entire kitchen was on fire.

"What happened? Did the oven catch fire?" Jordan could barely hear herself over the roar.

"I think something burning flew through the window." Violet pointed over at the window by the door, where a breeze was now coming through, fanning the flames higher.

"Where's the fire extinguisher?" Jordan yelled.

The smoke was getting thick, rapidly. They both pulled their shirts over their faces to try to help them breathe.

"It's by the back door," Violet said. They looked at each other. There was no way they could get to the fire extinguisher through the flames.

"There's one out front, too, right?" Jordan ran for the door leading to the front of the house—but was knocked back almost onto her ass when she pushed on the door.

What the hell?

"What the hell?" Violet echoed her thoughts, rushing over to help push on the door. This door couldn't be locked; there wasn't a lock on it. Something was blocking it. They both pushed on it together but whatever was holding it wouldn't budge.

They were trapped in the kitchen, and it was on fire.

Oh God, had Allan and his friends followed her here and done this? This went way beyond throwing rocks through a window. Fire was engulfing the whole back wall now. They were going to be lucky to get out of this with their lives.

"Call 911, and let's get in the cooler," Violet yelled. "We should be able to keep the smoke out until the fire department arrives."

"If we do that, the bakery will burn." She couldn't stand the thought of her friend losing the shop that meant so much to her. But the flames were getting higher. This was her fault, damn it. She needed to fix it. "I can still get to the fire extinguisher by the door."

Violet grabbed her arm. "No. Those flames are too high. It's not worth you getting hurt."

"Yeah, well my phone was hanging by the door." She could see her jacket burning on the hook, where her phone was in the pocket. It was probably a melted pile of goo by now. "Where's yours?"

Violet shook her head, and Jordan knew the other woman had left her phone upstairs in her apartment.

There was no getting to it. The fire extinguisher was the only option.

"We have to go for the extinguisher," Jordan said.

Violet began gathering dry materials—baking powder, salt—stuff they could throw on the fire. Using water might make the fire worse.

"You throw it," she yelled. "I'll run through the flames."

There was no way in hell. Jordan shook her head. "Sorry, boss, but even with your workouts, I'm taller and can jump higher. It will be easier for me to get over the flames and grab the fire extinguisher."

She could tell Violet didn't like it, but she gave a brief nod. They were out of options and Jordan had the better chance of making it. The smoke was getting higher, the heat more oppressive.

Violet had her supplies ready to throw. Jordan tried to figure out if she could actually clear the flames that were climbing higher every second. Oh God, she hoped so.

"On three," Violet yelled. "Jump high.. One… two… three!"

Flour and salt flew everywhere as Jordan leapt as high as she could. She felt the heat from the flames on her legs, but it wasn't burning her.

She rushed to the extinguisher.

"I got it!" Jordan yelled. She couldn't stop her cry of pain as the extinguisher's metal burned her hands. But she held on. If she didn't, she and Violet were going to die.

She sprayed, tears streaming down her face from the searing burn on her hands as Violet continued to pour the last of the flour over the flames.

They got it under enough control to be able to run out the back door. She was grateful when Violet took the extinguisher from her and continued using it on the fire. “Go get help.”

Did Violet know what she was asking? Jordan had always said if she was on fire, the town of Oak Creek would go inside and make a sandwich. She hoped she wasn’t about to prove that true.

But she ran toward The Mayor’s Inn anyway. Her hands were burned, so she couldn’t keep using the fire extinguisher. Maybe Violet could and possibly save the bakery.

When she rushed inside, she found some college-aged kid she didn’t recognize working the desk.

“I need your fire extinguisher. And call 911. The bakery is on fire.” Her voice sounded hoarse and brittle. Her breathing didn’t hurt—probably a good sign—but her hands were killing her.

The kid jumped up, and after a shocked second, he grabbed the fire extinguisher from under the counter and thrust it at her. She had to cradle it in her arms to carry it. The kid was already on the phone when she ran back out.

Jordan ran back to the bakery and handed the extinguisher to Violet. “That’s from The Mayor’s Inn. They’re calling the fire department now.”

She watched, gritting her teeth against the pain, as Violet used the extinguisher to further fight the flames. Within a few moments, the bakery was surrounded by people who’d heard the ruckus, bringing extinguishers of their own and shooing Violet out of the way. Soon the fire trucks arrived, moving everyone back.

Jordan kept silent about her blistered hands as Violet came to stand beside her and they watched the firefighters work. The other woman had enough on her mind without worrying about Jordan. Once the fire was under control, the fire chief insisted both women get looked at over at the hospital.

Jordan was exhausted and almost whimpering by the time they were escorted into the examination room. Violet, on the other hand, looked like she was ready to go door to door to figure out who had set fire to her beloved bakery.

Jordan didn't have the heart to tell her it was probably not someone trying to hurt Fancy Pants at all. It had been someone trying to hurt Jordan.

Violet had just had the bad luck to hire her.

Two nurses escorted them down a long hall. One kept glaring at Jordan every few seconds while typing something on her phone when the older nurse wasn't looking.

They stopped in front of a door and the older nurse opened it. "Ms. Collingwood, if you'll come in here with me, Nurse Estes will take Ms. Reiss to a separate room."

Violet nodded, then pulled Jordan in for a hug. "Are you okay?" she asked.

Jordan was careful not to touch Violet with her palms or fingers. "Yeah. I'll be fine."

She didn't want to mention that she didn't know how she was going to pay for this. The minimal insurance she had wouldn't cover much. She just wanted to go home, but now she didn't even have that.

Nurse Estes continued to glare as she pulled away from Violet, which didn't help her feelings of unease. Obviously, she was just letting things overwhelm her because of exhaustion and pain. But when the woman texted someone again without apology or explanation—just making Jordan wait awkwardly there in the hall—and looked back up, her eyes were icy.

"This way." The woman tilted her head toward a smaller hallway and crossed her arms over her chest.

Jordan followed along beside her as they turned down

another hall farther from the emergency section. "Look, maybe I should just go home," she said. "I'm sure I'll be okay."

Although she didn't have a home to go to and definitely couldn't drive with her hands in this shape.

Nurse Estes raised an eyebrow. "We have a room for you. Things are a little hectic in the hospital today, but you'll be fine here."

Hectic? Things hadn't looked busy when they'd come through a few minutes ago. A lot of hospital staff had been standing around talking.

"Oh, okay." Jordan knew she sounded skeptical, but hell, she *was* skeptical.

"My dad turns seventy next month," Nurse Estes said.

What did that have to do with her? "Oh, happy birthday."

"It probably won't be much of a birthday because he has to work full-time. He was supposed to retire years ago but couldn't."

Jordan's stomach cramped. She knew what was coming next. She'd heard too many versions of the same statements.

"Your father stole my parents' retirement money. My father will be working for years now rather than retiring. You have a lot of nerve even showing your face in this town, much less *living* here."

There was nothing Jordan could say that would make this right. But she had to try. "I'm sorry for—"

Nurse Estes cut her off, opening the door. Both of them stepped inside. "I'm sure you are. Here's your room. Someone will be back to see you as soon as we can get to it."

Before Jordan could say another word, the door shut with a resounding click and Nurse Estes was gone.

She looked around. The room was tiny and filled with boxes. It had been an examination room at one time, based on the table, counter and small sink. But it obviously wasn't used that way regularly.

The only place she could sit at all was in a hard plastic chair along the far wall. With the state of her hands, she couldn't move the boxes to sit or lie on the examination table.

She couldn't grasp the doorknob to open the door and get out.

Jordan sat, staring at the blisters that had formed on her palms and fingers, and waited.

And waited.

Chapter 10

Gabe was ready to rip someone's head off.

Of course, anyone who'd been around him for the past two months, since the night he'd made such an ass of himself with Jordan, would say that ripping people's heads off had just become his ops normal.

Getting the call that Violet's bakery had caught on fire, and that she'd been *inside* when it had happened, had not helped his temper.

Listening to Edward Appleton, family friend and vice president of Collingwood Technology, talk about how he hoped this fire would help bring Violet back to the company all the way from Idaho Falls to Oak Creek had not helped his temper.

And now sitting in his sister's hospital room, arm around her, listening to Sheriff Nelson explain that this hadn't been some kitchen fire at all but someone trying to hurt *Jordan*?

There wasn't enough temper in the world for him to lose.

Not a day had gone by for the past two months that he

hadn't thought about her. That he hadn't wanted to kick his own ass for what he'd said to her.

He didn't blame her at all for refusing to speak to him after that.

And now someone had thrown a damn *bottle bomb* into the bakery and could've killed both Jordan and Violet? Jordan had had to leap over goddamn flames in order to put the fire out?

He couldn't even wrap his head around it.

Someone setting a building on fire went way beyond righteous anger over money Jordan's father stole a decade ago. And not just on fire, but, according to the sheriff, dousing the place with accelerants to make sure the flames would destroy everything and blocking the door so no one could get out.

Hell. No.

Gabe was not going to sit back any longer. And not just because this was now affecting his sister.

Somebody needed to help Jordan.

She may not be willing to give him another chance, but he could still help her from afar, be that guardian angel she'd once mistaken him for. Maybe make up for some of his own asinine behavior while he was at it.

When the sheriff excused himself to go see Jordan—and Violet invited herself along—Gabe knew he wasn't going to miss the opportunity to make sure Jordan was okay with his own eyes. She might tell him to go to hell, but that wasn't any more than he deserved.

"I'm coming too," he told Sheriff Nelson and Violet. "If there's trouble, I want to know about it. And that woman is the epitome of trouble."

Especially for him.

* * *

Sheriff Nelson came back with his brows furrowed to lead them to Jordan's room. Evidently there had been some difficulty locating her in the hospital.

The second he entered the room, Gabe understood why. The place they'd put Jordan was a fucking *supply closet.* It had been an examining room at one time but obviously hadn't been used for that purpose in a while.

Jordan sat on a hard plastic chair, quietly crying.

Somewhere deep in his chest, Gabe's heart cracked.

As soon as she saw them, she tried to pull it together. Violet rushed over to her, but Gabe just stood in the doorway, caught in helpless fury.

As Violet crouched down next to her, Jordan tried to wipe her face on her shoulder awkwardly rather than use her hands. The fury grew inside him as he realized what was happening.

Her hands were burned. He couldn't see them, but he could tell just by how she was holding them loosely, making sure they didn't touch anything else.

They were burned so badly she couldn't even blow her own nose. She was trying to wipe her eyes and face on her own shoulder.

Gabe was going to kick someone's ass for this. But first, he was going to make sure Jordan was okay.

He grabbed some tissues from a box lying haphazardly on top of a stack of supplies and walked over to her. Leaning down, he tipped a finger under her chin, wiping her cheeks gently with the tissue, dirt and flour coming off with the wetness.

Those gray eyes looked at him with such heartbreaking thankfulness that he felt like his chest was being ripped open. He crouched down in front of her and held another tissue over her nose.

"Blow," he said gently. She did.

Violet just looked confused.

"Her hands are burnt." He explained to his sister what she hadn't noticed. "She can't do it herself."

He wanted to trail his fingers down Jordan's cheeks. Wanted to kiss her. Wanted to go into this goddamn town and slay every single person who'd ever been cruel to her. Wanted to sweep her up in his arms and carry her away from here forever.

But he couldn't do any of those things. He'd given up the right with his stupid words about Allan Godlewski two months ago, so he just wiped her face again, overjoyed when she didn't pull away. Instead, she rested her face against his hand.

Gabe's eyes narrowed as he studied Jordan more closely. Her face was pale, her lips pursed and bracketed, her body stiff. Why? Violet had already been at the hospital nearly three hours, that meant Jordan must've been here that long also. More than enough time for them to have gotten her pain under control.

Looking into Jordan's eyes from his crouched position, he reached for her wrists and gently turned them over so he could see the extent of her burns.

He heard his sister's sharp intake of breath and the sheriff whistle through his teeth as they saw her wounds. There was no hospital anywhere in the entire country that wouldn't have already treated these burns and had them wrapped to avoid infection.

Instead, this town had put Jordan in a fucking *closet.*

"Oh my God!" Violet crouched down next to him. "You burned yourself when you picked up the fire extinguisher, didn't you?"

Jordan nodded. "I'm sorry." Her tears were threatening to fall again. "It just hurts more than I thought it would, and I can't drive, and I'm not sure what to do."

Violet looked over at him, agony for Jordan's pain radiating in his sister's eyes. She rubbed Jordan's shoulder. "I'm sure the pain medicine the doctors gave you will kick in soon. Or maybe they need to give you something stronger if it's still hurting you this badly."

"No, I just want to go home." Jordan's words were barely a whisper.

"They haven't given you anything at all, have they?" Gabe hoped he was wrong. Prayed he was wrong.

Those big gray eyes stood out starkly in cheeks that were too pale. "I—I . . ."

He wasn't wrong.

He stood and tucked a strand of Jordan's hair behind her ear, burying his fury. That wasn't what Jordan needed. "You hang in there a few more minutes. I'm going to handle this for you."

Confusion battled relief in her eyes, breaking his heart further. When had this woman ever had someone to fight a battle for her? He wanted to kiss her so badly he could taste it. But he wanted to tend to her needs even more.

Sheriff Nelson gave Gabe a nod of approval as he walked out the door and straight down to the nurse's station.

He was well aware of how to use his height to his full advantage when the situation called for it.

The situation damn well called for it now.

The two women there looked at him very attentively. Smiling.

"I want to know who's responsible for Jordan Reiss."

They both stiffened and looked away, saying nothing.

He stepped up to the counter and leaned over it, completely into their personal space. "You're going to tell me what the hell is going on with her, right damn now.

Why was she put in that closet, and why hasn't she been seen yet at all despite her wounds?"

One nurse shot the other one a sly grin. "I don't know what you're talking about."

Gabe turned away, refusing to spend another second on them. These women were petty and spiteful. He would make sure they got what was coming, but right now he needed to find someone to help Jordan. She was what mattered most.

"Who's the doctor in charge here?"

"That would be me, Mr. Collingwood. How can I help you?"

Gabe spun to find Anne Griffin standing behind him. Shit. Maybe this explained part of the problem. He'd always liked her. She'd been one of the first people to reach out to Violet and help her through the aftermath of her abduction.

That didn't mean he was going to let Jordan's treatment in this hospital stand.

"You're Zac Mackay's woman."

She raised an eyebrow. "You're Violet Collingwood's brother."

"Are you the one purposely blocking Jordan Reiss from getting the treatment she needs? Is it because of what happened to Zac's family?"

One of the nurses actually snickered. Until Dr. Griffin turned and glared at them.

"I would never stop *anyone* from getting treatment in my hospital, regardless of what they'd done." She was obviously offended at the suggestion. "I took the Hippocratic oath to ensure that."

"Then do you want to explain to me why Jordan is in a room barely bigger than a fucking closet right now? And has been here for three hours with second-degree burns and hasn't been treated?"

Silence fell over the entire emergency room at Gabe's roar. He didn't care. He was just getting started.

Anne stiffened, and he expected an argument or excuses out of her. Instead, she let out a blistering curse that would've made his Navy SEAL brothers proud. She jabbed a finger at the nurse who had snickered.

"Get a wheelchair. If what I think has happened is the case, both of you will be lucky to have a job by the end of the day." She turned to him. "Take me to Jordan."

Chapter 11

Forty-five minutes later, Gabe finally felt like he could breathe again when Jordan's beautiful gray eyes found his and her mouth curved into the tiniest smile.

The hellfire Anne had rained down on the nurses responsible for ignoring Jordan would've had his SEAL comrades reaching for the bell to ring out immediately. Hell, the entire town had probably heard Anne's righteous indignation. Good. They needed a wake-up call.

Jordan was at least now lying in a bed—a *real* hospital bed—attached to an IV. Color was returning to her cheeks, and she'd actually smiled at something Violet said a couple minutes ago.

Gabe stood guard at the door, like he had been for the past forty-five minutes, ready to take down anyone who dared make even one disparaging remark in Jordan's direction. He'd been ready to pounce every time she'd winced over the pain in her hands as they'd been cleaned. The fact that Anne had done the work herself had been the only thing that had kept him from literally growling.

The kindness, professionalism, and respect the doctor

had shown Jordan had restored a little of his faith in this town. But not much.

Anne moved to the door after talking to Violet for a minute. "Again, I'm so sorry, Jordan. How you were treated was completely unprofessional. If you'd like to write up a formal complaint with the state, I would understand."

"No," Jordan said softly. "I'll be fine. I just want to go . . . I just want to get out of here."

"There's no reason for you to stay overnight. I'll give you a prescription for pain medication and an antibiotic ointment. But you're going to need someone to drive you. You won't be able to drive with your hands in this state."

Jordan looked panicked for just a moment, like she was going to try to argue that she could do it herself.

"I'll get her home safely," he said without looking at Jordan. There was no way he was going to be able to let someone else do it. "I've set up triage care for burns before when I was in the military. I'll make sure she has everything she needs and is able to access it before I leave."

Anne nodded and he turned to look at Jordan, waiting to see if she would argue. "Okay, um, thank you."

Her voice was still too quiet. Too traumatized. But at least she'd agreed.

He didn't even try to hide the relief he felt that she hadn't turned him down. Maybe she'd forgiven him for what he'd said or maybe she just really needed someone to lean on.

How long had it been since she'd had someone like that? The intensity with which he wanted to be that someone for her caught him off guard, but he'd learned not to fight his instincts.

She needed a guardian angel. He could be that. Her Gabriel.

The knot that had become such a part of him over the

past two months eased. He wasn't letting Jordan out of his sight. He would take care of her and make sure no one hurt her again.

Of course, his sister was staring at him like he'd grown two heads. He couldn't blame her, given the fact that she had no idea anything had happened between him and Jordan. Obviously, Jordan had kept his asshole-ish behavior to herself.

Not surprising. He was learning Jordan kept everything to herself.

He was a little relieved when Aiden Teague entered the hospital room a few minutes later, and Violet all but threw herself at him.

Gabe didn't even kill the other man for sucking Violet's face off since, one, his sister was positively beaming at him, and two, he took Violet away before she could start asking questions about Gabe and Jordan.

Gabe ignored the fact that Aiden and Violet looked like they were going to tear each other's clothes off the second they made it home. Violet may be an adult, a strong, smart, and capable one, but she was also the baby sister he'd helped raise. Some things Gabe just did not need to see.

But he had to admit, Violet had developed such an inner core of strength over the past two months, Gabe wasn't sure his sister needed anyone to protect her. She could protect herself.

He looked over at Jordan lying against the propped-up hospital bed with her eyes closed and realized how much things had changed. Two months ago, he'd thought Violet needed protection and Jordan could look out for herself. Now the opposite was true.

He moved closer to the bed until he was standing right next to her. The urge to stroke the side of her face was strong, but he resisted, not wanting to wake her up if she was sleeping.

But those gray eyes opened a moment later.

"Hi," she whispered.

Now he didn't even try to stop himself from touching her. He stroked her cheek. "Hi, yourself."

"Thank you. I—"

He moved his fingers till they were covering her lips. "No need to thank me. Just rest for right now."

"I know you're busy," she said. "You don't really have to give me a ride. I can call an Uber or something."

"What about once you get home?" he asked, one eyebrow raised. "You're going to need help. You're not going to be able to cook for yourself, or even open a door. I can at least get things set up for you at your house."

The skin across her cheekbones was drawn tight, her eyes darting around the room. "It's just . . . I know you don't really want to be around me. I don't want you to feel like you have to."

His face was only inches from her own. "Why would you think I didn't want be around you?"

She shrugged. "After the last time . . ."

"Last time I acted like the biggest asshole on the planet."

Now those gray eyes flew to his. "But you said you were sorry, even sent me those flowers, and I still didn't talk to you. I figured you'd pretty much written me off. I don't really blame you."

Gabe stared at her for a long minute. He'd made a tactical error with her, not something he was used to doing. Yes, he had apologized and sent her flowers. When she'd refused to talk to him, he'd thought it was because what he'd said had been totally unforgivable.

Bile pooled in Gabe's gut as understanding clicked in his mind.

Jordan *believed* all this stuff about herself. Believed the town had a right to hate her. Believed it was only someone like Allan Godlewski who would really want her. What Gabe said two months ago had just reconfirmed that in her mind. What had happened here today had just reconfirmed that.

And it was bullshit.

She was quiet and stoic. She tried to not draw attention to herself in any way. That was how she lived her life here, just staying in the background. She acted like she didn't care or notice how people treated her, but she really did.

After what he'd said, he should not have left her alone. But she'd been very clear. Forcing himself to respect her wishes made Hell Week seem like a tropical vacation. He'd wanted nothing more than to keep pursuing her. Keep apologizing. Keep letting her know he couldn't get her out of his mind, and she was beautiful.

He kissed her forehead. "I never wrote you off. I just figured you had the right to stay angry with me after what I said. But no more arguing right now. Just rest and let the meds soak in." Her eyes were already drooping. "Sleep. When they release you, I'll take you home and make sure it's set up so you can manage."

And by that he meant he'd be staying there with her for the next few days. He had a business to run, but he'd do it remotely for a while.

"There's something we need to talk about . . ." Her words were a little slurred.

She'd said something similar last time, but he'd ignored her, blindly assuming he knew what was best. He wouldn't make that same mistake again.

He brushed a piece of her soft brown hair off her for

head, and touched her cheek smudged with flour and smoke. "We will. Whatever it is, we will. But for right now just go to sleep. I'll be right here when you wake up."

Confusion, doubt, and hope battled in those gray eyes before they slid closed.

Chapter 12

Jordan had never been on a roller coaster. She'd never really desired to go on one, but she imagined the experience would be similar to what she was feeling now. Unpredictable, exciting, scary, out of control, thrilling, and a little bit painful.

All these feelings at once were a lot. And utterly overwhelming.

She wasn't exactly sure what had happened at the hospital. One minute she'd been trapped inside that little closet of her room in so much pain, the next Gabriel had swooped in.

And the next . . . honestly, a lot of it was a blur. All she'd known was that when Gabriel had crouched beside her and wiped her nose with that tissue, she'd believed him when he said he was going to handle it.

And he had, because now she was sitting here in her truck that he'd gotten from Fancy Pants. He was walking around to the driver's side. She'd gotten out of the hospital with no mention of payments and no questions about minimal insurance. She would fight that battle when the bill came. Right now, she had other things to worry about.

Like the fact that she couldn't go back to her house because of the damage that had been done. Explaining this to Gabriel wasn't going to be easy. Maybe she shouldn't try at all.

"Thank you again for all your help," she said as he got in the truck.

"I'm sorry my help is necessary at all, but you're more than welcome."

His easy smile—one she thought she'd never see again—sent her over another steep hill on her emotional roller coaster.

"I hope it's okay," he continued, "I had them fill your prescriptions at the hospital to make sure there was no delay."

He cranked the truck, which, once again, started with no problem since he was the one behind the wheel. *Bitch.*

Jordan nodded. "Yes, that's perfect. Annie said I should try to keep ahead of the pain, to take them as directed, not to wait for it to start hurting too badly. She said it will hurt to touch anything for a couple of days but then should be more generalized." She was rambling, but she couldn't seem to stop herself. "Actually, I was thinking maybe I would just stay in town at a hotel. Just survive off junk food for a few days during the worst of it with my hands."

But, crap. What if they wouldn't rent her room at The Mayor's Inn?

"Or," she continued quickly before he could make a comment, "maybe I'll get a room outside of town. Just call it a mini vacation. Veg out in front of the TV."

A vacation she couldn't afford, especially given the damage to her house and computer system, not to mention the fact that her place of employment had just caught on fire. She didn't know when the bakery would open again, if ever.

Her heart sank as he turned the truck off.

"I'm going to ask you something, and I want you to be honest." He shifted his body so he was facing her.

She nodded slowly.

"I would like to come to your house for the next few days and help take care of you. Not just because you need help—and you do need help, Rainfall—but because I would like to spend time with you. Trust me when I say not a day has gone by in the past two months that I haven't wanted to see you."

"Oh."

"But if you're not comfortable with me being around you and helping you in some pretty intimate ways, then I would be more than happy to hire a nurse to come stay at your house until you can get by on your own."

She was touched at the thought. It was more than anyone had ever done for her. "Oh," she said again. "Thank you."

"I'd like to take care of you, but I'll understand if you want a nurse." Her breath blew silently out of her mouth as he reached over and cupped her cheek. "But nurse or not, you're not getting rid of me easily again, Rainfall."

"I-I'm not?"

That smile of his sucked the rest of the oxygen out of her lungs. "No, you're not."

She didn't really want a home healthcare professional. Particularly since she didn't have a functioning home to bring someone to anyway.

She needed help.

She'd never been good at asking for help, mostly

because she'd always known there was no one she could count on help from. Could she count on Gabriel?

She hoped so. She was about to find out.

"I don't mind you helping me."

"Good. Then I'm coming home with you. And if you want to veg out, you can do it in the comfort of your own home."

She flinched. "I can't go to my house. There are some repairs that need to be done."

He processed that for a moment before his eyes narrowed. "What sort of repairs?"

She didn't want to tell him. She couldn't seem to force the words out.

His thumb trailed across her cheek again. "The same kind of repairs I helped you with last time?"

She looked away from him but nodded. He let out a blistering curse under his breath.

"When did it happen?"

She shrugged. "Late last night. That was why I was at the bakery in the middle of the night to start with."

He turned back and gripped the steering wheel so hard his knuckles turned white. "How many windows?"

His fury was almost a tangible thing, but it didn't scare her because she knew it wasn't directed at her. It was directed *for* her.

"I don't know. Most of them, I think. I couldn't stay there."

Gabriel started the truck again. He didn't say anything besides asking her to stay in the car while he stopped at the local hardware store. He was in there for a long time, and she expected him to come out with plywood to cover the broken windows at her house. But when he came out, his hands were empty.

He didn't say anything, just gave her a smile and drove them to their next stop, the Oak Creek grocery store. This time after he parked, he held the door open and helped her out of the truck.

"I don't usually shop here." She wanted to drag her feet when he gripped her elbow gently to escort her inside. This was one of the places that had been hit hardest by her father's theft. The last time she'd tried to shop here, when she'd first gotten back home, they'd told her to stay away.

He stopped and looked down at her. "If you tell me the food here is poor quality and you prefer to go somewhere else, I will be happy to take you wherever you would like to shop." He raised an eyebrow. "But if you don't shop here because the owner has some beef with your dad, and you're trying to make them feel more comfortable, well, to hell with that."

"But . . ."

He kissed her on the top of the head. "No. Thanks to some of the people in this town, you're in a lot more pain and a lot more tired than you should be. Thanks to some of the people of this town, we've still got a lot of work to do to repair the house they damaged. So the people of this town can damn well sell you a few basic products without it harming their delicate sensibilities."

He didn't understand. Gabriel couldn't possibly understand. He wasn't from Oak Creek, hadn't lost all his money, didn't know what it was like.

But she let him escort her inside because what he was saying was also correct.

They did their shopping, and the world didn't end. A few people stared, but nobody said anything. When they got to the front to check out, the cashier, someone Jordan didn't recognize but who obviously recognized her, pressed her lips together in mutiny.

Jordan knew what was coming. It was the very reason she'd refused to go out with Gabriel in the first place, because she wanted to avoid something like this.

But before the scene could even get started, Gabriel's arm wrapped around her waist and slid her until she was standing behind him, placing himself between her and the cashier.

"How much for my groceries?" Gabriel said.

Something about him—His deep voice? His air of authority? The fact that he roughly resembled Thor?—made the cashier forget whatever argument she'd been planning and begin scanning the groceries. Gabriel paid, grabbed the bags, and they were back out the door without incident.

Jordan was afraid he was going to want to talk about it. But he didn't. Instead, as soon as he helped her back into the truck, he started arguing about the lack of radio station choices in this area.

It was an absurd conversation.

And perfectly normal.

She tucked her feet under her legs and turned to the side so she could study him while he drove.

"I don't do country music," he said. "Give me rock any day."

"I like Tim McGraw and Sam Hunt. But mostly I like classic rock. Like real classic rock, not eighties hair bands like you probably listen to."

"You're wounding me, Rainfall. Mötley Crüe? Def Leppard? Twisted Sister? Those are some great bands."

"Twisted Sister?" She couldn't hold back her giggle.

He laughed out loud. "I will definitely concede that they were the bottom of the eighties hair band pool. When you say 'classic rock,' what are you talking about?"

"Stones. Pink Floyd. But mostly I love Jimi Hendrix."

He reached over and ran a finger down her arm. “Then I think you and I are going to do just fine.”

Chapter 13

Anger boiled to the surface as Gabe surveyed the damage. Using all his military training, he managed to tamp it down. Barely. Those assholes had really done a number on it this time. She hadn't been kidding when she said nearly every window was broken.

The first thing he did was take her in and get some food into her. He liked the feeling of feeding her from his hand way too much, since she couldn't do it herself, and then he made her take her pain medication. She hadn't said she was in pain, but he hadn't missed the way her jaw had started to tighten as they got closer to her house.

Or maybe it was seeing all the damage in the daylight that made her tense. There was no way she could've repaired this by herself, even if she wasn't injured.

Gabe wasn't going to repair it by himself either. Jordan had friends in this town, and it was time she started accepting that. It had only taken one call to get more than enough people here to have these windows replaced by nightfall. He'd made that call while he was at the hardware store. With the number of prefab windows the store had in stock, all Gabe needed was the measurements from Jordan's house. He'd prepaid for the windows and told the manager to be expecting a call and someone to pick them up.

The weather might have been mild for the past few weeks, but it was winter in Wyoming, and mild could change to ugly overnight. Not a time you could stay in a house with most of the windows knocked out.

He wrapped her in a blanket and set her on the couch. Her drugs had kicked in, and she was drowsy, but she still resisted.

"I have to help you with the windows," she said despite the big yawn she couldn't stop.

He raised an eyebrow. "And just how do you expect to do that, gimpy? You can't do much with those bandages."

She scrunched up her features in an adorable pout that made him want to kiss the hell out of her. "Well, you're not going to be able to get the plywood over the windows by yourself. I don't have enough wood anyway."

He heard the sound of multiple vehicles pulling up the driveway and kissed her on the top of her head. "I'm not going to be fixing the windows alone or using plywood."

"You hired people?"

"No. I called my friends. Actually, I called *your* friends. They were happy to help out."

The look on her face would've been comedic if it wasn't so heartbreaking. "My friends?" she asked slowly.

He just smiled at her.

"Jesus, Jordan," Charlie yelled from the front door as she stormed her way in. "What did you do, have batting practice in here?"

The petite blond gave Gabe a nod and a small smile from behind Jordan's back and mouthed *thank you*. Gabe knew the two women had been roommates for a few weeks before Charlie had moved in with her fiancé Finn.

"Charlie?" Jordan tried to get up from her perch on the couch, but she got tangled up in her blanket. Charlie came around and sat by her.

"Don't get up. I've got huge news to tell you."

"About the wedding?"

"About the fact that the wedding isn't going to be a moment too soon. Guess who's having a baby!"

Jordan sat straight up on the couch, staring at Charlie's completely flat belly. "You're pregnant?"

"Yep! Just took the test—okay, *three* tests—today." Charlie moved around and sat on the couch, dragging Jordan in for a hug.

"I'm so excited for you," Jordan whispered, a huge smile on her face.

"Let's just sit here on the couch, and I'll tell you all the latest about the wedding, and we can let the guys go to work. Although you might have to share your blanket with me. It's cold in here."

"Is Finn here too?" Jordan asked. "Is he going to help Gabriel board up the windows?"

Gabe watched as Charlie tucked a strand of Jordan's hair behind her ear. "Finn. Zac. Dorian. Gavin. The whole gang. So you sit here with me and let them work for a change." She made a shooing motion with her hand toward Gabe and started talking about wedding dress fittings. He smiled as he walked out. Jordan didn't have a chance against Charlie and her overwhelming personality.

Outside the guys were unloading the windows Gabe had bought.

"Thank you for picking them up." He shook Zac's hand, then the other men's.

"Not a problem," Zac said. "What the hell happened?"

They carried the replacement panes to the six windows that needed swapping. The process wasn't terribly hard, but it took two people.

"Evidently this isn't a new occurrence." Gabe and Zac carried the window around the side of the house. "A couple of months ago, she had a window broken, and some guy named Allan Godlewski was here harassing her."

Finn and Zac both cursed. "I know that asshole," Finn said. "Lives in Reddington City. Why the hell was he here?"

"He's buddies with Adam DiMuzio, isn't he?" Zac asked. When Finn nodded Zac turned to Gabe. "The DiMuzios own the pizza place in town. Mr. DiMuzio has been one of the biggest pot stirrers when it comes to Jordan. Every time it seems like it's going to die down, he'll remind people about the past."

Zac helped Gabe clear out one of the broken panes so they could replace it with a new one. "In Mr. DiMuzio's defense, his family was one of the ones Michael Reiss hit hardest. Plus, he and his wife were good friends with Carol Peverill, my late-mother-in-law. When Becky and Micah died, they took it hard."

"Enough to condone something like this?" Finn asked from the next window he was working on with Gavin.

Zac shrugged. "I wouldn't have thought so."

Gabe helped Zac secure the new pane into the frame. "Jordan said the windows were broken in rapid succession last night, and the people who did it were drunk and loud. So it wasn't Godlewski acting alone. We know that much for sure."

Gavin shook his head. "Jordan is so isolated out here."

Finn slammed his palm against the wall. "But that shouldn't make any difference. It's one thing not to like the

Reiss family. It's one thing to ignore Jordan when she comes into town or even refuse to serve her in your place of business—although that's crappy enough—but to deliberately do this to her house? To deliberately not give her the care she needed at the hospital today? That shit has got to stop. Charlie just about blew a gasket when she heard."

Zac nodded and continued to work on the window. "I'll talk to Godlewski myself. That should at least stop the window breaking."

Gabe nodded, then noticed Dorian was standing at the trucks, looking out into the woods. "He okay?"

Gabe had worked with the men at Linear Tactical to get Violet away from her kidnappers a few months ago. The team—Dorian included—made no secret of the fact that Dorian had been captured by enemy combatants and tortured for weeks during his time in the Army Special Forces.

The man still struggled. Being around people was difficult for him. He was much more comfortable roaming in the wilderness and often headed out there for days or even weeks at a time.

Gabe didn't know the man well enough to know if him staring out into the trees was the sign of some sort of impending breakdown, but the behavior seemed odd.

"Ghost, you good, man?" Zac's use of Dorian's call sign from the military wasn't an accident. He was trying to bring him back if Dorian was heading down a bad mental path.

"Yeah, I'm okay," Dorian said. "There was someone out there watching us. But he's gone now."

Everybody immediately set down the windowpanes and rushed to Dorian, looking in the same direction he'd been studying.

"Where?" Gabe asked. "Do you think it's Godlewski?"

The big man shook his head. "No. I would've known about him long before now. There's no way he has the skills to keep his presence hidden. This was someone else."

"Someone else, like we need to set up a guard?" Gavin asked.

"No. He's gone now." Dorian looked away from the forest area and grabbed a pane from the truck. "Whoever it was wasn't here for Jordan. I'll check it out more closely myself when we're done."

When Dorian didn't say anything else, the men got back to work without any more talk or questions.

Gabe grabbed Zac's arm. "I'm not trying to disrespect your friend, but how reliable is his intel? If there's someone out there watching Jordan, I need to know about it."

Zac pulled him closer and lowered his voice. "I trust Dorian's instincts. If he says there's no danger out there, you can trust him about that."

"But . . ." Zac didn't have to say the word for Gabe to hear it.

"No buts. I do truly trust Dorian." Zac grimaced. "But he's been catching glimpses of someone out in the woods for weeks now. Thinks someone is watching him. Watching Linear Tactical as a whole."

"What do you think? Have you spotted anyone?"

"No, I haven't found any trace of anything. I don't think Dorian has found much either, to be honest." Zac shrugged.

"But he's convinced someone's out there." Gabe looked out at the woods again. He didn't doubt that Dorian's senses were unparalleled. And his prowess in the woods was legendary. If there was someone out in the surrounding wilderness watching, Dorian would be the one to sense him.

But this could also all be the sign of some mental deterioration.

Zac shook his head. "I know what you're thinking, and I've thought it too. Hell, Dorian has thought it. We're watching for any other signs of PTSD. Together."

PTSD could be insidious, striking in ways someone least expected. But it sounded like Dorian was aware of the possible problems. And Zac and the other Linear guys had their friend's back.

Zac slapped him on the shoulder. "Now let's get the rest of these windows fixed."

"Thank you for doing this, Mackay. A lot of people in town would say this is going above and beyond, especially for you."

He shrugged, walking back toward where they'd been working. "Well, a lot of people in this town are proving themselves to be idiots. Jordan isn't responsible for her father's sins. And what happened with Becky and Micah was an accident of the most tragic kind. I can't make Oak Creek change their minds or their actions, but I can damn well make sure they know I won't be condoning them or acting in the same manner."

"Glad to hear someone in this town has some sense."

They resumed working on the window. "This town is good people, Gabe. Your sister didn't make a bad choice by moving here, I promise. They just close ranks around their own, and unfortunately, they've lost sight of the fact that Jordan used to be one of those very own. They need to be reminded of what their values truly are."

Gabe hadn't seen anything that made him think that was going to happen, but he hoped Zac was right. Because there was a lonely, injured, young woman inside this broken house who needed a community she could call home.

They finished within the next hour and went inside to clean up the mess in there. Charlie was still sitting with Jordan, but Jordan was sound asleep.

Finn kissed Charlie on the top of the head. "Obviously, you were talking to her about wedding stuff."

She reached back and thumped him in the stomach. "Just because you fall asleep every time we talk about the wedding doesn't mean everyone does," she whispered.

Charlie got up to help them clean the inside of the house. Within thirty minutes, they had the glass swept up and everything put to rights as best it could be. Gabe built a fire in the fireplace and turned up the central heating to chase the chill from the house.

"Any word on the fire?" Gavin asked. "That involved a window too, right?"

Gabe's nod was curt. "Sheriff Nelson thinks that attack was aimed at Jordan. He'll definitely be questioning Adam DiMuzio and Allan Godlewski. I have Kendrick Foster looking into it on his own."

"It's one thing to break windows on a house. Another thing altogether to start a fire. Jordan got hurt. She or Violet could've been killed," Zac said. "Another reason this all has to stop."

Everyone was silent for a moment, watching the sleeping Jordan. She looked so young lying there. So defenseless.

They all nodded at Gabe before moving toward the door.

"Throwing the rocks in here had to have scared her," Charlie said as she walked with Finn. "Obviously, the fire was tougher on her physically, but what happened here is what's going to have the potential to leave the most scars. To be alone in your home that you love, sound asleep, and most of the windows getting smashed like that? It would've scared the shit out of me when I lived here."

"Did anything like this happen when you were here?"

The small blond woman shook her head. "No. God knows trouble has followed me around enough in the past few months, but nobody messed with me, or Jordan, when I lived here."

Probably because of the massive man behind her with his arms crossed over his chest. Anybody who messed with Charlie Devereux was very definitely getting Finn Bollinger as a package deal.

"I'm not going to let anything else happen to her," Gabe said. "And Zac is going to make sure word gets around town that anybody who tries something like this again is going to answer to someone a lot tougher than Jordan."

Charlie reached out and squeezed his arm. "I was a little pissed at you because you were so overprotective of your sister. Violet doesn't need it. She can take care of herself. But Jordan . . . she needs a champion. She's not weak. She knows how to fight, but—"

"She doesn't know she's worth fighting for," he finished for her.

Charlie gave him a nod before wrapping her arm around Finn's waist. "Don't screw it up, Collingwood, or you'll answer to me."

It should've sounded ridiculous coming from someone as small as Charlie. She was nearly a foot shorter and probably a hundred pounds lighter than either he or Finn.

For the first time, Gabe could see the iron strength that had kept her alive when a vicious terrorist had tortured her to try to get information. Had she broken, it would've meant both her death and probably Violet's also. But she hadn't.

And it was that same iron strength that was focused on him now.

So hell yeah, he believed she would kick his ass if he screwed this up with Jordan. But she wasn't going to have to.

"Believe me, I won't."

Chapter 14

Jordan nuzzled into her pillow, not quite ready to face the world. She willed her eyes to open as she stretched, careful of her hands. They still hurt, but not with yesterday's agony.

But her house . . . that was almost more than she could understand.

The last thing she remembered yesterday was talking with Charlie on her couch while Gabriel and the Linear Tactical guys had been working all around her. Charlie had been in the middle of a sentence about her wedding when Jordan had interrupted her.

"Why are the guys helping with the windows?"

Charlie rubbed Jordan's leg through the blanket. "It's freezing in here. You couldn't live in this house with so many of the windows broken out."

"You know that's not what I'm asking."

Charlie gave her a gentle smile. "They're here because you're a neighbor who needs assistance. And because this never should've happened in the first place. And because if the roles were reversed in some way, you'd be the first person on her way to help."

"Zac too?"

"Zac was the first one to volunteer, sweetie. Now shut up and let me talk about my wedding and my pregnancy."

Jordan hadn't meant to fall asleep, but she had been lulled by her friend's sweet voice and the soothing sounds of the others replacing her windows.

Now she awoke alone in her bed, wrapped in so many blankets she was about to overheat. She managed to make her way out from under the pile, her brain struggling to put together the pieces from yesterday.

Why wasn't it dark in here? It should be if the guys had boarded up all the windows. She blinked as she realized light was flooding in the whole room, but no cold air was coming in. The windows hadn't been boarded up with plywood; they'd been replaced altogether.

She pushed the rest of the blankets off with the backs of her hands so she could go investigate further and discovered that except for her sleep shirt, which barely came down to her hips, she was completely naked.

"Do you need help getting to the bathroom?"

She jerked her head up to see Gabriel standing in her doorway.

"You replaced all the windows? I . . . Thank you. That must've cost a lot of money." Money she couldn't really afford.

He crossed his arms over his chest and leaned against the doorframe. "There's nothing for you to worry about. The guys who did this are going to help pay for the damages, rest assured."

The way he looked standing there, as if everything in the world would bend to his will, she had no choice but to believe him.

"Bathroom?" he asked again.

She hadn't thought this part through when she'd agreed to have him come stay with her rather than a nurse. Her hands were feeling better, not nearly as painful as yesterday, but she didn't want him in the bathroom with her. Charlie had helped her last night, and that had been bad enough.

"I can manage by myself, if you can just rip off some toilet paper for me." She couldn't look at him as she said it. Damn it, she would just sit there and drip dry if she had to.

"Fair enough."

She made it through using the bathroom relatively unscarred, finding she had more use of her hands now that they weren't so painful. She could actually wiggle her fingers. Thank God, because there was just no way she would survive if Gabriel had had to follow her into the bathroom.

When she came back out, she wrapped herself in the blanket to keep from giving him a peep show.

"You look a thousand percent better than yesterday," he said with that smile that did something to her insides.

"I feel so much better."

And she really did. The pain medication, a good night's sleep, knowing that the windows had been taken care of—and they'd been taken care of much better than she ever would've dreamed—had relaxed a part of her that had been tense for so long she was surprised it could even be loosened at this point.

But mostly she felt better because when he'd turned to her at the hospital and told her he was going to take care of the situation, she'd believed him. Maybe she hadn't had a choice at that exact moment, but she'd believed him.

And he'd come through in spades.

"Hungry?" he asked, turning back toward the kitchen. He didn't wait for her answer. He pointed to one of the chairs at the kitchen table. "Sit."

She did, telling herself it was because there wasn't much she could do to help him anyway.

Not because nobody had ever taken care of her like this. Either way she might as well enjoy it while it lasted.

He cooked omelets, telling her she was getting a Denver omelet, and she could either eat it or be a little whiny baby, thus proving people from Wyoming weren't as tough as they claimed.

She would've eaten battery acid after that remark just to prove him wrong, but then he checked with her to make sure the jalapeño peppers he was about to add were okay.

"Bring it on, Collingwood." She raised an eyebrow at him. A few peppers didn't scare her.

Him, on the other hand? She didn't fear for her physical safety. Gabriel was not a man who was ever going to use his considerable strength to hurt someone smaller than him.

But there were other ways she could be hurt.

They made it through breakfast, her matching him bite for bite. The omelet was delicious although definitely spicy, though not enough to stop her from defending the honor of all Wyomingites.

He cleaned up, brushing her aside when she tried to help, then sat back down at the kitchen table with the supplies to clean her hands. He unwrapped the loose bandage. She was a little afraid to look at the wounds since yesterday all she'd been able to do at the hospital was stare at them and cry at how much they hurt.

Gabriel's fingers were gentle as he rubbed the antibiotic ointment onto the blisters.

"Never again." He brought her hands up to his mouth and kissed the top, uninjured side of each finger.

"I can't promise I'll never get burned again. I do work at a bakery."

"No, never again do you sit inside a room hurting, believing that you deserve to be there."

She flinched at words that hit a little too close to home. "The situation with Oak Creek is complicated."

"I know it is. But still, never again."

Jordan just nodded. She wasn't a masochist, but Gabriel just didn't understand the extent of the havoc her family had wrought on this town.

And besides, she didn't want to think about that right now. She would much rather focus on the feel of his lips against her fingers.

He carefully rewrapped the loose bandage around her hands, leaving her pinkies free since they hadn't been burned. The rest would need to stay wrapped a few more days until the blisters healed or popped. At least the burns on her thumbs were superficial. They didn't even need ointment.

The pain was peripheral. All she could seem to feel was Gabriel. How he stroked her wrist as he wrapped the bandage. How his big strong legs were on the outsides of hers, their knees touching.

She was being ridiculous. These were just casual touches between one person doing the decent thing and helping another. They didn't mean anything. But when his eyes met hers after he finished the last of the wrapping, they were filled with the same heat she could feel coursing through her own veins.

"You're hurt," he said. "I shouldn't touch you."

"I'm not that hurt," she whispered. "I want you."

The heat flared in his eyes. He reached for her, pulling

at the edge of the blanket wrapped around her until their faces were just an inch apart. The fact that she was naked under the blanket except for the short T-shirt moved to the forefront of her mind.

"When I was putting you in that shirt last night—*naked*—it damn near killed me. All I could think about was that picnic table two months ago and how good you tasted. How sexy it was when your thighs clenched around my head like you were never going to let me go."

His lips nipped at hers, and she gasped.

"Every night for two months as I've tried to fall asleep, it's been with the taste of you on my mouth, the smell of you in my nostrils, the sound of you crying out my name in my ears." His voice was almost guttural.

"I thought about you too. Remembered." Way more times than she should have.

"Last night, putting that sexy body of yours into that shirt, all I could think about was hearing and smelling and tasting you again."

She let go of the blanket and it fell open, exposing her from the waist down. But she didn't care, she just wanted what he was saying.

"Yes."

He was looking down at her now, at the flesh between her legs. The place no one but him had ever seen before in a sexual manner. But hell if she was going to stop this to have a talk about her virginity. She'd learned her lesson the first time. Maybe he wouldn't even notice.

He actually licked his lips, and she couldn't stop her squirming. "Gabriel . . ."

His fingers trailed up her thigh until he was cupping her intimately. She didn't even try to hold back her groan. When his own groan echoed hers, she couldn't help but smile.

But then he withdrew his hand and moved all the way back until they weren't even touching.

"I put you to bed last night and didn't lay a finger on you."

She blinked up at him rapidly. "I believe you." The thought that he would take advantage of her while she was sleeping had never occurred to her.

He trailed his finger down her cheek. "I know that. And your trust means everything to me. I would never abuse it like that."

She smiled at him. "Well, I'm not asleep now. I'm not exhausted, frightened, or on any pain medication stronger than Tylenol. So I think we're okay."

That heat was still raging in his eyes, but he didn't move any closer.

"Gabriel, what's wrong?"

"Last night, for the first time as I tried to fall sleep, it wasn't what happened at the picnic table that filled my mind. It was what happened once we got back here."

She cringed. She'd been such a bitch that night, refusing to explain or give them a chance. She gathered the blanket back around her, feeling cold where a moment ago she'd been burning. "We fought. It happens. Can't we both let it go?"

He shook his head. "I'm not talking about that. I'm talking about what you were trying to tell me before I said all that stupid stuff."

She reached out and wrapped her arms around his neck. She didn't want to think about that night, just wanted to focus on now. "Who cares? I don't. It wasn't important. Kiss me."

He let her pull him in by her forearms and kissed her briefly, but then stood all the way up, out of her reach.

"I'm an engineer who works in advanced math all the

time. But last night all I needed was simple subtraction to figure out what you'd been trying to tell me."

She cringed. He'd figured it out. She shouldn't be surprised.

"You went to jail when you were seventeen. You'd lived in this house alone a year before that. I can imagine your father's activities didn't make you the most popular high school student."

"No, they didn't." There was no point in denying it.

"So that talk you wanted to have. I assume it was to tell me that you're a virgin."

No point in denying this either. "Yes."

Chapter 15

Gabe wasn't surprised. He'd already known it had to be true.

He'd stayed up most of the night thinking about her and wondering if the best thing he could do for her would be to leave, to just get her the nurse they'd talked about and hightail it back to Idaho Falls.

He could still do that right now. But not if she kept looking at him that way and whispering in that husky voice of hers that she wanted him. Because he damn well wanted her too.

But Jesus, it had to be because she honestly wanted him, not because of any sort of misguided thanks or obligation. He scrubbed a hand over his eyes. He wasn't sure how to explain his concerns without insulting her. Again.

She'd just been through so much, and he didn't want to add to her burden. He wanted to take some of her burden away.

But he wasn't a goddamned saint. He wanted to sink inside that body of hers so badly he could practically taste it. *Literally* taste it.

"I just don't want to be someone else who hurts you."

That was it in a nutshell.

"Geez, Gabe, is your penis so big that it needs a warning label?"

If he'd had coffee in his mouth, he would've spewed it everywhere. Instead, he laughed at her impish little grin.

This woman. She had strength and grit and spunk that most of the people in this town were too blind to see. She had lived through circumstances that would've broken most people.

And had done it completely alone.

She tried to act like she wanted to be alone, that she was okay with it. But Jordan was alone because she had to be, not because she wanted to be.

Behind those smiling eyes of hers, there was pain. And fear that he might reject her now, fear that for some reason he might not appreciate the gift she was willing to give him. He would be stupid not to see that her virginity really was a precious gift.

Gabe had never been stupid. He wasn't going to start now.

"If it hurts for more than a second, then I'm definitely doing something wrong."

Her eyes widened just a fraction, and he realized she'd been preparing for his rejection. He took a step closer.

"You still want me?" Her voice was hesitant. "Even though I don't know what I'm doing?"

He leaned his hands on the arms of the chair on either side of her and kissed her gently. "I know you're generous, passionate, and the sexiest woman I've ever seen. Knowing that I am the only man who's ever touched you? That is definitely not a turn-off. The opposite, in fact."

A feminine smile fell over her features, softening the tension and adding to her beauty. "We better do something about that then." She held her hands out in front of her. "But I can't touch you."

"It won't be long until you can get those little hands on me. Until then, I'm more than happy to take the lead when it comes to touching."

A happy smile lit those gray eyes. Gorgeous. He just had to stare into those happy eyes for a moment.

But she wasn't having any of that. "Then what are we waiting for? Get out of the way, mister, so I can get to the bed and see this legendary penis."

He laughed and bent down to kiss her again. But what he'd meant as a brief, playful touch became much more when her little tongue began dueling with his.

He had to taste her. Right now, right here, again, before anything else. He had to know if she tasted as good as he remembered.

His lips broke off from hers, and she started to stand, but he pushed her back down into the chair with one finger on her chest.

"Stay." He crouched down in front of her chair and moved the blanket aside, blessing that short shirt that had already ridden up to her waist.

God, she was so damn beautiful.

"G—Gabe? Aren't we going to . . ."

"Oh, we are. But first, this. I've got to taste you again."

He dropped down and licked her slit from bottom to top.

He hitched one leg over the arm of the chair, shifting her torso sideways and down further.

"But you don't get any pleasure this way."

He licked her again before using his tongue to tease her clit, loving the little gasp he elicited. "Oh sweetheart, hearing you call my name is a pleasure unto itself. And there's plenty of time for me. Later."

* * *

AFTER JORDAN LAY BONELESS IN THE CHAIR FROM THE onslaught of Gabriel's mouth, he picked her up and carried her into the bedroom.

When he peeled the T-shirt off her body, she gave herself over to him. He kissed his way up her belly to her breasts, then up her shoulders to her neck, then back down to her breasts.

Gabriel was all big shoulders and heavy muscle. Incredibly powerful, but also impossibly gentle. His lips and hands were everywhere, kissing over her hips and under her breasts and behind her ear. And while he was arousing her again to a fever pitch—which honestly she'd never dreamed possible so soon after what he'd done to her in the kitchen—she wanted more. She wanted to touch *him*, stroke him with her fingertips, drive him as crazy as he was driving her.

When he bit her nipple and fire zinged straight to her core, she rubbed her thighs together in need and let out a frustrated grunt when she could only hold his head to her by her forearms.

Gabriel laughed and lifted his head to look up at her. "What was that sound? That didn't sound like pleasure."

"I want to touch you. It's not fair that you get to drive me crazy over and over, and I can't reciprocate."

Humor lit those green eyes as he lifted himself onto one elbow beside her. "I'm sorry. Are you bored? Maybe I should try a little harder." His fingers trailed down her torso and began strumming her clit. Jordan couldn't stop her gasp or the way her hips shot off the bed.

"For God's sake, don't try harder. You might give me a heart attack."

His deep chuckle was a beautiful sound. "And what

would you do to me if you could use those hands of yours?"

She could barely think around the workings of those clever fingers. Whatever focus she could find was shot to hell when he leaned over and began nibbling on her ear.

"Focus, Rainfall," he whispered in her ear. "Tell me what you would do to me. If you don't, I'm going to make you come again. And then one more time. And that's before I even get inside you."

His thumb continued its onslaught against her clit, while his fingers slid inside her, deep.

"You don't play fair." She gasped. "Also, you need to work on your threatening skills, if the most menacing thing you can come up with is orgasms."

He chuckled again. "Don't think I don't know you. You hate the fact that I haven't come yet. It goes against that generous nature you have."

Damn it, she did hate that she hadn't been able to give him his turn yet, although she wasn't sure it had anything to do with any generous nature on her part. She just wanted to see if she could make him lose control the way he so obviously did her.

His fingers thrust deep, and her hips shot off the bed again. She tried to close her legs, but he hooked one of his jean-clad thighs over her naked one, opening her even farther to him.

Even as soft as the material was, it was an irritant. She wanted to feel his skin.

"I would get those damn jeans off you, that's for sure," she got out through gritted teeth.

His fingers stroked her for a second more before pulling out of her completely. She didn't know whether to cry or be relieved.

But as he stood up next to the bed and pulled off his jeans, she could only stare.

"Better?" he asked.

"Boxers too." She wanted to see all of him.

A second later the boxers were gone too, and he was gloriously naked in front of her.

If she had thought he was unaffected by what they'd been doing, she'd been terribly wrong.

She wanted to touch him all over, that massive chest, that trim waist, that hard length of him. Somehow looking at him so gloriously naked and confident was turning her on just as much as his touch on her flesh moments ago.

She *ached* with need.

She scrambled forward, desperate to get closer to him. Forgetting about her wounded hands, she hissed in pain when she put her weight on them.

He was immediately beside her, lifting her weight off her hands. "Hey, be careful."

She didn't know how to explain what was happening inside her. She didn't understand it herself.

"I hurt," she whispered. It was the only way she could explain the ache inside her.

His eyes immediately turned compassionate. "Okay, we can stop. This can wait until later."

"No!"

His eyes widened just slightly at her forceful response. "I was just kidding about reciprocal orgasms. We have plenty of time if you're hurting."

She took the back of her bandaged hand and pressed it against her lower belly. "No, I hurt here. The ache, Gabriel. Make it go away." He was the only one who could. She needed him inside her now. No more games.

She thought he didn't understand as he cupped her head and laid her gently back against the pillows.

"Shhh, Rainfall. I've got you." And then she saw that deep heat in his eyes. Like he understood. Felt the pain himself. "I'll make the hurt go away."

There was no more teasing.

He grabbed a condom and rolled it on before his big body covered hers completely, skin touching skin from head to toe. He took his weight on his elbows on either side of her head, wiping the hair from her forehead with his thumbs. There was no jest in those emerald eyes now, only heat.

"I just want you to be sure," he said.

That he would stop and ask her that when she could feel the length of his erection pressing against her meant everything.

"I'm sure."

She was.

He kissed her, tongue dipping deep into her mouth. Slowly thrusting in, then retreating, then thrusting again.

"Yes." Her hips thrust up against his. That was what she wanted, what his tongue was doing.

He shifted his weight all onto one arm and slid the other hand between their bodies, between her legs, playing her with his fingers while his tongue continued to thrust inside her mouth.

It all felt so good. Hurt so good.

"Please, Gabriel."

He shifted and reached to guide himself to her opening. And slowly—God, so slowly—he worked himself inside of her a little at a time before easing back out and starting the process again.

The rocking of his hips against hers became her whole world. The feel of him inside her, stretching, burning with the most delicious heat, was all she could discern.

But he was holding back. She knew it. He didn't want to hurt her.

She didn't have the ability to use her hands to clutch him to her, but she damn well had her legs. Spreading them wider, they both gasped; she hooked her long legs around his hips and urged him closer.

He broke from their kiss and looked her in the eye, sweat beading on his forehead, a testament of the effort his control was requiring.

She didn't want his control. She wanted the opposite.

"Now, Gabriel."

He closed his eyes and yielded to her demand, thrusting all the way in until he was buried to the hilt.

Jordan let out a gasp at the slight burn, but it was gone a moment later as his fingers reached down between their bodies and began to drive her crazy once again.

Instinct took over, her hips moving of their own volition. Her leg hitched higher on his hip, giving him further access, and he groaned deeply, picking up the pace of his thrusts.

"Jordan."

The sound of her name on his lips had the tightness inside her building again. She clenched around him, loving how he snarled and thrust deeper still.

It was his lips sucking hard at the side of her neck and the hand clutching at her breast with no finesse that threw her over the edge.

The orgasm ripped through her, all the more powerful because it was both of them together this time. When his body jerked, and he shouted her name, it was the most beautiful sound she'd ever heard.

Chapter 16

Jordan wasn't exactly sure how relationships worked, but she was pretty sure what was happening with her and Gabriel wasn't normal.

The first four days after the fire, the two of them were barely out of each other's sight. They might not have left the bed at all if they hadn't needed to eat.

And even then, they rarely made it back to the bed without some sort of lovemaking on a different piece of furniture. She was never going to look at her kitchen table or couch or *especially* the ottoman he'd bent her over the same ever again.

As her hands had healed, she'd allowed her body to become drunk on their lovemaking to help take her mind off the fact that she didn't have a job, she'd lost all the coding she'd done on the computer, and she had no means of restarting since her computer had been destroyed.

And she didn't know how long Gabriel would be around. She woke each morning wondering if this would be the day he left.

On the fourth day, yesterday, he had. He'd gone into

Oak Creek to buy a few things, including, much to Jordan's embarrassment, the tampons she knew she would need in the next day or so.

Evidently, even Navy SEALs had undefeatable foes, and their name was tampons, because he hadn't come back. She hadn't heard anything from him yesterday or all day today.

She knew he would have to leave eventually; she just hadn't thought it would be so abruptly. She called herself all sorts of foolish and naive for letting his absence hurt her. They'd had no promises between them. He'd been kind enough to take care of her until she could do it herself, which now that her hands were almost healed, she could.

She couldn't accuse him of taking advantage of her. She'd been more than willing to participate in anything he'd suggested. She had suggested quite a few of their escapades herself. She didn't blame him for that.

She'd known this thing between them wasn't forever but had expected more from him than a disappearing act and thirty-six hours of silence.

The knock on her door caught her off guard. She reached toward her shotgun as she opened it.

Gabriel stood there. Her first thought was to lay into him for not coming back or at least calling. Then she got a good look at him.

His eyes were sunken, his skin almost gray with exhaustion. Pain and tension bracketed his full lips.

He held a box of tampons in his hand.

But it was the heartbreak inside those green eyes that had her opening the door for him and inviting him inside. She had firsthand experience with hopelessness and despair and wouldn't wish it on anyone, especially this proud warrior.

But he wouldn't come in, just stood there on her porch, looking, for all of his height and muscle, like he had no strength left. So she stepped outside into the cold with him. Whatever was or wasn't happening between them, this was obviously more important.

"What can I do to help?" She reached out and touched his arm, then realized he might not want her to touch him. But before she could move her hand away, he covered it with his own.

Gabriel stared at her silently for a long moment. "I can't believe you're asking me what *you* can do to help *me*."

Before she could even get another word out, Gabriel crushed her against his chest. She wrapped her arms around him, willing to do her damnedest to fend off whatever had put this look in his eyes.

"Is Violet okay?" It was the only thing she could think of that would affect him in such a way.

"Violet is fine now, at least physically. Emotionally . . ." He let out a deep sigh. "That's going to take much longer to heal."

He set down the box, wrapped his arms around her hips, and lifted her off the ground. She brought her arms around his neck, threading her fingers in his hair, and holding on to him as he buried his face in her neck and breathed.

"The whole way here I thought you would turn me away," he said after a long minute. "You have every right to turn me away. I have a good reason for disappearing, but that doesn't mean that I don't know that I'm just another person who let you down."

He finally lowered her feet back to the ground, and she noticed his wince.

She stepped back, studying him more closely. "Are you hurt? What the hell is going on? I thought you got scared off by a box of tampons. That you weren't ready for whatever implied commitment that entailed, not that you'd run off and gotten yourself punched in the gut."

"Shot, actually, but through Kevlar, so yeah, it's like a really bad punch to the gut." He gave her a smile, but it didn't wipe the sadness from his features, nor did it come anywhere close to meeting his eyes.

She had so many questions, but she didn't want to pry. Even though he had a good reason, his sudden departure made her question exactly where they stood. Maybe he wouldn't want to talk about this.

So she just kept it simple and told him the truth. "I'm sorry for what happened to you, but I'm glad you're here."

He ran a finger down her cheek. "I hurt you."

"It's okay. I—"

"No, it's not okay. Yes, there was an emergency. I thought for months that the man who had orchestrated Violet's kidnapping had been eliminated. But I was wrong. He was closer than either of us could've believed. I didn't even know I had an enemy, and he was right next to me all along."

She took him by the hand and led him inside. "Sometimes knowing your enemies doesn't soften the blow. Sometimes it just hurts no matter what."

She knew her enemies in Oak Creek, and that didn't do much to make their hatred easier to bear.

She sat him down at the table and made coffee for them both, the box of tampons sitting between them, and just listened. Listened as he told her about Stellman, the man behind Violet's kidnapping and human trafficking, being back from the dead. How his sister had been taken again yesterday and how she and Aiden Teague were almost killed.

He grabbed her hand and told her how if he hadn't

been at that drugstore to buy her tampons, Violet would probably be dead. That the fire at the bakery hadn't been someone from Oak Creek at all, but this Stellman guy trying to capture Violet.

And although she wished it hadn't happened at all, she was glad at least nobody from Oak Creek hated her enough to try and kill her.

As far as excuses went for not showing up, Gabriel's was a pretty damn good one. More than anything, Jordan was glad everyone was safe.

"The last day and a half have been a complete madhouse. That doesn't excuse the fact that I didn't get in touch with you. You needed me, and I wasn't here."

She reached over to cup his cheek. "You're here now. That's what matters."

* * *

Gabe slept that night wrapped in Jordan's arms. Sleeping with a woman wasn't new to him. He'd never been the type of guy who cut out after sex. Feeling a woman's soft curves against him, holding her against his chest in silent thanks for her being so open with her body, had always been part of intimacy for him.

He was well aware of his own strength and size. He had to use care to make sure he never hurt a woman. He'd been brought up, first by his father and then by the navy, to understand he was a protector. He was meant to stand between those who would cause harm and those who didn't have the means to fight. He'd always accepted the role of guardian, cherished it, even.

But instead of him holding her, it was her smaller body sheltering him. As if she would stand guard and protect him against his foes even though she didn't have nearly his size or strength.

The next morning, he sipped his coffee as he watched Jordan through the kitchen window. She sat outside on the porch in the rocking chair, like she had every morning. Once again, she was wrapped in a blanket, this time over a loose sweatshirt, yoga pants, and warm socks, which she had been able to manipulate herself now that her hands weren't wrapped anymore.

He wasn't sure he'd ever seen such a look of peace on anyone's face as she stared out at the land in front of her.

He was finally understanding why she stayed in Oak Creek despite everyone disliking her so much. This place—the land, the house—was in her very *bones*. She drew strength from it, in what she was doing now: sitting there and soaking it all in.

To anyone else, it would just be Wyoming in the middle of winter. Cold, somewhat barren, not much to see or experience. But not for Jordan.

She'd told him about her mother, who had died of a brain aneurysm when Jordan was ten. She'd told him how the house and land had been passed down from daughter to daughter, never actually being put in husbands' names. That was why she'd been able to keep it when law enforcement had frozen any accounts or finances associated with Michael Reiss after he'd stolen all the money and disappeared.

She'd told him how hard being away from here had been while she'd been incarcerated. How she'd taken to drawing pictures of the fields and trees surrounding her house from memory—not that she was much of an artist—in order to keep sane.

The thought of this beautiful, sensual creature totally in love with her land and home being imprisoned for something that could've happened to anyone, hurt even his rusty heart.

The next three days, they spent cocooned with each other like they had at first. Finding out she was a virgin had supercharged every possessive, alpha instinct Gabe had. He hadn't been able to stop touching her, pulling her close, caring for her.

Not that she seemed to mind. She reveled in it, moving closer to him whenever he reached for her. She snuggled up against him when they talked, when they watched television, when they slept. And while he'd been delighted to explore with her the different aspects—and positions—about sex she liked most, he realized it wasn't just sex that was new to her.

It *all* was new to her, right down to the slightest friendly touch.

She soaked in every hug, kiss, stroke. She leaned into him every time he pulled her to his side or down onto his lap.

She was starved for touch, and he didn't even think she was aware of it. Regardless, he had no intention of making her ask for it. He wanted her close as much as she seemed to want to be close. Which was fine with him; touching her healed hardened parts inside him too.

But all the healing—physical and emotional—meant it was time for him to leave.

He didn't want to. But things couldn't stay the way they were, with both of them holed up in her house, ignoring the real world.

Case in point, the way she came inside now, getting dressed for the day.

"Where are you going?"

She held her hands out in front of him, wiggling her fingers. "They're all better, so it's time for me to look for a new job, at least until Fancy Pants reopens. With Aiden's injuries, Violet may not be in such a hurry for that anymore."

He grabbed her hand and kissed the palm. The blisters weren't as pronounced, but they still had to be a little tender. "Are you sure you don't want to stay here and play hooky with me?"

She leaned over and kissed him. "Maybe we can play a little something else when I get home later. But the bills have got to get paid."

This woman. Her quiet strength was staggering. It was easy to forget that she was so young—not even twenty-four. When he'd been that age, he'd been a hotshot SEAL with all his arrogance and stupidity swinging freely for anyone to see.

This woman could've been a SEAL. She was smart enough, strong enough. And she damn well wouldn't ever have walked around acting arrogant; it wasn't in her nature.

Jordan had the most enduring of strengths . . . the kind that could bend. Reshape itself. The kind that withstood. Sustained. Battened down until the storm blew over.

The kind of hushed strength many people would mistake for weakness.

They'd be wrong.

"I can make it worth your while if you decide to stay."

Her fingers trailed along his temple. "I have no doubt that's true, but unfortunately, that's still not going to pay the bills."

He got up and walked in with her. He rinsed out their coffee mugs as she went into her room to get dressed. A sticky note on her refrigerator caught his attention, as it had multiple times before, although he'd never asked her about it.

$622,000.

That was all it said on the yellow paper.

Jordan came out a few minutes later dressed in a pair of khaki pants and a blue shirt, her thick brown hair pulled back in a braid.

He tapped the note. "What costs $622,000?"

She stiffened before shrugging a shoulder. "The amount of money I need for the life I want."

He crossed his arms over his chest, leaning against the fridge, waiting for her to elaborate, but she didn't.

Quite a vague answer for such a specific amount. Definitely more than this house and land were worth, although since she already owned both, she shouldn't need to buy it.

Maybe a house somewhere else? Starting over in a different country? A share in a yacht?

What was the life she wanted to live? Gabe had no idea.

"What sort of job are you looking for?" He didn't even know what skill sets she had. He knew she liked computers. She'd been working on something—he wasn't sure what—on the old laptop he'd lent her, since the vandals had destroyed hers.

She put a piece of bread in the toaster. "I'm not picky. Whatever is available. Hopefully, the bakery will reopen soon. I just need to keep a positive cash flow." She held up a piece of bread in question. He nodded.

"I guess cash flow is important to get to $622,000."

He hoped she would explain more, but she just laughed. "That's for sure."

"Are there a lot of available jobs in Oak Creek?"

She rolled her eyes. "I stopped looking for jobs in Oak Creek a week after I got out of prison. Nobody here is going to hire me. Your sister was the only exception, since she knew Charlie. It will be hard enough with my criminal record in Reddington City, but I'll be able to find something."

Frustration ate at Gabe. Jordan was smart, well spoken, and friendly. She should be able to do so much more than just whatever she was able to find. But hell, he had his own business problems to work out, big changes he was thinking about after what had happened with Violet. He probably shouldn't be offering life advice to anyone else until he got his own shit together.

They ate their toast, neither of them talking much.

"If I get offered something right away, I might not make it home all day," she told him. "Were you going to stay here?"

"If that's okay. There's a lot of stuff I need to work through. A lot of changes for my company that I need to figure out. And I've got my laptop here, so I'll use that."

"You don't have to stay here if you don't want to, Gabriel. I'm not going to be upset or anything."

"Trying to get rid of me?" He cocked his head to the side and gave her a casual smile, but he was hanging on her response.

"Not at all. I just don't want you to feel like you have to stay if you don't want to."

"I want to," he said. And he meant it.

She winked at him. "Okay, but don't steal any of my stuff. I'll see you when I get home."

Chapter 17

Hours after Jordan left, Gabe settled into the rocking chair on her front porch. The more time he spent here, the more he could understand Jordan's connection to the land.

There was something healing about it. He'd been raised in Idaho Falls, and Idaho wasn't all that different from Wyoming in its topography and landscape. But there was something about this particular place that soothed the soul.

Its beauty was like Jordan, he realized. So quiet and unassuming that you almost missed it. But once you did see it, it was inescapable.

He'd gotten a text from her just after lunch. She'd found some work for the day and wouldn't be back until after dinner.

What was he going to do about his own company? The week's events were forcing him to take a much closer look at his overall goals. Collingwood Technology had been his parents' brainchild —they'd both been engineers—and had never actually been Gabe's passion. It was only after they'd died, when he'd been forced to leave the military and come home to raise Violet, that he'd put his focus into the company. And for twelve years, it had been fine. Maybe not what he would've done with his life had the situation been different, but certainly not something he dreaded each day.

Even though he enjoyed the business aspect of running the company, he hadn't had much of a chance to spend time doing the research and development parts he loved the most. When was the last time he'd been in a lab and used his engineering skills? Or even the coding and computer work that he loved so much? For the past few years, there had been less and less opportunity to do what he enjoyed as more and more of his time was taken up with the daily grind of running a multimillion-dollar business.

But now he was at a turning point.

God knew he already had all the money he needed. He could sell the company and live the rest of his life in luxury. Although that didn't interest him either.

The challenge had always been what interested him.

It was time for him to take a good look at why he was staying at Collingwood Technology. Violet had already gotten out to follow her passions in baking and build a life here in Oak Creek.

Maybe he needed to find his passion and do the same.

What did he want?

Gabe walked back inside, his attention drawn again to that sticky note on the fridge.

$622,000.

Jordan obviously knew what she wanted and the exact amount she needed. She just didn't know how to get the money.

He, on the other hand, could have that sort of money

at almost any time, but didn't know what he wanted to do with it.

The battery from his laptop was dead, so he grabbed the computer he'd lent Jordan. Once he answered a few emails, he would be free to spend time with her when she got home in a couple hours.

When he woke up the screen, it showed what Jordan had been working on last. Not surfing the web or browsing social media like he'd expected. It was open to Java, a pretty complex computer coding language. If someone wasn't familiar with it, the words on the screen would look like gibberish.

Jordan was obviously familiar. She'd been coding. Interesting. Maybe this was part of her $622,000 plan. Maybe she wanted to have her own business.

He'd only planned to glance at it, since he was definitely familiar with Java and coding, but once he started, he couldn't tear his eyes away. This was high-level work. What she was working on was nothing short of brilliant from a cybersecurity perspective.

And dangerous.

She was working on robotic process automation. A way, in essence, to fool a computerized machine inside a corporation into learning what Jordan wanted it to learn, in addition to what it was programed to do.

On the one hand, it could be a fantastic way to increase the functionality of basic robotic devices within a business. A computerized coffee maker could be connected to a company's network to not only make coffee at a certain time, but also to turn on lights, control temperature, lock or unlock computerized doors.

Or, as proven with this coding, provide someone outside access into a closed system.

Depending on what type of access she was going for,

Jordan was either working on something brilliant or highly nefarious.

Realizing the sun was beginning to set, he closed the laptop. He needed to give Jordan a chance to explain her work. Maybe she didn't even realize the ramifications of what she was doing.

The sound of a soft thump hitting the front door drew his attention. He shut the computer down and heard another similar sound on the side of the house. What the hell?

It was only when he heard the noise again and then saw something dark splatter against the kitchen window that Gabe realized what was going on.

Someone was throwing shit against Jordan's house.

Gabe was out the front door in just a matter of seconds. The three males—teenagers with slingshots in their hands at the tree line of Jordan's property—obviously hadn't expected anyone, especially Gabe, to be inside.

They immediately turned and ran into the woods.

"Oh, hell no," Gabe muttered and took off in pursuit.

They had a big lead and were more familiar with these woods, not to mention Gabe wasn't one hundred percent healed yet since taking that hit a few days ago, but there was no way he was letting them get away with this.

The oncoming darkness played to his strengths, as did the cold. The boys were weighed down with their bulky winter jackets while he ignored the cold and moved much more easily.

When he'd gone through hell week to finish his SEAL training, he never thought he would use the deadly skills Uncle Sam had taught him to track down some teenagers in the woods. But that was exactly what he was doing.

They were a half mile into the woods when the boys got smart. They must've realized they weren't going to be able to outrun Gabe, so they slowed down, trying to outwit him.

A good plan in theory.

He slowed his speed but continued to track them on silent feet. Just because he'd been in the navy rather than the Army Green Berets like the Linear guys didn't mean Gabe wasn't just as deadly in the wilderness.

He heard some sort of animal-type call and realized the boys had split up and were signaling each other. Gabe moved in the direction of the call.

As he proceeded through the trees, it wasn't long until he spotted two of the guys.

They obviously thought that they had lost him or that he'd gone after their other friend—or maybe they were just damn lazy—because they were no longer doing a very effective job of hiding their tracks or moderating their breathing. Gabe remained silent as he moved around behind them. He needed to get these two incapacitated so he could go after the third kid. He wanted to make sure he had the undivided attention of all three while they "talked."

The two boys were keeping an eye out for him in the other direction when he stepped out from behind a large tree.

"Looking for me?" he whispered.

The bigger of the two guys squawked in surprise. The smaller one took a swing at Gabe. Gabe blocked the punch without any effort whatsoever, then stepped to the side as the bigger guy found his courage and decided to help his buddy out.

Neither of them got in a hit. Gabe kept himself on his best behavior, not doing any damage to them either. Although when he thought of what these kids' actions would do to Jordan, reinforcing the town's rejection, he was tempted to give them both a couple of cracked ribs.

Instead, he used the bigger guy's forward momentum when he rushed Gabe for a second attempt, stepping out of the way and giving him a push as he went by. He flew to the ground. A moment later, he grabbed the smaller guy and threw him into his friend.

Before either kid could get their bearings, Gabe had ripped their shoes off and was taking the laces out.

"What are you doing, man?" The smaller kid asked. He tried to scoot away, but Gabe grabbed his shoulder and threw him back onto the ground.

Once he had the laces out, he began tying the boys' hands behind their backs.

"What the hell?"

Gabe ignored the bigger one and made sure the bindings were good and tight. It would hurt like a bitch in this cold, but Gabe didn't give a shit.

"You two stay put while I go find your friend. Then we're gonna have a nice chat."

Finding idiot number three wasn't terribly difficult either. Instead of making a beeline for wherever they had parked, he'd decided to circle back around and try to help his friends.

Gabe could almost respect the loyalty if it wasn't for the fact that these were three cowards attacking a lone woman's house.

This one was smarter, quieter, listening for Gabe rather than assuming he had the advantage. Gabe didn't try to get behind him like he had the others. This time when he saw his prey, he pursued. The kid's eyes got big when he spotted Gabe, then he turned and ran.

The kid was fast and surefooted, but Gabe was relentless in his pursuit. A couple of minutes and a flying tackle later, and the kid was on the ground.

"You can come with me so we can have a talk with your friends, or I can rough you up a little bit and *then* we can go have a talk with your friends. They're waiting."

The kid wisely started walking. They reached the other two, who were still cursing and trying to get themselves untied, when Gabe looked around, eyes narrowed.

There was someone else out here. And that person wasn't friendly.

Chapter 18

"Who else came with you?" Gabe asked, allowing the menace he was feeling to leak into his voice.

All three of them shook their heads, but it was the big one who spoke. "It's just us three. We were just messing around, man. Chad told us the bitch had gone to work."

Gabe's fist clenched at the slur, but he ignored it for now to focus on the danger at hand. All three of the kids looked like they were about to piss their pants—they were telling the truth.

He looked around again. Every instinct was telling him someone else was out there. Someone dangerous. Those instincts had kept him alive in enemy territory more than once.

He ripped off the third kid's shoes and tied him the way he had the other two. Now all three of them were crying and moaning.

He narrowed his eyes and pointed at them.

"Shut the fuck up." His voice was barely more than a whisper. "Someone is out there, and if that person isn't with you or with me, then that's a damn problem. Be quiet so I can find out where he is. Because if something happens to me, you three dumb asses are going to freeze out here."

They shut up.

Gabe disappeared into the woods, trying to get a better feel for what he was sensing. Whatever it was, *whoever* it was, wasn't a teenager up to some mischief.

Gabe could almost feel crosshairs on him. And he did not like being prey.

He made a wide circle around the kids. There wasn't much he could do about a sniper who was willing to take a shot in cold blood.

Although he'd never been his team's best distance shooter, Gabe had spent time staring down a scope at a target. He had even taken a life that way. In a way, the distance had made the kill easier.

That did not make him feel better right now.

Twenty minutes later, by the time he'd moved around to the east side of the kids, the feeling of being watched—being *stalked*—had passed. He understood why a few seconds later.

Dorian Lindstrom stepped out from behind a group of trees, far enough from Gabe to not be taken as a threat, a half-unconscious man over his shoulder. He dumped the guy onto the ground with little finesse.

"Jesus Christ, Dorian. You spooked me, man. Was that you who had me in your sights?"

"No. This guy did."

Gabe walked closer and realized it was Allan Godlewski moaning on the ground. Dorian had obviously beaten the shit out of him. Gabe wasn't going to lose any sleep over Godlewski taking a beating, but it looked like his nose was broken, and half his face was swelling. Dorian obviously hadn't held back.

"He attack you?" Gabe asked him.

The big man shook his head. "No, I didn't do this. He was like this when I found him."

What the actual fuck? "Well, it wasn't me. I was running those punk kids to ground. So who did it?"

"Dorian crouched down next to Allan. "The person I've been tracking. The same one I mentioned last week."

Gabe took a step closer. "Is that who had me in his sights?"

"No. Godlewski had you in his sights."

"How do you know it was him and not your ghost?"

"Because if you'd been in that person's sights, and they'd wanted the shot, you'd be dead already. Godlewski had a rifle next to him, and I think he intended to use it. That's why the wraith stepped in."

Wraith? That was a ghost, right? "Are you sure your… wraith is any safer than Godlewski? I'm beginning to have concerns "about this guy roaming free around Jordan's house."

Dorian grabbed Allan by the arm and threw him back over his shoulder in a fireman carry. "I've got to get him to a hospital. Jordan is safe. The ghost is dangerous but isn't after her. Or you."

"Is he after you, Dorian?"

"Yes and no."

He let out a sigh. "Don't talk in riddles, man. Is he hunting you or not?"

Dorian turned away. "Yes, I'm being hunted. But not by a him. Wraith is a she, not a he."

He faded into the darkness without another word.

Jesus.

Gabe let him go. He no longer had that dead-man-walking itch at the back of his neck. He had no idea why anyone, man or woman, would be running around

Wyoming's wilderness in the middle of winter. But if that person had just stopped Godlewski from going open season on Gabe, Gabe would assume that person wasn't an enemy.

He would have to leave Dorian to his mystery lady of the woods. Gabe had his own problems to deal with. He made his way back to the three punks he'd left tied up.

Untying their hands and allowing them to put their shoes back on, Gabe marched the kids back to Jordan's house, promising them that they'd regret it if he had to chase after them again. Since he'd taken their driver's licenses—or maybe they understood that he really was going to be pissed if he had to go after them a second time—they came quietly. Adam DiMuzio, Jeff McKeever, and Caleb Higgs. All between eighteen and nineteen years old.

Barely more than stupid kids. But old enough to know better.

When he made them clean off the shit they'd thrown at Jordan's house with their bare hands and paper towels, they weren't quite so amicable.

"Jesus, man," Adam said as he cleaned the front door. "What's your problem? Do you even know who Jordan Reiss is, what she did?"

Gabe crossed his arms over his chest. "I know she fell asleep behind the wheel and there was a terrible accident. I know that Zac Mackay, the man who lost his wife and child and has the most right to be mad, is not here like some immature douche shooting bags of shit at Jordan's house. As a matter fact, Zac Mackay was here last week helping me replace windows that got broken. Which were, interestingly, broken by rocks thrown with a slingshot. A criminal offense, since someone could've gotten seriously hurt by the rocks or glass."

The color leached out of Adam's face, and he began to clean harder. The other boys worked silently.

"Do you know what her dad did?" he finally asked. "My family nearly lost our business because of the money he stole. My mom had a stroke, and we could hardly afford hospital care for her."

Studying Adam now, Gabe realized there was a hurt, scared kid inside him. He'd watched his parents go through some pretty rough stuff. And while that might incline Gabe toward a bit of leniency for the young man, it didn't change the fact that this shit—literally—with Jordan had to stop.

He stepped up to Adam and placed a hand on his shoulder. "How's your mom now?"

The boy shrugged. "She's fine, got back to normal. She's strong."

"And your family still owns New Brothers Pizza, right? Looks like it's doing well."

Adam shrugged again. "I guess. No thanks to her." He inclined his head toward Jordan's house.

"You want to get back at the person who stole from your family? Then you go find Michael Reiss's house and throw shit at it. Jordan had nothing to do with what her father did. She was barely sixteen when that went down. Younger than you are now. Do you know everything your father does?"

Adam shrugged. "No, but my father doesn't steal from other people."

"I know, and I'm glad. Michael Reiss is a bastard who should be rotting in prison for what he stole. Not Jordan."

"I know that."

"Then why do you think it's okay to punish Jordan like this?" Gabe gestured to the house. "All you're doing here is terrorizing a woman who lives on her own, someone who is trying to get her life back together after being dealt a pretty crappy hand. You got a sister, kid?"

Gabe could tell he was getting through to Adam.. "Yeah, two. One younger and one older."

"Would you want someone doing something like this to them? Breaking their windows in the middle of winter? Leaving something like this for them to find when they got home after working a long day? Worse?"

Adam shook his head. "No. Look man, I didn't have anything to do with that fire. That's taking it way too far."

"I know. We found out the people who set the fire weren't after Jordan."

"I'm glad. I was afraid it was Allan."

"Allan put you up to this?"

Adam shrugged again. "He's just always the one who knows when Jordan isn't here." Adam stared at the door for a long minute before turning back to Gabe. "But no, he's never really had to put us up to it. We've always been more than willing to jump on the bandwagon."

The kid looked a little embarrassed. Maybe there was hope for him after all. Gabe gave him a curt nod.

"Get your friends and get out of here. And Adam, don't come back. Jordan may not be willing to fight, but I'm willing to fight for her. And so is Zac Mackay and the rest of the Linear guys. You make sure everyone knows that."

Adam nodded, then turned to run down the steps.

"DiMuzio."

The kid turned and looked at him from the yard.

"Don't come back here just because of my threat, but because you're better than this. You're more than someone who would act this way toward a lone woman. Your family is too. You would want someone to look out for your sisters if you couldn't do it. I've got a sister here now too. I want to believe that the DiMuzios in this town—*everybody* in Oak Creek—is better than this."

The Adam that answered was more of a man and less of a boy. "We are."

Gabe nodded and watched the boy and his friends take off into the night. They wouldn't be back. Gabe was still smiling as he walked in the door and saw Jordan's laptop on the kitchen table where he'd left it.

That coding. He hoped he hadn't just protested Jordan's innocence when she might have devious plans of her own for Oak Creek.

Chapter 19

Washing dishes and busing tables at a café in Reddington City wasn't Jordan's idea of forward progress career-wise, but the owner had paid her fairly and said she could come back anytime. Jordan suspected Betty Mae might have been in prison herself at some point because the older woman didn't bat an eyelash when Jordan mentioned her own incarceration.

The work was hard, made more difficult by the thick rubber gloves she'd worn over her hands to protect the parts that were still healing, but Jordan had never minded hard work. She would be back the next day and as many days afterward as possible until Fancy Pants reopened. It felt good to have someone give her the benefit of the doubt for a change.

She forced herself not to think about Gabriel as she worked. He had a lot of crazy stuff going on in his life and might not even be at her house when she got home, even though he said he would be. But her pulse sped up at the sight of his car still parked at her house as she drove up a little bit after dark. The exhaustion from being on her feet for the past ten hours fled as she barreled up her front steps. She stepped in the front door and found him sitting at the kitchen table.

She couldn't remember the last time she'd come in the door and found someone waiting for her at the kitchen table.

"Hi." She knew her voice sounded breathless but hoped he would attribute it to running in from the truck.

"Hi yourself." He smiled. "I guess you found some gainful employment? Either that or you wanted to be alone and were too nice to chase me out of your house."

"Gainfully employed at a very nice café just outside of Redding City. Nothing too permanent, but at least enough work until Fancy Pants reopens."

"I made a little dinner if you want some."

"Oh my gosh, are you kidding? Yes, I want some."

He chuckled. "Don't get too excited. It's just some salad and pasta. I'm afraid all the culinary skills in my family went to my sister."

She grinned at him, then turned to the kitchen. "Nobody's cooked for me since my mom died, so anything beats the peanut butter and jelly sandwich I was probably going to throw together." She grabbed the pasta and salad out of the fridge and put the pasta plate in the microwave. When she turned back around, he was staring at her with an odd expression on his face.

"What?" she asked. "What's wrong?"

"Nothing. I'm just realizing you haven't had a very easy time of it."

She grabbed a fork and began attacking her salad. "It's not that bad. I'm alone a lot, but I don't mind being alone. It's in my nature."

"How do you keep from hating the people of Oak Creek and how they treat you?"

The microwave dinged and she got up to get her pasta. "Did something happen?" she asked, keeping her back turned. Her heart sank when he didn't answer right away. Finally, she turned back around, forcing a smile.

He studied her for a second before shaking his head. "No, nothing of consequence. I just meant not being able to get a job in town and stuff like that."

She sat down next to him at the table. "I can't really blame them for not wanting to hire me." She began to eat the pasta, letting out a sigh of pleasure. "It's amazing how good something tastes when someone else made it for you. Thank you."

The grin he gave her made her forget all about how tired she was.

"If you're this impressed with pasta out of a box and sauce out of the jar, I'd like to see how you'd react if I put actual effort into cooking."

She wagged her eyebrows at him. "That sounds like a very scientific experiment to me. We might have to try it multiple times to make sure the data is consistent."

His smile slipped just the slightest bit. "You're so smart."

She wasn't sure exactly how to answer that, so she just stuffed another forkful of pasta into her mouth.

"What did you do today?" she finally asked.

He sat back in his chair. "A lot of soul-searching. A couple of come-to-Jesus meetings. I went out for a little exercise in the woods. Found some teenagers getting into trouble but straightened them out. Ran into Dorian."

She nodded. "Dorian's around these woods a lot. He's said hello to me once or twice, and sometimes I just look up from the front porch and find him at the edge of the trees. The man is a little spooky."

She'd never feared for her own safety from him, the

opposite in fact, but the guy really did prefer being in the wilderness more than being around people.

"Yes, Dorian is a good man."

"You must have tied him up if you got him to talk to you for a long time. He's not one for talking."

Gabe smiled. "No, it was a very short conversation."

She finished her last bite, then got up to rinse her dishes in the sink.

"I also did some work on the computers. I came across the coding you're working on."

Jordan stiffened. She couldn't help it. Collingwood Technology was at the forefront of certain computer applications and programming. Gabe would certainly know what he was doing in that regard. It would suck for him to tell her that what she was developing wasn't any good.

"Oh? What did you think?" she forced herself to ask.

"I thought it was dangerously brilliant."

The word brilliant had her breaking out into a grin. She finished washing her plate, trying to get her juvenile reaction to his praise under control before she turned back around.

When she did, she was surprised to see a look of tension on his face. "I don't understand. Brilliant means good, right?"

He stood up, eyes pinned on hers, but didn't walk over to her. "It's nothing short of brilliant. It's a method of accessing closed systems coming from directions most corporations wouldn't even think of."

"I've always loved computers. Even back in high school, I did some coding in my spare time."

He leaned up against the counter. "You've obviously got a talent for it. I mean that. I would immediately hire someone with your skill at CT."

"While I was in prison, there was an education initiative. We were able to take some classes to see if we had any special skill sets. Ended up I was very good at coding and cybersecurity in particular. I'm good at finding holes and back doors."

He rubbed a hand over his face. "You know that's what hackers do, right? Find areas to exploit."

She smiled at the pained look on his face. He was trying his best to stay neutral and non-accusatory. She grabbed a towel to dry her hands, then walked over and kissed him on the cheek.

"Hackers—people who want to cheat the system and others—are who I want to stop. That's what I've been working on, new and different methods of combatting cyber warfare. Theoretically, I'm pretty successful at it."

"And you've got to think like a criminal to beat a criminal. That's what it is you've been working on."

She gave a one-shouldered shrug. "I guess thinking like a criminal is part of my genetic makeup. But my plan is to open my own cybersecurity business, or at least sell the programs I develop."

His arm wrapped around her.

She buried herself into his side. "I'm probably naive to think that anyone would want an ex-con anywhere near their security systems."

"Actually, you'd be surprised what many forward-thinking companies want when it comes to that. As a matter of fact, CT has its own cybersecurity issue I've been dealing with. Maybe I'll get you to take a look at that."

Something warm and tingly went through her at his words. The CEO of a highly regarded technology company wanted *her* opinion. She didn't even try to stop the smile that cracked her face wide open. "I would love that."

He ran a finger down her cheek. "Look at that smile."

"This might be the most excited I've ever been in my whole life."

Those green eyes narrowed. "If that is the most excited you've ever been, I have definitely been derelict in my other duties."

She spun around so she was pressed up against his chest and wrapped her arms around his neck, rubbing up against him. "Oooh. I never thought the word *derelict* could be sexy. You better see to securing your reputation."

He reached around her waist with one arm and lifted her with almost no effort. "You know what else I'm going to be seeing to?"

"What's that?"

"Taking you on a date."

She stiffened. The way he was holding her, he couldn't help but notice.

"It doesn't have to be in Oak Creek." He kissed her nose. "We can save that battle for another time."

She smiled again. "Okay. I'd like that. Not to sound completely pathetic, but this will actually be my first real date."

"First real date?"

She felt like an idiot, but he was looking at her with such boyish excitement, the feeling faded away.

"I went out with someone once a few months ago, but it ended up he was just using me to get information to hurt my friends. So that doesn't count."

His forehead touched hers. "It very definitely doesn't count."

"I guess you're the first of a lot of things for me."

The possessive grin should've scared her, or at least set off her feminine alarms. But his hand slipped into the hair at the base of her neck and gripped tightly. "That pretty much makes me the luckiest guy on the planet. I'll take it."

He began walking them both toward the bedroom.

"You just leave it to me. I might not be very romantic, but I bet I can come up with a pretty impressive first date."

He was pretty impressive in a lot of ways, especially the speed and finesse he used his 200 pounds of muscle to whisk her effortlessly into the bedroom. His lips moved down her jaw to her throat, and when his teeth bit down on that place where her neck met her shoulder, every other thought—past, present, future—disappeared from her mind.

Chapter 20

It took two weeks to set up the date the way Gabe wanted it. He certainly could have taken her somewhere else. Somewhere nice, maybe in Reddington City, but that wasn't what he wanted. After all, you only got one first date. He had no doubt she'd be happy and thrilled with almost anything. That was just her default setting: appreciative.

She'd known so little for so long that any luxuries or extra niceties in her life were sources of joy. Gabe found he wanted to spoil her. It was easy to feel that way about someone who could have rightfully been angry or bitter over the hand she'd been dealt in life. But she chose to embrace the joy of the little things instead.

What he had planned was way over the top, Gabe realized that, but he didn't care. Jordan deserved to have somebody go over the top for her.

She worked hard, driving every day to Reddington City without complaint to work at the café. He'd thought she was waiting tables and had forced himself to say nothing when he found out she was bussing tables and washing dishes. Jordan seemed to like the woman she was working for and argued that it was only temporary anyway, until Fancy Pants reopened, so he'd left it alone.

He'd had enough of his own work to do and hadn't been able to stay with her as much as he wanted because he needed to take care of things at CT. The first couple of days he'd been tempted to pack her up and move her to Idaho Falls with him. He certainly knew enough people to be able to get her a job similar to the one she was working now. But those damn parole restrictions meant she couldn't come live with him in any other state for at least another fifteen months.

But she was never going to anyway. The more he saw her around her house, the more he realized that. This house, this land, was her fortitude. She could survive somewhere else—as she obviously had—but this was where she belonged.

And that fact had him thinking in directions he'd never thought in before. Because every time he spent a night away from her back in Idaho Falls to deal with Collingwood Technology, he liked it less and less.

He didn't know what that meant long-term, but he knew better than to ignore instincts when they were screaming at him. Even if it scared the shit out of him a little bit.

Of all the women he'd thought he might fall for, an ex-con with a smart mouth who lived in a tiny town in Wyoming hadn't even entered the realm of possibility.

An ex-con with an excellent eye for coding. He'd watched her work in the evenings and realized how gifted she really was.

Definitely talented enough that he could offer her a high-paying job at CT. Hers was the type of mind he looked for, the type that had kept his business on the forefront of technology for so long. But he hadn't made her an offer because he wasn't sure what direction he was going in with his company. He just knew it was time for a change.

Plus, even a well-paying job wasn't going to get her $622,000.

That damn sticky note was becoming the bane of his existence.

He'd asked her about it again, but her response stayed the same: it was the amount that would get her the life she wanted. Nothing about that response fit into everything he knew about her. What would $622,000 provide that she didn't already have? She didn't want a new house or to live somewhere else. Maybe it was to start the business she'd mentioned—although that was way more than she needed.

And why wouldn't she just tell him that? Why keep it a secret?

But that was a worry for another day. Today it was time to take a special lady out on her first date.

Planning it had been complicated, but he'd finally gotten everything he'd needed three days ago. Ironically, getting Jordan to agree to ask for the day off work had been one of the hardest parts.

She was nervous. It wasn't difficult to see the tension radiating through her body as they drove from her house toward Reddington City. It was just past noon.

"This is a lunch date, right? We're not going anywhere fancy, because I'm not really dressed for it. Actually, I feel a little ridiculous."

"What you're wearing is perfect." He'd already assured her of that more than once, since she'd gotten so upset when he'd asked her if she could wear a dress or skirt. Evidently, her wardrobe was quite limited.

When she'd walked out wearing the skirt she'd worn to

their picnic, Gabe nearly swallowed his tongue. The memories swamped him. Would *always* swamp him.

"Are you sure? This is really more of a summer-weight skirt."

Even though the weather had been mild, it was still winter in Wyoming. He understood her concern.

"I promise you it will be absolutely perfect." He took her hand where it rested on her thigh. "I'm never going to lead you into a situation where you're not prepared if I can help it. I promise."

So many things have been out of her control in her young life. He never wanted to add to her burdens.

She took a deep breath, then blew it out, relaxing. "Okay. I trust you."

His heart clinched at those words. She didn't say them lightly, and he didn't take them that way.

But truly, where they were going, the skirt would be perfect.

"Since we're on our way, can't you at least give me a hint about where we're going?"

He smiled. "Well, I have to be honest, a little bit of our date involves a business meeting for me."

All her tension was back. "Business?"

He stroked a finger across the back of her hand. "Nothing big."

That wasn't completely true. His business meeting today was just an initial, informal, get-together with a potential buyer for Collingwood Technology. But it allowed him to justify chartering a private jet. As they took the exit for the Reddington City airport, Jordan realized what was going on.

Now her tension skyrocketed.

"Gabriel, I don't want to ruin anything, but if we're going on an airplane, I just need to remind you that I have to stay in the state of Wyoming according to my parole limitations. And although I'm sure they probably wouldn't find out, I can't take that chance." He could hear the shakiness in her voice and knew she was close to tears.

"Hey." He squeezed her hand. "I would never do anything that might jeopardize your future."

Those big gray eyes stared up at him. "I just thought you might have forgotten. Most people take for granted the ability to just go where they want whenever they want. So we're going to stay within the state lines?"

She looked puzzled, and he couldn't blame her. There weren't a hell of a lot of places to go in Wyoming, especially for business and a date. Particularly in a lightweight skirt in the middle of winter.

He drove the rest of the way and parked in the airport's one parking lot. Unlike Idaho Falls, there were no short-term versus long-term parking lots at the Reddington City airport. He reached in the back seat and got his black leather portfolio, which held some of the papers he needed for his meeting today…as well as one paper that would prove most important to Jordan. He handed it to her.

"Actually, we'll be going out of state."

She read the paper, then looked up at him. "You got permission from my parole officer for me to leave the state with you?"

He winked at her. "That's part of the reason this is both a date and a business meeting. Yes, I did need to meet with someone briefly today." Although he certainly could've met with Ian DeRose at another time or by another means. "But that was a way for me to legitimize getting you on this plane for our first date."

"Mr. Patterson really approved this?"

"Getting Patterson to approve it was much easier than getting you to agree to take the whole day off of work. He wasn't surprised in the least to find out that a technology company was interested in your skills. As a matter fact, he had nothing but good things to say about you."

"Oh."

Oh. Of course she was surprised someone spoke nicely about her. She was always so quick to believe the bad things about herself but much slower to believe the good.

It was time for that to change.

Her tension began to disappear as her excitement about this new adventure overshadowed her concerns. When she broke out into a big smile, Gabe knew he'd made the right decision. No matter how the rest of this day went, that smile right there was worth every bit of effort he'd put into their date.

"I've never been on a plane before."

He reached over, grabbed her hands, and brought her fingers to his lips. "Another first." He was fast becoming addicted to providing her firsts.

"Where are we going?"

"Someplace where that skirt will be absolutely perfect."

Chapter 21

"Don't get too used to this," Gabriel said as they walked up the steps into the jet he'd chartered. "Generally speaking, I fly regular airlines like everybody else. But what the hell, I am the CEO of a multimillion-dollar company; I might as well claim some of the perks. Before I met you, I hadn't even taken vacation days in more than five years."

"What's a vacation day?" Jordan quipped. They were as foreign to her as this luxury jet.

Admittedly, she didn't have much basis for comparison, but the plush seats and champagne in her hand, provided by the first mate who served as both flight attendant and backup pilot, made her almost giddy. Even if Gabriel wouldn't tell her where they were going.

She'd never dreamed it would be Los Angeles.

Actually, a small airport outside of Los Angeles. It was a long way to go for just a few hours, less than a full day, but since this was a business trip for him, she just let herself enjoy it.

Because she was in LA!

They drove around downtown in the rental car before

Gabe parked and announced that everyone should have a couple hours on the Hollywood Walk of Fame their first time in LA.

She'd been a little nervous that he would take her to some office or business dinner where she would feel out of place and underdressed. But instead, he just played tour guide, dragging her from one place to another in the balmy sunshine. The skirt really was perfect for the location.

"I never knew how empty my life was without a picture of Elvis standing next to Predator," she said as they drank a frozen lemonade and headed back to the car.

He shrugged. "Yeah, well, you're young. So it's to be expected that you wouldn't actually know the truly fine things in life yet."

He snickered at his own joke as he opened the car door for her. Jordan knew she was in trouble. How was she supposed to not fall in love with this man? He used his strength to protect her. His wealth to spoil her. His intellect to challenge and engage her.

But what did she have to offer in return?

He went around and started the car. "Okay, to make this a legit business expense, I've got to stash you somewhere for a few minutes so I can have my meeting."

"Sure. I can hang out at a coffee shop, or heck, I can just sit in the car and enjoy the sunshine. God knows I'm not going to see temperatures in the seventies in Oak Creek anytime soon."

"Don't worry, I've got just the place. And then we'll go on our date."

"This isn't the date?"

"Elvis impersonators and frozen lemonades?" He huffed as he raised one dark brow. "No, this is not the date. I'm offended." He returned his attention to driving, and she couldn't help but giggle.

"Sorry I offended you."

"You did. You really did." He winked at her.

Yeah, she was in so much trouble.

When she saw the signs for where they were going, her eyes filled up with tears.

Santa Monica Pier.

"Gabriel . . ." She couldn't even get any other words out.

"I thought maybe you could dip your toes in the Pacific while I had my meeting. It won't take me too long, then we can have dinner on the pier itself."

Her throat seized; she couldn't even speak, but she grabbed his hand and squeezed.

A few minutes later they were pulling up to a parking lot near the Santa Monica Pier.

"Are you okay on your own or do you want me to help get you situated?"

All she could do was stare out at the ocean she'd never dreamed she'd be looking at today. She finally found her voice. "I am more than okay."

He leaned over and kissed her on the cheek. "I'll come find you when I'm done. Will probably be about an hour."

"Take all the time you need."

* * *

GABE WATCHED AS JORDAN WALKED THROUGH THE SMALL parking lot until her feet hit sand. She stopped, obviously unsure what to do, then did what anyone in her position would: crouched down and took off her shoes.

When, miracle of all miracles, a parking spot opened up right there in the tiny lot, Gabe didn't question it, he just pulled the rental into the spot. His phone was in his hand a second later, and he was texting Ian DeRose. The location of their meeting—a coffee shop a couple of miles away—needed to be changed.

Because there was no way in hell he was going to miss seeing Jordan touch the ocean for the first time. He and Ian could damn well have their meeting right here in the parking lot.

A few minutes later, Gabe was still watching her from a distance, watching her reach down to trail her fingers in the sand or to pick up a shell that had caught her interest, when his friend walked up beside him.

"You know I would've come out to Idaho Falls, right?" Ian slapped him on the shoulder. "One of these days, I'm going to get your sister to go out with me."

Gabe reached over and shook Ian's hand, not taking his eyes off Jordan. "Afraid you're too late. I think she's gone and found herself a permanent-type guy." After Aiden Teague had almost died to protect Violet, Gabe no longer had any problem with the man.

"Damn it. That's what I get for being a gentleman and waiting."

Gabe rolled his eyes. Ian DeRose, billionaire investor and philanthropist, had never been a gentleman a day in his life. And Gabe was glad he wouldn't be sniffing around Violet anymore.

Gabe asked the question that had allowed him to justify all this as a business trip. "You still interested in buying Collingwood Technology?"

And then she did it. Something in Gabe's heart clenched as Jordan took those final steps that put her feet in the waters of the Pacific. He smiled as she jumped back —that water was probably damn cold—but then she stepped back in again.

He realized Ian was saying something.

"What?"

Ian's eyes narrowed. "Is this because of what happened with Violet? The whole Stellman situation? Because you're acting weird. Since when do you like the beach?"

Gabe pointed to Jordan. "Since she wanted to put her toes in the Pacific."

Jordan was standing there now, long brown hair falling down her back, her face turned up toward the sun, that skirt floating gently around her knees.

Jesus, he was in trouble.

Ian gave a dramatic sigh. "Well, since we were on the same SEAL team together, I guess I won't take advantage of your lovesick dopiness to offer you some obscenely low price for your company."

Gabe rolled his eyes. "Thanks. You're a peach."

"I've been trying to get you to sell for years. Why now?"

Gabe looked back out toward the ocean again. Jordan. "I'm just not sure my heart is in it anymore. My heart is . . . other places. Being hit so hard by someone I trusted has me rethinking everything. I'm not sure what I want, but I don't think Collingwood Technology is it anymore."

"What are you going to do if you sell? I can't see you just sitting around counting your money."

No, Gabe was well aware he needed something to keep him challenged and focused professionally. He thought of Jordan's plan to open a cybersecurity consulting business.

And suddenly he knew exactly what he needed to do.

"Actually, I wouldn't be selling you all of the company, just about eighty-five percent of it. I would keep the cyber division and clients. Focus only on that."

Because it was something he and Jordan could do together. Not just do, but thrive at. He could help Jordan get her damned $622,000, then get her to tell him what it was for.

Get *her*.

Ian leaned back against the car. "Yeah, brother. I've always been interested in acquiring CT. It's a solid company that would be a great part of my portfolio. My people have to look over everything, of course, but as far as I'm concerned, I'm in."

Gabe had known this would be the case, and he could've confirmed it with a simple phone call to Ian. Ian knew that too but was wise enough not to point it out.

The two of them had fought side by side on missions that were so top secret they would never be allowed to talk about them with another living soul. Those missions had formed a bond that wasn't easily shaken.

Ian would do anything to help Gabe, and the feeling was mutual. The fact that he was a billionaire and could buy Collingwood Technology multiple times over was just an added bonus.

"I think you have better people to play with than me," Ian said. "So I'll leave you to it."

"We'll talk soon. Next time you can fly out to see me."

Ian slapped him on the shoulder. "And why do I have a feeling that might be in Wyoming rather than Idaho Falls?"

Gabe shot him a grin. "Don't worry, they have airports in Wyoming. Just not as big."

Ian shook Gabe's hand and wished him luck before fading into the crowds of tourists and cars behind them.

Gabe had no doubt if he turned now, he wouldn't be able to find his friend. Ian had a way of disappearing even when surrounded by dozens of other people. It had made him invaluable as a SEAL.

Gabe wasn't exactly sure what his friend did now, but he knew it was way more than just sitting around counting his money and buying businesses every once in a while. It was dirty and it was dangerous.

But Ian DeRose could take care of himself.

And right now, Gabe had more interesting things to focus on than an old team member.

Jordan was surprised to see him this early, but he distracted her with a few splashes, and soon they were walking up on the pier itself.

He bought them hotdogs, and they went to the end of the pier to eat them, sitting on a bench, surrounded by fishermen and seagulls and a briny smell that was unique to the ocean. He turned to her.

"This," he reached over and wiped a smidge of mustard at the corner of her mouth, "is a date."

Her smile rivaled the California sun. "I dare say it's the best date that I've ever had."

He poked her in the side. "By that measure, it's also the worst date you've ever had."

But those worry lines that often took root between her brows were completely gone. This really was a good time for her.

She tucked a strand of her long brown hair behind her ear. "The cost of chartering that flight notwithstanding, I like this more than I would eating at a fancy restaurant. That just intimidates me. Eating hot dogs on a bench, on the other hand . . ."

"Well, we might have to go to a few fancy places, but I've found that some of the best food in the world is from tiny spots where you're welcome in your jeans and a T-shirt. That's my kind of place." And he wanted to take her to all of them. All over the world.

They made their way back along the pier, to the car and back to the regional airport. Once they were in the air, the first mate reported he would be up front unless they needed him, leaving them alone.

"So does this first date end with a kiss?" she asked.

"Maybe." He wagged a brow at her. "Maybe if you're lucky, a lot more than that."

"Actually, I think it's your turn to get lucky."

"Is that so?"

She unbuckled her seatbelt and was soon straddling his thighs. "I don't know what you've heard about me, but I definitely put out on the first date."

He'd always been the more sexually aggressive one. But not now. Jordan wanted to be in charge, and he was more than willing to let her.

"I want to taste you," she whispered, voice husky, as she reached underneath to unbutton his jeans.

They'd never done that, first because of the injuries to her hands, and then because he just hadn't been able to keep his hands off her body. But he didn't want her to feel like he expected that.

"Rainfall." He hoped he would get a special spot in heaven for what he was about to say. "You don't have to do this. As sure as I am that your hot little mouth would have me coming apart in an embarrassingly short amount of time, I don't want you to feel like I expect it."

She licked her lips, a smile of feminine confidence lighting her features. "Oh, I know you don't expect it. I want it."

She slid down until she was on her knees between his spread legs. Normally that sight would be one of the sexiest things he could think of. But not right now, not with Jordan.

He reached down to pull her up. "I don't want you on your knees in front of me. You've had too much of your power taken away from you. I don't want to be another person who does that."

She shook her head and slid down his zipper. He couldn't stop the groan that fell from his lips as her hand wrapped around him and pulled him out from his boxers.

"You're not taking my power." She licked him from base to tip; his hips jerked of their own volition.

He watched, mesmerized as her small pink tongue began to lick around his head, exploring, learning, playing.

"Who really has the power here, Gabriel?"

Those gray eyes blinked up at him as she took him deep in her mouth. She was right; physical positioning had nothing to do with power in this situation.

Jordan was the one kneeling at his feet, but she very definitely had all the power.

Her hand wrapped around the base of his cock. She licked him like he was her favorite-flavored lollipop. "Fuck, Jordan." He nearly shot off the seat. The sight of her with that dark hair falling around his thighs, her hungry mouth working him—exuberance making up for any lack of experience—meant he wasn't going to last long.

He threaded his fist in her hair as she rubbed against his shin and knew this was turning her on too. And fuck if that didn't just turn him on even more.

He would make sure she got hers too.

He forced himself to let her set the pace, to explore as much as she wanted, but soon he was sweating with the need for release.

"Take me deep, Rainfall. Hard."

She did, and within just a few moments he shouted her name and exploded into her mouth. She swallowed every drop before slowly releasing him and easing her head down to rest against his thigh.

His hand was still wrapped in her hair as he began to stroke it. She gave him a sleepy, satisfied smile, as if *she* were the one who'd just had a mind-blowing orgasm.

He reached down and scooped her up into his lap, more than ready to make sure she did. "Your turn."

"Just hold me," she whispered into his neck. "This has been the single most fantastic day of my life, and I just want to end it right here."

"You sure? I certainly don't mind returning the favor."

"You already have."

Chapter 22

"You're going steady with my brother," Violet said in a singsong voice. She wagged her eyebrows at Jordan as she walked from the back kitchen of the newly reopened Fancy Pants through the swinging door—the same one that had been blocked and almost gotten them killed a little over two months ago.

Jordan nearly dropped the tray of pastries she was boxing, trying to think of a response before Violet returned to the kitchen as they both completed their Thursday afternoon closing duties.

Over the past few weeks she'd done her best to keep her relationship with Gabriel under wraps, although she hadn't been successful at all in keeping her happiness under wraps. The time since Los Angeles had flown by in a sort of daze of contentment and passion.

Everything had seemed to fall into a beautiful sort of balance. Gabriel went back and forth between Idaho Falls and Oak Creek, balancing his work there with time with her. In her bed.

And shower. And couch. And kitchen table.

And Jordan had loved every second of it.

But was Violet mad at the thought of Jordan and Gabriel as a couple? The bakery had only reopened a couple of weeks ago, so they hadn't had much chance to talk.

Not that Jordan would know exactly what to say, anyway. She and Gabriel hadn't mentioned anything permanent. Stuff was going on with his business—he'd mentioned selling part of it. But neither of them had talked about where their relationship was going, if anywhere.

"I only mention it because he asked a couple of weeks ago about you using a computer with system access to CT," Violet continued as she came back through the swinging door and began wiping down the counters.

"Oh. Is that okay with you?"

"Of course. You've been holding out on me on how good you are with computers. I knew you had skills after you modified the bakery accounting software. But Gabe says you're impressive. And for him to use the word 'impressive'? Well, that means something."

It meant everything to Jordan.

There were multiple Collingwood Technology computers at her house now. Some were for his use since he was there so often.

He'd explained to her that he was considering selling off most of the company and focusing on what interested him professionally, some of which happened to be cybersecurity. And he was amazing at it. Between the two of them, him with his years of experience and her with her new eyes and perspective, they made a pretty daunting team.

But he was also letting her enhance and develop her

skills on her own. When he'd offered her the use of one of the CT computers, with functionality far greater than anything she could afford, she'd been in awe.

And she didn't take it lightly. The operating system was proprietary to Collingwood Technology, and the computer itself probably cost more than her house. Moreover, it was a huge measure of trust on his part. Not even all his employees had access to what she did.

When he'd shown her the desk where he'd set up the computer in her living room, she'd just stared. "I'm not sure I know what to do with this."

"I think you know exactly what to do with it."

She tore her eyes away from the system to stare at him. "I don't understand why you're giving me access to this."

He bent forward and kissed her on the nose. "Maybe I want to see what you're capable of when given the right tools. You're pretty fantastic even on that crappy system you were using. Let's see what you can do with non-crap. Maybe we can get you closer to your $622,000."

He wanted to know what that money was for, but she couldn't bring herself to tell him. She'd told Charlie when she'd lived with her, but that was all. Charlie hadn't really understood and had tried to talk Jordan out of it. But Jordan didn't really expect anyone to be able to understand *The Plan*.

It wasn't something anyone could understand unless they'd lived it. Gabriel wouldn't understand either. That's why she evaded him every time he asked, trying to make it seem like it wasn't a big deal.

Jordan looked at Violet now. "Thank you for allowing him to provide system access to me. Coding comes pretty naturally, but I'm inexperienced, which means there's a lot I don't know. Gabriel has taught me so much."

The door to the kitchen swung open as Jordan finished

the last sentence. Charlie walked in, grinning. "Oh, please tell us more about what that big Navy SEAL has taught you. I bet a lot more than just about computers."

Peyton Ward followed behind Charlie, shaking her head at her friend's outrageous statement. Peyton's four-and-a-half-year-old daughter, Jess, was already zooming past her mom and Charlie to Jordan's side.

The little girl smiled up at Jordan, the perfect mix of angelic and impish. "Got anything extra up there?"

Charlie walked over and tried to shoo Jess out of the way with her hip. "Get in line, kiddo. Pregnant ladies get the leftover treats first."

Jess scrunched up her little face. "Aw, c'mon, Aunt Charlie, you said that yesterday."

Charlie grinned down at her. "And guess what? Still pregnant today."

"Fine. But only because I'm going to be this baby's sister-in-law one day." Jess leaned over and kissed Charlie's still nearly flat stomach.

Jordan looked over at Peyton, then Charlie, who both just shrugged. Jess and Ethan, Finn's eight-year-old son and soon to be Charlie's stepson, had already decided they were going to marry each other.

Those kids were so damn serious when they talked about it, no one had the heart to tell them it might work out otherwise. Not that they would listen anyway.

Jordan handed Charlie and Jess each an éclair. Peyton leaned up against the wall, looking tired as she always did. Jordan offered her a pastry too, but Peyton shook her head no

They all moved to the front of the bakery so Jordan and Violet could finish their work. Peyton and Charlie both started to help but were shooed away. Jess was allowed to wipe down the cabinets at her height with a wet washcloth.

"Tell me more about your Navy SEAL," Charlie said with a grin as she licked cream filling from her fingers. "And all he's *teaching* you."

"Please don't," Violet begged. "He's my brother, you know."

"Yeah, but look at her smile!" Charlie yelled. "That's a smile of a woman who's getting what she wants and needs."

Jordan could feel the heat covering her face, but she still couldn't wipe off her smile. Charlie was right; she was getting what she wanted and needed.

Plus, she was getting stuff she hadn't even known she wanted and needed. Companionship, respect, intellectual stimulation. And dates. None that involved another chartered jet or trip to Los Angeles, but still just as perfect.

They'd gone to some extravagant places that had made her a little uncomfortable, but also a lot of fun places. Bowling. Movies. Hikes. She'd loved all of it mostly because it was time spent with Gabriel.

And all those dates had mind-blowing sex at the end.

But yeah, she wasn't going to talk about that out loud, even if Gabriel wasn't Violet's brother. Jordan just wasn't ever going to be a sit-around-and-gossip-with-her-girlfriends type. That had been so distant from her life over the past ten years that she didn't think she would ever develop the habit.

But it was nice to have girlfriends. People who noticed when you smiled.

"Let's talk about the wedding. Less than two weeks to go," Jordan said as she began to close out the register.

"Ten days," little Jess chirped. "Mommy made me a countdown calendar. I'm going to be a flower girl. Ethan's going to be a junior groomsman because he's too big to be a ring bear."

"You'll be beautiful." Jordan didn't correct her mispronunciation of "bearer." "And Ethan will be a handsome groomsman."

"I'm still mad that you won't be a bridesmaid," Charlie muttered.

Jordan just shook her head. She and Charlie had talked about this multiple times since Charlie and Finn had gotten engaged. Everyone in the entire town would be there. Jordan would be there too, but she didn't want to take a chance on messing up the beautiful day by standing up in the front of the church.

Hopefully, no one would do anything thoughtless to ruin a wedding just to humiliate her. She had to admit that people hadn't been as actively hostile over the past two months. Even the weekly poop throwing against her house had stopped.

She didn't think it was anyone truly changing their tune about her; more likely it had to do with the fact that every time she stepped foot out of Fancy Pants, one of her friends or the Linear guys was with her. They wouldn't let her go to the next town over to buy gas or groceries anymore. Instead, they marched her into the local shops.

They never made a big deal out of it, never rubbed it in the shop owner's face or confronted them. They just quietly moved with Jordan as she shopped, then stood and talked with her as she paid.

Jordan didn't like it. She was uncomfortable and would rather just leave it alone.

"Why are you doing this?" she'd whispered to Zac and Anne the first day they'd patiently walked her into Oak Creek's grocery store. Except for the one time with Gabriel, Jordan hadn't stepped foot in there.

Zac put a hand on her shoulder. "It's like I told Gabe. The way Oak Creek has treated you is not who we really are. The people here know that, but they'd rather hang on to their anger than do what's right. You've been nice enough not to force them to deal with it."

Quiet Doctor Anne took Zac's hand. "But they have to. They're the problem in this town. Not you, Jordan."

She had ended up with a bunch of groceries she didn't even need in an effort to just get out of there. But Mrs. McMillian, the owner of the store, hadn't said anything—negative or positive—as Jordan paid. When Jordan had gone back the next week, this time with Aiden as her escort, it had been a little easier.

She was finally feeling like this town was home again. She was on the inside for once, instead of being the kid outside with her nose pressed up against the window, looking at all the happy people inside.

An "us" rather than a "them."

For the first time, she was feeling like she had something like a family.

She finished her duties at the bakery, laughing and talking wedding plans the whole time, before driving home. It was early afternoon and Gabriel was gone until tomorrow night, but she had lots of stuff to work on. For the first time, everything in her life seemed to be working *for* her rather than against her. Her already huge smile grew as she bounded up the steps; she knew she must look like an idiot, but she didn't care.

It was the smile of a woman who was getting what she wanted and needed.

Maybe things really had turned around. And maybe the women were right; she did deserve some happiness for once. The past was behind her. It was time to look to the future.

She balanced the piece of French opera cake she'd kept

aside especially for Gabriel in one hand as she unlocked the front door and went inside.

A figure sat at her kitchen table. The dessert fell from nerveless fingers.

"Hello, Jordan. Daddy's home."

Chapter 23

Jordan watched in horror as her father walked over and picked up the box she'd just dropped. "Now, now, don't waste those lovely desserts you make at your little bakery."

"What are you doing here?" The question came out weak and hoarse. She'd never expected to see her father again.

"Can't I come visit my daughter?" He reached out to touch her, but she jerked away.

"No." Her voice was stronger this time. She owed absolutely nothing to this man. She had family, but this man was not it.

She reached for the phone in her bag. "I'm calling the police."

She wasn't prepared for his backhand to her face. She tasted her own blood as the phone fell from her hands.

"I'm your father. Show some respect."

"You haven't been my father since I was fourteen years old. Haven't been my father since you stole from the people in this town that Mom and I loved so much. You're nothing but a selfish asshole."

Jordan had never spoken in that way to anyone her entire life. But she'd never been this angry in her whole life.

How dare he? How dare he come back here and expect any loyalty from her. Even looking at him made her sick to her stomach.

She expected another blow at her words, but instead his gaze filled with a sort of begrudging respect.

"Look at you, all grown up, complete with claws. I should've come back here months ago. But honestly, I didn't have any use for you until you started hanging out with Collingwood. Is he your target?"

"My target?"

"He has millions. Much more than anybody in this town ever had. If you're smart, you're thinking about how you might get your hands on some of that."

Jordan wiped the blood from her lips, shaking her head vigorously. "I'm not trying to steal from him. I love him."

Michael threw back his head and laughed. "Love him? You really think someone like him is going to get serious about someone like you?"

She flinched, saying nothing. She couldn't deny that she'd had those very thoughts herself.

"Although . . . he does love to take you out, doesn't he? I've been watching, Daughter. Lots of dates. Fancy places." He spun around and gestured to the computers. "And he certainly has been generous with what he's brought you here."

"What do you want?" she whispered. She just wanted to get him out of here so she could call the police. Maybe she couldn't stop him right now, but she could at least let law enforcement know that Michael was in the area, and maybe they'd be able to track him.

He turned from her and started pacing. "I always hated this town. I did love your mother, that's why I forced myself to put up with it. But when she died, this place became unbearable for me."

"So you just decided to steal everyone's retirement funds and run off?"

He let out a sigh. "If I had known how pitifully little I would get, I probably wouldn't have wasted my time. Half a million dollars doesn't last as long as you would think. Especially when you're on the run."

"It was $622,000."

Michael's smile was slimy. She hated that she was related to this man.

"I saw your little sticky note. I thought you were on the straight and narrow until I saw that. Then I figured you were just trying to get more money from Collingwood. I set the standard for you, and you want to surpass it."

She shook her head. "I've been working to pay back that money to the people of Oak Creek. You've ruined some of their lives. I wanted to make it better. To replace the bad you've done."

Michael rolled his eyes. "Jesus. You sound just like your mother. I guess I shouldn't be surprised you took after her. I had hoped being in prison would have given you a more realistic outlook on life, but apparently not. I guess we'll have to do this the hard way."

She was tired of playing his games. She wanted him out of her house. "What are you talking about?"

"I was hoping you were using Collingwood as a mark. Actually, both of the Collingwood siblings as marks. I was impressed. Now, knowing you actually care about them, I'm not so impressed."

"I don't care if you're impressed or not. I just want you to leave."

Michael shook his head. "I came here hoping to help you with whatever scam you were pulling with Gabe."

"I already told you. I'm not pulling any scam with Gabe."

He rolled his eyes. "Yeah, I see that. What a waste. But you've got access to him, so you're going to help me run a scam instead."

Now it was Jordan's turn to laugh. "I wouldn't help you scam a terrorist, much less someone I care about."

"Oh, I think you will."

A chill settled on her skin. "I won't do it. I don't care what you do to me, I still won't do it."

"Oh, I think you will. I've been watching you with them."

"You've been following me? Following my friends?"

He crossed his arms over his chest. "Do you think I would really come back here without some sort of plan? And you were key, one way or another. Although, I'll admit, I was sort of hoping we could work together."

"Like I said, there's no way in hell I'm going to help you steal from Gabe."

Michael walked over and opened the kitchen drawer with a familiarity that chilled her even more. He grabbed a picture of Charlie.

"This is Charlotte Devereux, isn't it? I hear she's pregnant."

Jordan felt like she was walking through a minefield. "What are you doing?"

Michael picked up her phone from the ground and held it out to her. "Why don't you text your friend and make sure she made it home safely from the bakery."

Oh God. She snatched her phone and began texting Charlie.

Are you all right?

She waited for a reply, tension radiating through her body. Then, finally . . .

How does everybody in this town find out stuff so damn fast? I'm fine. My brakes went out, but I got the car under control before I hit anything. We'll chat later when Finn isn't about to lose his mind.

Jordan couldn't hold back her cry and brought her hand up to cover her mouth. "What have you done?"

"Nothing." He shrugged, the epitome of innocence. "Like your friend said, she's fine." He turned and began to pace. "Do you know what's wrong with having loved ones, Jordan? Those feelings can so easily be used against you. We'd all hate for something to happen to Charlotte or her unborn baby. Just like we'd all hate for anything to happen to Violet or Anne or little Jessica. But accidents do happen. You know that better than anyone, don't you, Daughter? I mean it *was* an accident, what happened to Becky and Micah Mackay. Wouldn't it be terrible if something happened to Zac Mackay all these years later just as he's found love again? My God, that's the sort of thing Greek tragedies are written about."

Fear gripped her heart like a vise. "What do you want?"

"I want the same thing you do, for nobody to get hurt. Believe it or not, I haven't just been sitting around here taking pictures and playing Peeping Tom. A colleague discovered a potential weakness in the Collingwood Technology computer system, a back door that will allow me to drain some of their accounts anonymously. I was hoping to make this a long-term gig in which you and I could work together. We could've taken the money more slowly, and they never would've realized what we were doing. We would've gotten a lot more that way. But it doesn't look like that's an option. We'll just have to do a grab and run."

"I'm not going to help you steal from Gabriel."

"That's your choice. I'll just make a quick call to Allan Godlewski. He's a pretty helpful guy."

Her stomach clenched. "Allan is working with you?"

"Godlewski isn't my normal caliber of partner, but after someone attacked him in the woods and broke his nose a couple of months ago, he pretty much hates this town as much as I do." Michael studied his fingernails. "But the guy is a little unstable. Violent even. That's a shame."

Michael looked up, eyes narrowed. "One call to him, Jordan, and someone you love will die today."

A sob bubbled up inside her. "What do I have to do?" She would make sure her friends were safe, then worry about the money.

"You'll have to get into the operating system at Collingwood Technology. Shouldn't be difficult for someone with your computer skills—or hell, use *other* favors to get access from Collingwood if you need to. I'm sure if you show up, he'll be very glad to see his sweet girlfriend, and you'll figure it out from there."

It never occurred to her father—because he thought like a criminal—that Gabriel had trusted her enough to provide her Collingwood Technology system access from *here*. She didn't have to go all the way to Idaho Falls. But she wasn't about to let Michael know that. If he knew, he might think of all sorts of other ways for her to harm Gabriel's company.

She just had to buy as much time as possible, then figure out what to do from there.

Michael snatched her phone out of her hand, threw it on the ground and stomped on it. "Just in case you were getting any ideas. It doesn't have to be Anne Griffin my partners go after. What about Bollinger's son . . . what's his name? Ethan?"

She looked at the man whose DNA she couldn't believe she shared. "Why are you doing this?"

He shrugged as he turned away. "Just business. That's all it's ever been. Get ready to go. We're driving to Idaho Falls."

Jordan shook her head, knowing the fact that this man cared so little about her shouldn't hurt her, but it did. Some part of her—the little girl in her, the *daughter*—had always held on to the hope that there had been some mistake, that maybe Michael hadn't robbed the people who knew and trusted him.

That hope was now dead.

She looked over to the fridge for her shotgun. She would have no problem using it against him. But it wasn't there.

Michael turned. "Why are you still standing there? Do you want your friends to get hurt? It's completely up to you."

She had no way to warn them. All she could do was go along with her father's plan and hope she could stop it before it damaged the business Gabriel had spent most of his adult life building.

"Let's go."

Chapter 24

Every time Gabe walked into the CT office, there were a thousand fires to put out. But it was worth it, considering he was commuting long-distance and only coming in three days a week at most. The rest he handled via email and correspondence from Oak Creek.

Ian DeRose's offer to buy the company, split just as Gabe had wanted it, had been sitting on his desk all day.

He was about to sign it. A few minutes from now, he'd be going into a meeting to let his core team know what was coming, putting the rumors to rest. Collingwood Technology—under a new name—would be in very capable hands, but those hands would no longer be Gabe's.

In a few weeks, for the first time in his adult life, he was going to be free to go wherever he wanted and do whatever he wanted.

And the only place he wanted to be was back at Jordan's house.

He wanted to do everything with that woman. Build a company with her. Build a life with her. Travel the world with her. Be a part of every first she ever had for the rest of her life.

The good thing about being in your mid-thirties? When you finally decided to settle down, you knew what you wanted.

Gabe wanted *her*.

When he got a call from the security desk in the lobby announcing Jordan was here to see him, Gabe felt like he'd almost conjured her out of his thoughts. He rushed downstairs to meet her, wondering the whole time why she would be here. He knew how seriously she took her parole restrictions.

As soon as he saw her, he knew something was wrong. She was standing in the middle of the lobby, tense, both arms wrapped around her middle. As he crossed to her, she stiffened even further. He wanted to grab her, pull her to him—everything inside him demanded that he do that—but she looked so brittle, so breakable, he stopped without touching her.

He hadn't seen that look in her eyes for months now. What had put it back there?

He kept his tone low, soothing. "Hey, beautiful, didn't expect to see you here. What's wrong?"

"Nothing's wrong," she said brightly. Way too brightly. "I just wanted to see you. I should've called first, I'm sorry."

"You're welcome here whenever you want, Rainfall. Were you feeling like a rebel?"

"Something like that. I-I . . ."

He stepped closer and wrapped his hands over her hunched shoulders. She immediately stepped away.

"What's going on, Jordan?"

"Nothing! Nothing." She smiled that smile again, it was

almost painful to look at. "I just wanted to see you. Get a tour around or something."

Maybe she was just nervous because she was here. He didn't care if she broke her parole, but he knew she did. "Is everything okay at the house? Did something happen?"

Her eyes shot up to his. "No, everything is fine."

Things obviously weren't fine. He reached over and cupped her neck. "Tell me what's going on. We'll deal with it together."

She swallowed, her eyes darting frantically around the lobby. He could almost feel the panic rolling off of her. Jesus.

"Jordan . . ."

Her eyes fell to the front door before she finally seemed to pull herself together. Her shoulders straightened. Her chin came up. She met his eyes and held them. "I'm fine. You know me, just nervous that I might get in trouble, I guess. I thought being here might give me some inspiration or something."

"Can you give me an hour? I have a conference room full of people that I need to deal with, and then I'd love to show you around."

She gave him a tight smile. "Okay, that's no problem. I'll just stay here until you're done."

He wrapped an arm around her shoulder and led her toward the elevator, giving a small nod to the receptionist. "No, you can stay in my office. No need for you to stay in the lobby."

Because as soon as he could wrap up this meeting, he was damn well going to figure out why Jordan was really here. Inspiration, his ass.

She didn't say anything as they exited the elevator and walked down the hallway, but something was wrong.

"Give me twenty minutes, and I'll be back."

"I thought you said you needed an hour."

"I'll cut it short. Whatever's going on . . ."

"Nothing's going on." She gave him a smile he didn't believe for a second. "Take your time, I'll be fine in here." She sat down in the chair across from his desk.

He gave her a curt nod and left his office. He definitely wouldn't be taking his time. But at least he knew she would be safe in his office. Whatever had hurt or scared her couldn't get to her now. She'd come here for a reason, he knew that much. She wouldn't have risked it for nothing. Whatever it was, they would figure it out.

And goddammit, if someone from Oak Creek had broken her windows again, Gabe was going to take a much more drastic approach than Mackay's "wait for the town to remember who they really are" plan. It had seemed like things were getting better.

But something had her here in a panic. And it wasn't something good.

Despite his efforts, the meeting took longer than he wanted it to. It was nearly forty minutes before he got back to his office.

Jordan was gone.

He checked his phone but found no messages from her. He sent her a text.

I'm back. Where are you?

No response. He was just about to go check the restrooms, although he had one attached to his office, when Kendrick came bursting in.

"We've got a huge problem."

* * *

It took less than twenty minutes for her to gain entry into Gabriel's computer—since he'd already trusted her enough to give her system access—and install the code that would let Michael worm his way into the CT financial system. She fought not to vomit with every keystroke.

This back door into the Collingwood Technology system would put the whole company at risk. But Jordan forced herself to push that thought to the side. She would tell Gabe as soon as she could. As soon as she knew her friends were safe.

This was going to change everything. How could it not? How could he ever trust her again knowing that she'd lied to his face and put everything he'd ever worked for at risk? He might understand, even forgive her, but he wasn't going to be able to ever truly trust her again.

She rubbed her chest to try to ease the pain there. But it wouldn't go away.

She swallowed a sob as she pressed the last key to run the program, then stood and rushed out of his office, taking the elevator down to the lobby and walking out the door. Maybe she'd handled this all wrong. Maybe she should've called the police from his office. But what if they didn't believe her? It certainly wouldn't be the first time.

No, she would have to handle this herself.

As soon as she got home, she could get on the other computer linked to CT and hopefully undo the damage she'd done here. That would work.

For the first time since Michael had made his demands, she felt the slightest bit of hope. Yes, she could just rewrite the code once she got home. Maybe even stop her father before he could make his move against Collingwood Technology, or at the very least shut it down before he did much damage.

Gabriel wouldn't even have to know.

She wasn't going to hide Michael. She had to warn her friends so they could be on watch. After all, Linear Tactical was in the business of protecting and teaching people how to protect themselves. They would want to know. They had a *right* to know about the danger in front of them. And then law enforcement. Hopefully, they could pick Michael up before much damage was done.

But she wouldn't have to tell Gabe what had happened. She could fix this without him ever knowing. Things wouldn't need to change between them.

She rushed through the lobby and out the door to where Michael sat waiting in her truck. She didn't hesitate, walked straight out, and got in, smiling at her father like nothing was wrong. The sooner she got rid of Michael, the sooner she could put her plan into action.

"Call your people now and tell them to back off my friends. It's done."

"Do you think I'm just stupid enough to believe you? We'll get somewhere where I can check, and *then* we'll see about your friends' safety."

They drove all the way out of Idaho Falls before he finally pulled over to a café with internet access and took out his laptop.

Her heart sank. Michael was quick, good. Some of her coding ability must have come from him. She would have to move fast in order to keep him from accessing accounts before she could stop him.

The happy look on her father's face—the pride he felt from stealing from others—made her want to throw up.

Michael grinned at her. "I'll be honest, I didn't think you'd be able to hack their system in that short amount of time. Your skills are either better than I thought, or Collingwood's security is much weaker."

Or Gabe had trusted her, and she'd just used that trust against him.

"You got the access you wanted. Now call off Godlewski."

She listened as he called Allan. "We got what we wanted. You guys stand down."

Allan said something she couldn't hear. That sickening grin came over Michael's face again.

"Yeah, well don't worry. I'm sure there will be a next time."

Allan said something else, then Michael disconnected the call.

"Your friends are safe. For now. And Godlewski said to tell you it didn't have to be this way. Could've been much easier."

If she didn't already know she had to turn him in, that sentence would've clenched it for her. Michael knew he could get her to do what he wanted. There was nothing stopping him from forcing her to do it again.

They drove back to Oak Creek in silence. Michael, giddy with his win, actually tried to engage her in conversation, but she ignored him.

As they came up on the outskirts of town, he stopped the truck. "This is where you get out. I think a nice walk back out to your house will do you good since, sadly as Allan reports, you don't have many friends here who will give you a ride."

He took out his phone, a much nicer one than the one he'd broken, and spun it around so she could see the picture on the screen.

It was her standing in front of Collingwood Technology. "That's you very clearly outside of the state of Wyoming. If you warn any of your friends or decide to tell the police you've seen me, then I will send this picture to your parole officer. I'm sure you'll have an interesting time explaining why you broke parole."

Years of practice keeping her feelings locked inside helped her hold her tongue now.

Michael smiled at her. "Don't worry, Daughter. I'm sure I'll be seeing you again soon."

Chapter 25

Jordan ran to the bakery as soon as Michael drove away, but no one was there, and Violet wasn't in her upstairs apartment. Jordan ran to Aiden's house next, since it was closest, but no one was home there either.

She decided to run to the hospital to see if Annie was working. But the closer she got to the building, the more her stomach clenched. The last time she'd been here, she'd been in terrible pain, and nobody had cared.

By the time she reached the emergency room door, her hands were visibly shaking. She had to force herself to keep moving forward. This wasn't about her. This was about keeping her friends safe.

She walked up to the nurse's station closest to the door, relieved when she didn't recognize the young nurse working there.

"Is Dr. Annie Griffin working right now?"

The nurse shook her head. "No, I'm sorry. She's off tonight. Are you injured? Do you need to see a doctor?"

"No. Would it be possible for me to use the phone?"

The nurse shook her head. "I'm sorry, but this phone isn't for public use."

Jordan braced herself when two nurses walked around the corner. Nurse Estes, the woman who'd almost gotten fired rather than treat Jordan, glared at her. But thankfully, Riley Wilde was with her. Jordan had known Riley in high school. They'd never been friends, but at least Riley never treated her badly.

"Jordan, is everything okay? You look very pale. Are your hands bothering you?"

"I need to get in touch with Charlie or Violet or Annie. Or just call Linear Tactical. Can I use your phone?"

Nurse Estes just huffed and walked off in the other direction. Riley rolled her eyes.

"Don't pay any attention to her. Here's my phone, but if you need them, I think they're all at dinner at New Brothers right now. At least that's where Anne was going when she got off work about an hour ago."

Relief flooded her. "Thank you." She felt like she should say more but didn't know what. "Thank you," she said again before turning to leave.

"Hey, Jordan!"

Jordan turned back to the other woman.

"There are a lot of people in this town who like you. Or would like you, if they had a chance to get to know you. Don't forget that."

Again, Jordan wasn't sure what to say. "I . . ."

Riley shooed her with her hands. "Go find your friends. I just wanted to make sure you knew that."

Jordan nodded, trying to take it all in, as she turned and ran back out the door. A new friend was something she would have to think about later. Right now, she needed to keep her current friends safe.

She dashed down the two blocks back to New Brothers Pizza, slowing as she reached the door. God, she didn't want to go in there. All the nervous energy that had been coursing through her system was gone. Now, she just felt ready to fall over. She definitely didn't want to face what was in front of her.

But that wasn't an option. She did have these friends, and they had stood up for her. She was going to protect them, even though she was probably about to be publicly humiliated.

Jordan pushed the door open to the pizzeria and walked inside. Conversation in the front half of the restaurant stopped. Someone rushed to the back, undoubtedly to get Mr. DiMuzio. Jordan didn't see her friends.

She was about to start looking for them when both Mr. DiMuzio and Adam stepped forward and blocked her way. Mr. DiMuzio crossed his arms over his chest.

Jordan had to clench her teeth to keep them from chattering. "I know you don't want me here. I'm just looking for my friends. It's important. But as soon as I give them the message, I'll leave."

To her surprise Mr. DiMuzio didn't argue the point. "Your friends are in the back."

"Oh, I—okay, thank you."

"Zac Mackay made it very clear to me that he has forgiven you for the accident. If he's let it go, then I'm sure I need to also," Mr. DiMuzio continued. "But seeing you here reminds me too much of what your father did. What we lost because of him."

Her throat dried up, making words almost impossible, but she forced them out. "I know. I'm sorry."

This was what she'd been trying to explain to Gabriel when she'd said the situation was complicated, and why she didn't want to try to go on dates in Oak Creek. These were not bad people. They weren't mean to her out of spite—usually. Many of them had lost so much at her father's hand, that seeing her just brought back that pain and misery.

"But you can rest assured there will be no more damages to your home." Mr. DiMuzio reached over and grabbed Adam by the ear. "His mother and I are ashamed of what Adam did. Even worse, he did it because he thought we would approve. We do not approve."

It was more than she'd ever thought she'd get from one of the families who'd been hurt the worst by her family. "Thank you."

Mr. DiMuzio gave one solemn nod of his head as if everything was now settled. "Go and see your friends. They're in the back room." He dragged his son by the ear back into the kitchen.

She didn't waste any more time. Every second she took now gave Michael more time to do damage to Gabriel.

She entered the private room, and just like out front, conversation immediately stopped.

"I—I . . ."

She rubbed her hand over her eyes. Was she doing the right thing? Even if she told them everything, would they ever be truly safe? Maybe she needed to run. Maybe the solution wasn't trying to get them to protect themselves, but to take herself out of the equation so Michael would follow. She looked around at all the faces staring at her.

"Want some pizza, Jordan?" Zac asked with a smile, his eyes compassionate, steady.

Annie slipped her hand into his. "Yeah, sweetie. We tried to call and invite you and Gabe, but your phone went straight to voicemail."

They were all looking at her with smiles and welcome. Not a single one of them—even Dorian, who sat mostly alone over near the window—had a hint of distrust or dislike in their features.

Jordan burst into tears. “I’ve put you all in danger.”

Chapter 26

When Kendrick had burst into Gabe's office and told him someone had attempted to access the accounts they'd been monitoring, Gabe had actually thought it was a good thing. Finally, they could make some progress on this vulnerable part of their system—something they'd been wanting to do for months—before the sale of the company to Ian was final. He'd stopped hunting for Jordan as he and Kendrick had pinpointed where the leak had come from.

When the results came back, the two men had looked at each other, then ran it again. Because that couldn't be right.

The IP address for the computer that had accessed the weakened account?

Gabe's.

When?

During the forty minutes he'd left Jordan alone there.

"How the hell were you on your computer while also in that conference meeting?" Kendrick asked.

Gabe slumped back in his chair. "Jordan came by. I left her here while I was wrapping things up."

Everything about his body felt numb as he tried to figure out a reason why Jordan would've accessed that account.

Kendrick was already on the phone, checking to see if Jordan had left the building. When the receptionist confirmed she had, he had all security footage streamed to Gabe's computer.

Gabe sat, grateful Kendrick was functioning on all cylinders because he certainly wasn't. "Why would she have accessed that account?"

There had to be a reason.

Kendrick clapped him on the shoulder. "That account and section of the system is vulnerable. Obviously, she didn't know we were aware of the problem and was trying to take advantage of it."

They'd only left it open in an attempt to ferret out any remaining system or employee vulnerabilities.

"But she could've accessed it at any time," he told Kendrick. "She's had access to a laptop with our operating system for weeks. Why would she come here today and use mine to access it?" It didn't make any sense.

"I don't know," Kendrick said. "Maybe she didn't understand exactly what she had at home. But hey, I'm willing to give her the benefit of the doubt. Maybe there's something going on we don't understand."

Yes, there had to be something going on they didn't understand.

"Oh fuck," Kendrick whispered, staring at the screen as the security footage came up.

"What?"

Kendrick tapped the screen with the tip of his finger. "This is right outside the lobby door."

Gabe angled the screen so he could see it better. It was Jordan's truck. "Who's that in the driver's seat? That's not

Jordan." Gabe knew the answer to his own question before he even finished it. "Michael Reiss."

"Yes."

Kendrick enlarged the security footage. Gabe watched, his whole world crashing around his feet, as Jordan came rushing out of the building. He studied the image, hoping to find some sign of coercion or struggle. Instead, he watched as a bright smile came over Jordan's face and she got in the truck with no hesitation at all.

Then he backed the footage up and watched it again just to be sure.

Kendrick shook his head. "Shit, man, I'm sorry. Want me to call the police? We can have her picked up before she even hits the Wyoming state line."

Gabe tried to wrap his mind around how his life had just completely changed in the past fifteen seconds. "Not yet. Keep the account open as if we don't know what has happened. Make it look like there's money available."

"It won't be foolproof for tracing. If she's smart, she could make it so we never find where she'd put it."

"I don't need to trace it. I just want to see what she does."

Maybe Michael was forcing her to work with him. Maybe that smile she'd given him was fake. Maybe there was some sort of explanation and she wasn't involved at all.

God, how he prayed that was true.

But an hour later, Gabe couldn't deny it any longer.

Kendrick knocked on his office door and stuck his head in. "Just wanted you to know we got a ping on the account, someone trying to filter out the cash they think is available."

"How much dummy money did you put in there?"

"I made it look like there's two million in the account."

Gabe rubbed his hand over his eyes. He'd spent the past hour trying to contact Jordan, just in case. Calling her over and over. He didn't know what he was going to say to her if he got her on the phone, but that hadn't been a problem. She'd never picked up.

"Did they try to take all of it?"

"No. Actually, a really weird amount: $622,000."

Jordan had found a way to get the money she needed for the life she wanted to live.

* * *

THREE HOURS LATER, GABE SAT IN A CHEAP FOLDING CHAIR in the southwest corner of Jordan's living room.

The blind corner.

He'd mentally labeled it that way because of how her front door opened. This corner was a vulnerability—you couldn't see potential danger here unless you deliberately checked for it.

Ingrained training and habit had always made Gabe look there as soon as he came through the door, to check for any potential threat and make sure it didn't blindside him.

Too bad he hadn't been able to see that the threat right in front of him, right beside him, wrapped around him, the entire time.

Evidently, he hadn't learned his lesson a few months ago, when someone close to him had betrayed him. Even worse, he'd blinded himself to who Jordan really was and who had raised her. He'd let himself be fooled by those big gray eyes and sob stories about things she'd never done and places she'd never been.

The people in Oak Creek he'd been most angry with—

the ones forcing her to stay away from them—had been the smart ones after all. The *right* ones.

And yet even with undeniable proof, some part of him still didn't want to believe it. That was why he was here, right? Because he was fool enough to hope there was some sort of explanation.

It was insanity to be here. He was too close to this. He couldn't think straight when it came to Jordan and this situation. He should've called in law enforcement or even the Linear guys to track Jordan and Michael. Hell, the local sheriff could've taken her into custody for a parole violation if she was still around. Nothing else even had to be proven right now. Gabe would be a hero in Oak Creek for providing the footage.

If she was still around at all.

He barely controlled the urge to slam his fist against the wall. Had she thought about the fact that she'd be giving up this place she loved so much when she got back in cahoots with her father? Was that worth $622,000?

Or maybe she thought she wouldn't get caught. The thing was, if she'd just used the computer here at her house, she might not have. It was still difficult to believe she hadn't figured that out.

Almost as difficult as it was to believe how asinine he'd been to give her unfettered access to his company.

No matter what, he had to see her face. Would she lie to him? Treat him as if nothing had happened?

Had she planned this all along, or had it been a crime of opportunity? Would she deny it when he confronted her? Beg for mercy? Try to seduce him?

Show any remorse whatsoever? He had to know.

The door clicked open. He was about to get his chance.

He remained hidden in the shadows, knowing Jordan

didn't have the combat-honed instincts to check for the vulnerability.

It was something he'd meant to go over with her, but he'd thought he had more time.

When she didn't turn on all the lights like she normally did, he stayed where he was.

Something in him broke apart when she rushed over to the desk with the CT computer. She turned on the small desk lamp and booted up the system. Moving silently behind her, like the warrior he still was, he positioned himself so he could see the screen clearly over her shoulder.

She was accessing the Collingwood Technology internal system again. Jesus, was she going to try to take more?

Her fingers flew over the keys, quickly gaining access to the heart of the system. The last tiny bit of hope he'd harbored that she wasn't involved in the illegal activities disappeared as she accessed the account once more.

His phone vibrated silently in his pocket and he took it out. A message from Kendrick.

Account accessed twenty minutes ago by somebody named Allan Godlewski.

Godlewski. Jesus. That pretty much told him everything he needed to know. Jordan's interest in Gabe had been a setup from the beginning. Hell, maybe they'd even planned the first day Gabe had driven in on Allan manhandling her.

Gabe's control snapped. "Going back to the scene of the crime?

Jordan shot away from the computer with a scream. She turned, all the color leeching from her face.

"Gabriel . . ." She held her hands in front of her in some sort of gesture of supplication.

He shook his head once. "Oh no, you don't get to call me that. I'm very definitely not your angel anymore."

She flinched, but he didn't care. He refused to let himself care, refused to be drawn in by those guileless eyes.

"What are you doing, Jordan? Didn't you get everything you came for this afternoon? Why did you stop with $622,000 when you could've gone for two million?"

"I can explain."

He took a step forward, and she took a step back. It was easy to see he was scaring her.

Good.

"You can explain how you used the access that I trusted you with to infiltrate my business and steal money from me?"

"Yes. You see, my father showed up earlier today. He forced me to—"

"Forced you to?" Gabe tsked. His voice was low, even. "It didn't look like there was any *forcing* going on when you ran back out to him in your truck, smiling."

She rubbed her fingers against her forehead. "Of course, you have security footage. I know it looks bad, but it's not what you think. Michael showed up today and told me I had to plant the code that would give him access to some of your accounts. He was going to steal money from you. You had some accounts that were vulnerable, and somehow Michael found out about them."

"Yeah. We were already aware of those vulnerable accounts. That's why we were watching them, trying to catch someone we thought would be stealing from us. I just didn't think that person was *you*."

Gabe clenched his fists. Never again. Never again was he going to trust an outsider. Hell, he couldn't even trust an insider. And he definitely couldn't trust his own instincts, which had told him Jordan was a good soul.

She was shaking her head rapidly. "No, it wasn't like that. I promise."

Gabe took another menacing step forward, unable to help himself. Fury coursed through his whole system. "I'll listen to everything you have to say, every single word, if you can explain to me why you headed straight to the computer without bothering to turn on the light. What were you doing?"

The remaining color fading from her face told him everything he needed to know. Keeping his eyes on hers in the dim light, he reached over and struck a key; the monitor lit back up. They both glanced over at the screen. They both knew what it held.

"Looks like you were going back in and covering up your tracks. Tell me that wasn't what you were doing, Jordan."

She had no earthly idea how much he wanted her to tell him that wasn't what she was doing.

"No, I was, but I was trying to get in and change the system before Michael could access the money."

"Why didn't you just call me? You've obviously been away from him for a while and yet my phone hasn't received a single message from you."

"My phone broke. I couldn't call you. I had to go into town. I was at New Brothers Pizza."

Now Gabe laughed, although there was no joy in the sound. "Jesus, Jordan, your father obviously has a lot left to teach you when it comes to cons. You're going to have to lie a lot more effectively than that. There's no way in hell Mr. DiMuzio let you inside of his restaurant. Everyone knows that."

"Gabriel—"

He slammed his fist down on the desk. "I told you not to fucking call me that. I am not your angel. Never again."

He steeled himself against the tears filling her eyes. She took a shuddering breath. "Gabe. I'm not explaining myself well. Just let me—"

"You know what? I'm tired of talking. I'm tired of listening to people who will look me in the face day after day, knowing how much I care about them, and lie without hesitation." He took another step forward, knowing he shouldn't touch her when he was teetering on such a thin blade of fury. He might not be able to stop himself from hurting her.

Even worse, he wasn't sure that he *wanted* to stop himself from hurting her.

She had the self-preservation to keep moving backward as he came forward.

"The people of Oak Creek were right to mistrust you, weren't they? They weren't stupid enough to get led around by their cocks. Were you even a virgin, Jordan?" Each question was punctuated by his step forward and her step back, until her back was against the living room wall. He caged her in with his hands on either side of her head. "Was it planned from the beginning? I just got word that it was Allan Godlewski who accessed the account—or attempted to access the account. I'm sure he was surprised when it ended up holding nothing."

She didn't say anything.

His body crowded in on hers. "That day I saw you struggling with Allan, was that part of your con? Was it acting? Do you like it rough, Jordan? Have I been too gentle?"

She pushed at his chest. "Fuck you."

He grabbed her wrists and slammed them back against the wall beside her head. "Come on now, I've been so soft and gentle, thinking you were new at this. Maybe I haven't been giving you what you need."

Before she could say anything else, he covered her lips with bruising force. It was less a kiss and more an act of war. Gabe felt himself getting hard. Who was he kidding? Not hard. *Harder*. He may not trust Jordan for a single moment, but he still damn well wanted her with a brutal force that ate at him.

Maybe he could fuck her out of his system. Maybe that would ease some of the agony clawing inside him at what she'd thrown away. She'd broken this beautiful thing that could've been between them.

But when she made a little whimper against his mouth, he pulled back, staring into those gray eyes. Eyes full of questions and confusion and hurt.

How fucking dare she pretend to feel hurt?

He muttered a curse and spun her around and thrust her face forward against the wall, shoving up against her back. He ran both hands down her shoulders, over her back, her waist, her hips, until he was cupping her ass. Groping. Squeezing.

"Is this how you like it when you're not pretending?"

"Gabriel, please . . ."

Goddammit, he *could not* listen to his name come from her lips like that—soft, sweet, gentle. He grabbed her wrists and slammed them up against the wall again.

"I didn't know what to do," she continued. "I'm sorry."

She sounded so broken. So defeated. She wasn't fighting him, wasn't struggling, wasn't saying no.

But she very definitely wasn't saying yes.

He looked at where he held her wrists so tightly in his hand. In a few hours she'd have bruises there shaped like his fingers.

What the hell was he doing?

He released her wrists and stepped back so that no part

of his body was touching hers, flinching when she just stayed in the same place against the wall.

"I apologize." He turned away, running a hand through his hair, the rage seeping out of him. This hadn't been what he wanted. "No matter what, I shouldn't have touched you like that in anger."

Her hands slid down until they rested at her sides, but she kept herself plastered against the wall, like she wanted to crawl inside it.

The rest of his anger melted away, leaving just a gaping wound in his chest. He shouldn't have come here. What closure had he expected to gain?

Seeing her defeated like this didn't make him feel any better.

Nothing would.

He wasn't sure what he was going to do. Leaving her here alone was stupid. She would run. Even though she wouldn't get far without the money she'd tried to steal, she would still run.

And then she'd be back in prison, away from this place she loved so much.

Why?

He couldn't stand to think about it. He had to get out of here.

He crossed to the door, not even bothering to get the computer he'd brought for her to use. Maybe she could sell it and buy herself another couple of days of freedom.

Hand on the doorknob, he turned back to her. She was still standing over against that wall. Goddammit.

"If you had just used this computer, I might have never known it was you. I at least wouldn't have known until after the money was gone."

He could've sworn she whispered, "I know," but that

couldn't be right. And he didn't trust himself to stay and find out.

He walked outside, shaking his head as lightning split the air overhead and small hail began to fall. Fitting. Thundersnow. A freak winter storm that produced lightning. They got them in Idaho sometimes too.

That lightning crackled through the sky, building and building, just waiting for a place to strike.

Gabe knew the feeling.

Chapter 27

Gabe knew he should start the drive back to Idaho Falls. It was late and besides, where the hell else was he going to go?

But he'd have to come back to Oak Creek tomorrow to tell Violet that the woman she'd trusted with her beloved bakery and her friendship had betrayed them both. Violet had been excited when he'd discussed letting Jordan use one of the CT computers with the network operating system. She'd wanted to see her friend succeed.

He slammed his fist against the steering wheel. He'd wanted to see Jordan succeed too.

So he'd have to come back first thing tomorrow morning. He wasn't going to give Violet this sort of news by phone or text.

When his own phone buzzed with a message from Aiden, Gabe pulled over to read it. Driving in this hail was bad enough; he definitely wasn't going to do it while looking at a phone.

Linear guys and women are talking strategy at Finn's house until we get a handle on this. V wanted to let you know she was safe, in case you were worried.

Gabe was still trying to decipher the first message when a second came through.

She agreed to close the bakery for two days. If we haven't got it under control by then, I'll be staying there with her while it's open.

Gabe didn't waste time trying to type. He called Aiden.

"Hey Gabe—"

Gabe cut right to the chase. "Does Violet know about Jordan? Is that why she's shutting down the bakery?"

"She doesn't want to, of course. But after what happened to Charlie today, none of us are taking a chance. We'd rather stay together and combine forces than be split and weakened."

"What happened to Charlie? Are she and the baby all right?"

"Jordan didn't tell you? Charlie was almost in a car accident today. Her brakes failed. Not failed, actually—they'd been cut. She's fine, baby too. Just shaken up."

Gabe's curse filled the car.

"Yeah, my feelings exactly." Aiden's background noise got quieter. "Listen, Violet didn't want to tell you this, but you've got a right to know. Dorian found evidence that someone was up in the apartment over the bakery after it closed, when everyone had left except Violet."

"What?" He bit out the word. "She doesn't even live there anymore."

"We're not sure what it's all about. But it's another reason we're all banding together. I just wanted you to know."

"I'm just outside of town. I'm turning around and will be at Bollinger's house in thirty minutes."

"You're not going to stay with Jordan?"

He started the car. He would still have to explain Jordan's betrayal. This was just going to make a bad day much fucking worse. "Jordan's not in any danger. I'm on my way."

He disconnected the call and swung the car back around the way he'd come. The sleety mixture of rain and snow made driving difficult, but he was pulling up at Finn's house less than thirty minutes later, once again trying to get his rage under control.

What the hell was going on? Charlie's brakes cut? Someone in Violet's apartment?

The door opened as he stepped up to it, his arrival obviously having been radioed ahead. Finn stepped aside for Gabe to enter, gazing at the storm for any further danger before closing the door again.

The men in this room were warriors. Gabe had known that years ago when they'd worked a couple of overseas missions together. Tonight, they were warriors once again. Active duty was just a piece of paper when it came to protecting the ones they loved.

Finn returned to one of the large chairs, lifting Charlie gently, then pulling her back down in his lap like he couldn't stand the thought of being away from her. One arm wrapped around her, his hand spanned protectively over her entire abdomen.

Zac was watching out a window, Annie close to his side. Aiden had his arm around Violet's shoulder, but she moved away to come give Gabe a hug.

"Aiden shouldn't have told you," she whispered. "You've already worried about me too much."

He pulled her closer. "It's my job to worry about you. Besides, there's something I need to talk to you about anyway."

God, he didn't want to have this talk with these people.

"You have men out in this weather?" he asked Zac, keeping one arm around Violet.

Zac nodded. "Gavin, Wyatt, Dorian—and a couple of the guys who do some work for us part-time. Finn's brother, Baby. Also, Boy Riley is in town and volunteered for some shifts. Most of them are in vehicles or shelters."

Gabe didn't know who a lot of these people were, but if these men trusted them to watch their six—more importantly, to watch for hidden danger to their women—Gabe would trust them too.

"Dorian's the only one out in the actual elements," Finn said. "The rest are in vehicles or shelters. This is one of the worst winter storms I've seen. Can't decide what it wants to do: thunder, lightning, rain, snow, hail . . . so it's just doing it all at once. Mother Nature is throwing a fit."

Gabe understood the feeling.

Charlie hooked an arm around Finn's neck and snuggled in closer to him. "I hope you rewarded your girl good and proper for saving our lives, Gabe."

Gabe let out a sigh and shook his head. "Jordan didn't save your lives."

Finn shrugged. "Maybe not outright, but getting to us as quickly as she did, and letting us know about her father and the others . . . she certainly circumvented what could've been some real danger."

Gabe shook his head. "You don't understand. Jordan is in on it with her father."

Violet stiffened and stepped away from him. "No, she's not."

"I know you don't want to hear this, believe me. But she is. She came to Collingwood Technology today and used the system access code I'd given her to backdoor into a vulnerable account."

They all stared at him for a long moment.

"She's guilty," he continued. "I know it sucks, but you've got to believe me. Jordan betrayed us all."

Everyone still stared, saying nothing.

"I have proof. Kendrick and I have been watching the accounts she accessed, knowing they were vulnerable. We thought we might catch someone trying to take advantage of it. Never dreamed it would be her."

"What did you do, Gabe?" Violet shook her head and backed away until she was next to Aiden.

"Jordan told us all that," Zac said. "She got to us at New Brothers and warned us of everything. Michael Reiss is working with Allan Godlewski and at least one other person. They were the ones who cut Charlie's brakes. Michael told Jordan if she didn't help him, Violet and Anne would be hurt also. Or maybe little Ethan."

Gabe stiffened, dread starting to work its way through him. "But . . ."

"She took Michael to Idaho Falls to try to buy time," Violet said. "For *you*. She knew if she used the computer at her house to access the system, Michael would've been gone with the money before you could have made a move to stop him."

"Going to the CT offices slowed Michael down," Aiden said. "Evidently, he'd broken her phone. She did the best she could in a pretty shitty situation."

He remembered Jordan's face when she'd shown up at CT, how her nerves had been strung out to the point of breaking. "Fuck."

"What did you do, Gabe?" Violet whispered again.

"She accessed the account, and it triggered an alarm for Kendrick. We found footage of her leaving voluntarily with Michael. *Smiling* at him."

Charlie shook her head. "She was protecting us. Buying time to warn us."

Which was why Jordan hadn't used the system access at her house. But what had she been doing tonight when she'd gotten home? "She accessed the system again tonight afterward. I caught her red-handed. She was going back in to cover her tracks. Why would she do that if she wasn't doing something illegal?"

Violet shrugged. "Because you mean the most to her. Charlie was teasing her about it earlier today at the bakery, about the smile that's been a permanent part of Jordan's features for the past few weeks that *you* put there." She shook her head again. "After she warned us, she told me she had to get back to her house so she could try to fix the damage. I told her to let me call you, but she wanted to try to do it without you knowing."

"But why? I would've believed her if she'd called and explained." It would've been so much less suspicious to him.

"Part of it was that she's young and she doesn't know how to deal with conflict," Violet continued. "But I think most of it was that she didn't want you to be disappointed in her. Didn't want to lose the bond the two of you have. I don't think she was planning to hide it from you forever. She just thought it would be easier to explain if she'd already stopped whatever her father was trying to do."

"She's always taken way too much responsibility for Michael's actions," Zac said, "and let Oak Creek beat her up because of it."

The thunder crashed outside around them, echoing the despondency growing inside him. He'd made a terrible mistake.

"I didn't believe it at first," he whispered. "Didn't believe that Jordan would do that. But when someone tried to withdraw $622,000 exactly, I knew it had to be her. That's the amount she's been working toward. Her *plan*.

She wouldn't ever tell me any details, just that it was the most important thing. When I saw it was that amount, I knew she'd played me."

"She never told you what that amount was?" Charlie asked.

He spun to look at her. "No. Just that it was how much she needed for the life she wanted. Seemed like such a specific amount."

Charlie shifted away from Finn. "Six hundred twenty-two thousand dollars is the amount Michael Reiss stole from the people of Oak Creek. Jordan has had that sticky note on her fridge since she got out of prison last year. It's the amount she wanted to make so she could pay everyone back."

Fear poured into him like the icy storm pouring from the sky outside. "Why didn't she just tell me that?" His voice sounded hoarse even to his own ears.

"Because she probably thought you would react like I did. Telling her that she didn't need to buy the town's approval. She hadn't stolen the money to begin with and didn't owe it to them."

Yes, he probably would've said something similar. Because it was true.

It all made complete sense now. Jordan had never wanted to leave Oak Creek. That was the piece of the puzzle that had never fit for him. She'd wanted the money because she thought it was what would allow her to *stay*.

"And attempting to withdraw that exact amount he stole before is a nice little fuck-you from Michael, isn't it," Aiden said. "Intended to hurt you, her, everyone."

He met his sister's eyes and this time she didn't have to ask it.

What had he done?

Chapter 28

"I have to get back to Jordan." Gabe nodded at Violet. "And yes, it's as bad as you think. Worse. What I said was unforgivable."

But, oh God, he had to try.

"Gabe." Zac held out a hand. "The time for groveling will come, but as long as Michael and his cronies are out there, nobody is safe. That includes Jordan. She didn't know you knew about the account. Did you block Michael when he tried to access it?"

Gabe scrubbed a hand over his face. "I waylaid access. Made it look as though the money would be available, but that it wasn't instant."

"That means Michael doesn't have any money yet," Aiden said. "How long before he figures out it's not coming? Because he may come back at Jordan when he realizes he's empty-handed."

Zac looked over from the window. "And Allan Godlewski is bad news. We looked him up after the window incident. He did time for aggravated assault, and over the past few weeks, he's developed a real hatred for this town."

"Might have to do with getting the shit beat out of him in the woods," Gabe bit out, wishing he'd been the one who'd done it rather than Dorian's invisible ghost.

Zac shrugged. "Whatever his reasons, he's pissed, and he's dangerous."

"Then get law enforcement involved. Arrest him, since they don't know we're on to them." Gabe just wanted to get back to Jordan, to figure out some way to make her understand how sorry he was.

Finn shifted Charlie on his lap. "We did. We were able to get a print from Charlie's car. Sheriff Nelson is running it, but in the meantime, when he went to bring Allan in for questioning, he was already gone."

"Obviously, Michael doesn't care about hurting people this time around to get money," Zac said, wrapping an arm around Anne and kissing her forehead. "The company he's keeping just proves that. We were talking earlier and the best way to get to Michael—"

"Is through Jordan," Gabe finished for him. He looked around at the three men standing beside the women who had brought such meaning to their lives.

Jordan should've been here next to him, part of this conversation, knowing she had someone to protect her too.

Instead, she was once again alone, believing yet another person in this town hated her.

"Yes," Zac said. "We've got to stop Michael and Godlewski before they know we're on to them and go to ground."

Gabe looked over at Violet, agony in his eyes. "I don't know if Jordan will listen to me at all. I wouldn't blame her if she never talked to me again."

Twice he'd accused her of not being much more than a

whore. Once—*amazingly*—had proven forgivable. Twice? He couldn't even imagine the circumstances under which she would forgive him for that.

He turned to Zac. "You have all my money and resources at your disposal. The most important thing is to keep Jordan and Violet—and all of you—safe.

Violet walked over and put her arm around his waist. "I want to kick your ass for whatever you did, but it looks like you're beating yourself up just fine. Jordan is one of the most kindhearted people I've ever known. You'll explain why you came to the conclusions you did, and how wrong you were—"

"Plus, you'll beg," Finn threw in. "Like literally, on the floor pleading for forgiveness."

The thought didn't bother Gabe. He only hoped it was enough.

Whatever it took, he would *make* it enough.

But first he had to make sure Jordan was safe.

"I'm selling Collingwood Technology," he told them. Violet knew and had agreed, a necessity since she was still part owner. "I'm going to focus on computer coding and cybersecurity since I have a very promising potential partner I hope I can still talk into starting a business with me.

"I want to expand her house because she loves it there. It's what I could never understand about the money she wanted when I thought it was to get away. If she could live in that house, on that land, every day for the rest of her life, she would. I want to add to it. Make her an office of all windows so she can look outside any time she wants to. She'll never have to be separated from her home and the land again."

"Oh my God," Violet whispered. "You love her."

He looked over at his sister, not even trying to deny it.

"The thought that she'd thrown away what we could have been? Jesus, Violet, it *gutted* me. That's why I said what I did. I should've known she was trying to fix it, that she was scared. I should've sat her down and had her tell me the whole story from beginning to end."

Violet squeezed his arm. "You'll make her sit down, and you'll tell her *your* whole story. She'll listen."

He put his hand over hers. "I hope so." He turned to everyone else. "I also started talks last month with Griffin Albert, owner of one of the banks in Oak Creek, about providing cybersecurity for some of the online features they want to offer. And . . . improving physical security in the safe deposit box room."

"That would be the perfect place to lure Michael in," Aiden said. "Probably Godlewski too, if he really wants to publicly stick it to the town."

Gabe nodded. "That's what I was thinking. If Jordan convinces Reiss she has a new target, I'm pretty sure he'd believe her and—"

He fell silent as the door slammed open. In the space of a moment, the three men around Gabe had hidden weapons drawn and had placed themselves between their women and the threat. Gabe didn't have a gun, but that didn't mean he was weaponless against their attacker.

But it wasn't an attacker at all. It was Dorian stumbling in.

"What in the actual fuck?" Finn said as he and Zac rushed to grab the huge man who was falling forward.

He had an arrow sticking out of his bloody jacket.

"Dorian," Zac said. "Is this an attack? Reiss or Godlewski?"

"No," Dorian said. "I was on my way back in. Wraith shot me."

Zac, Finn, and Aiden all looked at each other, obvious

concern in their eyes. Anne flew to Dorian's side, looking at the wound.

"Your same wraith person who beat the crap out of Godlewski a few weeks ago?" Gabe asked. "The one you said was hunting you?"

The other three men cursed.

"Who, Dorian?" Zac asked.

"Why the fuck didn't you tell us?" Finn asked at the same time.

Violet and Charlie were surrounding him now, too. He couldn't sit down because of the arrow.

"Yes." Dorian looked at Gabe, answering his question, ignoring the others. "The same person. She shot me."

"Well, honestly," Anne said as she unzipped Dorian's jacket and gingerly pulled it back to inspect his wound, "if you had to get shot with an arrow somewhere, this is probably the best place. The site will be sore once the arrow comes out, but there shouldn't be any long-term damage. She's either a very good shot or very lucky."

Gabe had no doubt it was the former. But he had no idea why someone would shoot Dorian. Even more, given everything Gabe knew about Dorian Lindstrom, he didn't know why D hadn't hunted down this mysterious wraith already and ended her.

Charlie gasped from behind Dorian.

"What?" Finn asked, rushing to her side.

"There's a note attached to the arrow."

"This shit just keeps getting weirder," Aiden murmured.

Gabe was surprised when Charlie looked at him with panic before looking back at the note again.

"What?" he barked, hackles already rising.

"It says, *Her house is burning and she's all alone.*"

Once Gabe realized the *her* mentioned in the note was Jordan, he hit the door running.

* * *

Jordan had been out of prison 249 days. She hadn't taken a single one of those days for granted.

The citizens of Oak Creek had done everything they could during that time to get rid of her, to make sure she knew she was unwanted here.

She couldn't say she didn't care. It had hurt a place inside that she'd tried not to let anyone know about. But she wasn't going to let them drive her away from the home she'd thought about every single day she'd been incarcerated. The home that had been in her family for generations.

One random lightning strike in a freak winter storm had accomplished what the people of Oak Creek had been unsuccessfully trying to do for nearly a year.

Get rid of Jordan.

She stood and watched—frozen both inside and out—as her beloved house burned. She'd thought things were as bad as they could possibly get when Gabriel had left her house in such a rage. The lightning strike about thirty minutes later had proved her so wrong.

She'd had no phone to call for help and once the blaze spread to the insulation in the attic, she knew the battle was lost.

All she could do was make trip after trip inside to pull out whatever she could save. Picture albums, her mother's quilts. She was wrapped in one of those quilts now, watching the fire.

From a distance she could hear the sound of cars

pulling up. Doors slamming. People talking—yelling—around her. She even thought she could hear a siren.

Not that the fire department could do much now anyway.

Arms wrapped gently around her from behind. "Rainfall, step back. The fire department is coming. Let them do their job."

Maybe she was broken. Her brain had finally snapped under everything that had happened today, because she knew it couldn't be Gabe talking to her. He hated her.

She didn't move, just continued to watch the fire. It was beautiful in its own brutal way. And it kept her warm. When it went out, she was going to be cold. So cold.

Distantly, she registered Zac and Finn moving to pick up the stuff she'd gotten out of the house, placing it farther back. The sirens were getting louder.

The arms around her tightened and pulled her much farther out of the way as the fire trucks pulled up. Soon they were spraying what remained of the building.

Jordan watched in a sort of vague fascination, arms still wrapped around her, as the firemen succeeded in putting out the blaze. As the flames died, it left them in darkness except for the headlights from the vehicles.

She should do something. Cry, scream, rail against the powers that be, powers that obviously decided she had done something horrible in a past life and deserved ample punishment in this one.

But she couldn't. She couldn't even open her mouth to say thank you when Zac and Finn moved the stuff into their cars.

Zac came and stood right in front of her, running a finger down her cheek. "There's nothing more that can be done here tonight. Charlie wants you to come stay with her at Finn's house."

"Violet's there too." That voice came from behind her.

Gabriel—*Gabe's*—voice.

She stepped out from the ring of his arms, twisting to face him, trying to figure out why he'd even been touching her in the first place. "Why are you here?" Her voice sounded scratchy, broken, as if it wasn't working right.

Nothing inside of her worked right.

"Because I never should've left in the first place." His hands were still at her waist, so she stepped back.

His touch right now, when it meant nothing to him, might speed up the crack that was coming. It was a fissure right now, her emotions held together by sheer numbness, but the chasm was inevitable.

She turned back to Zac and Finn. "Charlie and Violet are safe? Anne?"

"Anne went into the hospital," Zac said. "There was a . . . situation. Aiden is with Charlie and Violet, and yes, they're fine."

Finn reached out and squeezed her hand. "Come on, sweetheart. Your friends want you near them."

She glanced over at the charred remains of her house, barely discernible in the dim lighting. They were right. Nothing could be done tonight.

Nothing could be done at all.

She walked with Zac and Finn toward their cars without a word, away from the house, the land, the man who just yesterday had meant everything in the world to her. The yesterday that had held the brightest of futures.

Today there was nothing.

Chapter 29

Jordan woke up from a fitful sleep a few hours later. She had a blessed moment of sleep-dazed oblivion, then it all came crashing back on her.

Her house? Burned.

Her relationship with Gabe? Over.

Her reasons for staying here? Gone.

She slipped into yoga pants and a sweater that must have been Anne's since Charlie's and Violet's clothes would be way too short. Charlie and Violet had helped her last night after she'd arrived at Finn's house. They'd gotten her into the shower and into bed, then stayed with her until she'd fallen asleep.

Jordan had been trapped outside her own body, aware of everything going on around her but too distanced to really process it. She was recovered enough to process it now but didn't want to.

All she wanted to do was lie in bed and wrap her arms around herself, keep the gaping hole in her chest from growing any larger. Because right now, it felt like the hole would swallow her in its blackness forever.

But doing nothing had never been an option for her, and she wasn't going to start now. She was going to do what she'd always done: survive.

Just without the biggest, most important parts of her life.

She covered her face with her hands and took in deep, shaky breaths. She had to keep it together. She couldn't fall apart here in front of her friends.

She forced herself to get up from the bed and padded her way across Finn's big house toward the kitchen.

"She just lost the house that meant everything to her. She's not ready. She needs more time."

It was Gabe's voice, low and emphatic.

She rubbed her forehead, pain starting to thrum behind her eyes. He'd been at her house last night with Zac and Finn, but she didn't know why. He'd made it very clear how he felt about her and what she'd done.

She should've called him from New Brothers. The second she'd finished explaining to her friends that they were in danger, she should've borrowed Violet's phone and told him what had happened, explained her part, owned up to it, and how she hadn't been able to figure a way out of the situation.

She hadn't wanted to lose that closeness they'd developed over the past few weeks. He'd shared so much of his knowledge with her, and then she'd just rolled over when Michael had put pressure on her.

Or maybe she should've found a way around Michael's demands. If she was as good with coding and programming as she thought, she should've been able to figure something out. Some way to stonewall Michael. Stall him.

"We don't have more time," Finn said. "If we don't make a move now, we'll lose our chance."

"How much do you expect her to take, Finn?" Gabe

asked. "She's twenty-three fucking years old. You want her to just get up today like nothing happened? Because that's what we're asking her to do."

"Jesus, Collingwood, I'm not trying to be insensitive here, but it was just a house. We're talking about people's *lives.*"

A fist slammed against the table. "It wasn't just a house. Not to her."

That gaping hole was back in her chest. Gabe understood how much losing the house was gutting her. It had been so much more than just a house.

But Finn was also right. No house was worth someone's life. Charlie's, the baby's. Anybody's.

Jordan stepped into the kitchen. Both men stood up from their chairs.

"Good morning, sweetheart," Finn said, smiling at her. "Want some coffee?" Finn walked over to get some for her when she nodded. "Something to eat?"

Gabe stayed silent as he sat back down. Jordan didn't look at him but felt his eyes on her.

"No, no food yet." She cradled the coffee cup Finn handed her between her hands. Gabe pushed the sugar bowl in her direction. She muttered thanks without looking at him.

"The other gals are still conked out, and Ethan's over at his grandmother's, so you just get our ugly mugs. Zac should be here with Anne any minute," Finn said.

She clutched her cup of coffee, wanting to go back to bed and hide under the covers and never come back out.

"Jordan, I'd like to talk to you, if it's okay," Gabe whispered.

She really looked at him for the first time. Her first thought was to say yes. She knew she was wired to acquiesce, that it was her default setting to not make waves.

She'd been taking the blame for everything for so long that she didn't even realize now when she did it.

Blaming herself for not being able to stop her father and letting everyone in Oak Creek treat her like trash. Blaming herself for making a judgment call yesterday, a call that had ended up being the wrong one.

That wasn't the unforgivable sin. Gabe should've listened last night. He should've given her a chance to explain.

Not treated her like trash, like everyone else always had.

She was done being treated that way. She had nothing left to lose in this town, nothing left to lose in her relationship with Gabe. She'd lost it all yesterday.

But nothing left to lose also meant nothing left to fear.

"No," she said, just as quietly as he had. "I don't want to talk to you."

She felt a hand slip over hers where it rested on the edge of the table and another fall on her shoulder. Startled, she looked up to find Charlie and Violet standing behind her.

"That's right, sweetheart," Charlie said, glaring at Gabe. "You don't have to talk to him until you're ready."

"And if you're never ready," Violet continued, "then that's my dumbass brother's loss. For someone with a near-genius IQ, he's pretty damn stupid."

Even now, looking over at Gabe's grim face, she wanted to give in and at least listen to what he had to say. To give him the benefit of the doubt.

But that was yesterday, before she'd lost everything that had meant something to her in this world.

She expected Gabe to tell her friends to butt out of it, but he surprised her.

"They're right. You shouldn't talk to me. The things I

said to you yesterday were unforgivable. I have no defense. I was blinded by having been betrayed by someone close to me before. I couldn't see past the possibility of something like that happening again."

Jordan stared down at her coffee mug, a tear leaking out of her eye. Everything inside her wanted to reach out to Gabe, but she couldn't. Her life had been broken in a way she didn't know how to repair. She didn't even know how to start.

Gabe got up and crouched beside her, his height putting his face right next to hers. "You're right to feel angry," he whispered. "And you're right to take as much time as you need. But I'm going to be right here, every day, hoping you'll forgive me, that you'll let me try to make it right. That you'll call me Gabriel again."

He leaned down and kissed the top of her thigh, then stood and walked to the other side of the room.

Charlie and Violet moved fully into the kitchen and began making breakfast. Nobody tried to talk to Jordan, which was good. She couldn't manage it. When someone set two pancakes in front of her, she forced herself to eat them one small bite at a time.

Zac and Anne arrived a few minutes later, Zac announcing that Dorian was fine and back at his house.

"Whoever shot him used a practice arrow," Zac told Finn and Aiden, who'd also joined them.

"So even less damage," Finn replied. "Not exactly the best way to leave a message, but in terms of being shot by an arrow, almost the best of all possible circumstances. Practice arrows have the smallest heads."

There was other stuff the guys wanted to talk about but weren't because of her. She forced herself to look up from her empty plate. There would be time to fall apart later.

"What were you and Gabe talking about when I first came in?" she asked Finn.

Gabe spoke up from the doorway behind her and she turned to look at him. "You don't need to worry about it. It was a possible plan, but we'll find another way."

"A plan to do what?"

Gabe came and leaned against Finn's counter, where she could see him without turning. Charlie and Violet flanked her on either side of the table. The Linear guys were standing or sitting in various positions around the kitchen, one of them always keeping an eye out the window; Aiden currently on watch duty.

"We think we've come up with a way to trap your father," Zac explained. "But you would play a critical part."

Her eyes met Gabe's automatically. His lips were tight, face set in stone, but he didn't say anything. She looked back at Zac. "How?"

Zac gestured to Gabe to explain. "He's going to figure out in the next few hours that there's no actual money he can access from the account he tried to hack yesterday. The amount he attempted to transfer—$622,000—didn't go through to wherever he tried to send it."

Gabe had mentioned that amount last night. "I can't believe he would have the nerve to take that exact amount," she whispered. An unfamiliar rage coursed through her. Her father had no remorse whatsoever for what he'd done to the people of Oak Creek.

"He was testing the account with that. I'm sure if the transfer had gone through, he would have taken all he could get," Gabe said, his voice much more even than she could've managed. "The full two million."

"That was why you thought I was working with him. Because he took that exact amount."

Gabe gave a curt shake of the head. "It doesn't matter what amount was taken out of the account, or if you listed yourself as the recipient with 'Fuck you, Collingwood' in the signature line. I should've sat you down and listened to you from beginning to end."

Something eased the slightest bit. The man certainly wasn't cutting himself any slack or making any excuses for his actions. But knowing Michael had taken that exact amount explained why Gabe had been convinced his anger had been justified.

"When Michael realizes he has nothing, we're hoping you could offer him something better," Zac said. "A bigger prize."

"But what?" she asked. "He won't trust me to hack CT again."

"I recently contracted with Oak Creek Savings and Loan to handle their cybersecurity and develop stronger security for their safe deposit boxes." Gabe's green eyes pinned hers. "I've been moving all my business to this area. This is where I want to be. Where I still plan to be permanently."

She looked away, trying to process everything Gabe was saying amidst the chaos. Violet reached over and squeezed her hand but turned to glare at Gabe. "You're overwhelming her. Stick to the plan and do your crawling on your knees later."

Charlie wagged her eyebrows. "And while you're down there, make sure it's worth her while."

Charlie's outrageous statement broke some of the tension in the room. At least enough that Jordan no longer felt like she was going to break under it.

She thought about the plan. "I don't have any way of getting in contact with Michael, but I could relay a message to him through the account we hacked, warn him that you're on to him." She swallowed and forced herself to continue. "I could tell him that since the house burned down, I want to join him and get out of here."

"Then you would lead him, Godlewski, and anybody else he's working with to a meeting point where we'll have law enforcement ready to arrest them," Zac said.

"You're not safe as long as Michael is running around loose," Finn said. "He may go back into hiding for a while, but if he needs money, you're always going to be one of his few links back to society. He's got to be stopped. Because he's threatened one of ours."

She nodded. "When he cut Charlie's brakes."

"He threatened one of our own the moment he broke into your house and put you in danger," Zac said, coming to put his hand on her shoulder. "He was going down regardless. Now we just have an effective way to draw him out."

Gabe pushed himself away from the counter and walked over to her. "But I want it to be very clear that you don't have to do this. I know how much that house meant to you, and if you can't do this right now, then we'll all understand. We'll find another way to catch Michael and his cronies."

She looked around. Every single person was nodding in agreement.

"You have to do what's best for you, Jordan," Charlie said. "We support and love you just as much, either way."

She nodded. This might be the last thing she did for Oak Creek before she left, but she could do this. It wouldn't get the townspeople their money back, but it would put Michael Reiss behind bars. The next best thing.

"I'll do it. But we've got to move fast, or Michael will disappear again."

Chapter 30

Within an hour, Kendrick arrived with a CT computer Gabe and Jordan could use to get a message to Michael. As they worked side by side at the computer, Gabe was once again impressed by how intuitively this all came to her.

He was letting her take the lead, not only because she knew what would best entice her father, but also because Gabe wanted her to know he trusted her. He wasn't going to look over her shoulder. If she had a question, he'd be happy to help her figure out the solution. Otherwise, this was her show.

Behind them, Kendrick tried to talk the Linear guys into giving him a code name like they all had. Gabe knew the bickering was more to keep everyone—including Jordan, who was wound tightly enough to shatter—more relaxed. When it came time for the Linear guys to focus, they would.

Kendrick had been less than thrilled with the names the guys suggested.

"I still don't understand what's wrong with Kenny G as a call sign," Aiden said.

Gabe glanced over at Kendrick, who grinned as he flipped Aiden off.

"You've got to change your nickname anyway," Kendrick responded. "Since Shamrock doesn't apply anymore."

Aiden got the nickname Shamrock in the Green Berets because he'd been lucky enough to never have been captured or wounded on any operation—a near-impossible feat, given the missions their team had undertaken. But Shamrock's luck had very much died a couple months ago—as the man himself nearly had—when he'd been trying to save Violet.

Aiden crossed his arms over his chest. "Dude, I got the nickname Shamrock because of my luck with the ladi—"

"If you say ladies right now, you're not going to be getting lucky for a long, long time!" Violet yelled from the kitchen.

"Love!" Aiden yelled, grimacing. "I was going to say I was lucky with *love*."

Jordan snickered.

Kendrick grinned. "So Zac's name is Cyclone, Finn is Eagle, Aiden is Shamrock. And Dorian is Ghost."

"Gabe's call sign was Angel," Zac said, grinning. "People assume it's because of his name, but maybe he has some beautiful singing voice we don't know about."

"Is that true?" Jordan whispered.

"The part about Angel as my nickname, yeah. Because of Gabriel. The singing voice, not so much."

She smiled at him. He wanted to spend every day for the rest of his life putting that smile on her face as much as possible. He was going to do whatever it took to win her trust back. He couldn't help himself. He reached out and stroked his knuckles across her cheek.

And considered it a victory when she didn't flinch or turn away.

"I'm almost done," she said after a moment, and he dropped his hand. "Do you want to look it over?"

"Only if you think there's something I need to double-check to make sure Michael gets the message. Otherwise, no."

A pained expression settled on her face. "We are dealing with real money this time. The stuff in the safe deposit boxes is truly valuable. It belongs to the people of Oak Creek." She rubbed her fingers over her forehead. "Losing even more to the Reiss family . . ."

"They're not. It's never going to get that far. All we need is for Michael to show up for the meeting with you to hear about the bank. Once he shows up, he gets arrested. We'll worry about Godlewski and anybody else later. I'm sure Michael will be more than happy to turn on them to work out a deal."

Jordan nodded but the worried look didn't leave her face. Nothing was going to make that happen until this was over. At least they'd found her truck abandoned just outside of town, and she now had that back in her possession. That had made her feel at least a little better.

The debate continued behind them. "All I'm saying is that you guys are obviously not idiots when it comes to forming names. So how come the best you can come up with for me is Kenny G and Jackass?"

That just led to a slew of new and even more obnoxious suggestions.

"Okay," she whispered. "It's ready to send."

Gabe placed his hand over hers. "Do it."

With the click of one key it was done. "Now, we wait."

She didn't pull away, and he didn't let go of her hand as they turned and faced the ridiculous debate behind them. Kendrick was sprawled out on the couch, obviously enjoying himself despite all the comments. He ran a hand over his shaven head.

"Gabe, thank God you're done. Help me school these idiots on a better name for me. I'm a little surprised nobody has pulled out any racial suggestions yet."

Gabe rolled his eyes. "Probably because nobody can think of anything fitting for someone who's half black and half Chinese."

"Actually, I'm half black, one quarter Chinese, and one quarter Korean."

"So you're half black, half Asian."

"And one hundred percent awesome." Kendrick leaned back and grinned.

"Oh my God," Finn actually started clapping his hands. "He's black and Asian. He's *Blasian*."

Aiden sat up straighter in his chair, eyes all but glowing. "Blaze."

"Oh, hell no," Kendrick muttered.

Zac walked over and slapped him on the back. "Welcome to the team, Blaze."

Kendrick immediately started listing all the reasons why that would not work as his code name, but the guys were having none of it. They began gathering the equipment they would need to track Jordan when her father contacted her, everyone using the word "blaze" at least once every time they talked.

Gabe had worked with Kendrick long enough to know that the nickname didn't really bother the man. Sometimes he just liked to argue for the sake of arguing.

Everybody carrying on and talking all over each other the way families do—and that's what this was, a big, loud, obnoxious family—obviously amused Jordan a little. But at least her face had lost that pale, pinched look. She still had a lot ahead of her, even after her father was arrested, but she no longer looked like she might buckle under the pressure.

An hour later, the signal they'd been waiting for arrived.

"He's responded," Jordan said.

Even though she hadn't raised her voice much more than a whisper, everyone fell silent. For all their joking and sniping, the Linear guys were soldiers at heart and focused when there was a mission at hand.

Gabe sat next to Jordan, for moral support more than anything, as she returned to the keyboard to respond. She typed rapidly for multiple minutes.

"What did he say?" Gabe asked when she finally stopped typing. "Is he going for it?"

"It didn't look like it at first, but I think I convinced him."

"How?" He didn't want her putting herself in danger.

She stared at the screen. "I told him you hadn't trusted me and had been watching that account. I told him about how my house burned down and there was nothing left for me here, that this town has treated me like garbage since he left, and that it had only gotten worse over the past year. It's time for me to move on, and whatever we take from the safe deposit vault will just be severance pay."

If Gabe thought it had been quiet before, that was nothing compared to the quiet now. For the first time in his life, he understood the phrase *deafening silence.*

There was way too much truth in Jordan's words. It was almost impossible not to believe them.

"Rainfall . . ." Gabe wasn't sure what he could say to make this right, he just knew he had to try.

She finally turned and looked at him. "He bought it. That's what matters, right?"

No, that wasn't what mattered. What mattered was that there was something so damaged and broken in Jordan's heart. What mattered was that he had added to that. What mattered was that when she talked about there being nothing left for her here, she actually believed it.

But she was wrong. There was so much for her here. And he intended to prove that to her.

But before he could say anything or move any closer, she held out a hand to stop him. "He wants to meet in thirty minutes. That doesn't give us much time. Everything else will have to wait."

Gabe's jaw clenched. It was only because of the fact that Jordan wouldn't be safe until they handled Michael that he gave her a nod. "All right. But after, we talk."

He was very aware that she didn't answer him one way or the other.

Chapter 31

Thirty minutes later, Gabe was sitting with Kendrick, a.k.a. *Blaze*, a mile to the north of an abandoned warehouse. Zac and Gavin were in their vehicle on the southeast side.

Michael had chosen the meeting spot wisely, halfway between Oak Creek and Reddington City, nothing nearby. Views from the second floor of the warehouse would allow him to see anybody moving toward the building, plus gave him numerous points of exit if he needed it.

Jordan was going in with multiple disadvantages, and that did not sit well in Gabe's gut. If things went south, he and the guys might not be able to make it there quickly enough to get her out. Of course, no one could move quickly enough if Michael decided his daughter was a liability he had to take out right then.

"I don't like this." He pressed the button on the communication system that allowed them to all speak with each other and hear what Jordan was saying.

The guys didn't respond right away, probably because it was the thirty-sixth time he'd said the same thing in the past ten minutes.

"She has the recording device, she has the tracker, and Sheriff Nelson is standing by waiting for our call," Zac explained again.

Until they were sure they would be able to take down Michael, they hadn't wanted to get into the red tape of bringing in official law enforcement. If the cops took over, Gabe would have to trust Jordan's protection to someone else, and there was no way in hell he was doing that.

When he and the Linear Tactical guys just *happened* to drive by an abandoned warehouse and catch a fugitive inside, *then* they would call the police to move in.

"As soon as Jordan confirms her dad is there, we move in," Gabe said.

"Roger that," Gavin replied.

Through his binoculars, Gabe saw Jordan pull up in her truck. "I hope you guys can hear me," she muttered.

Gabe wished like hell he could reassure her, but the unit she wore only sent, didn't receive. "We can hear you, Rainfall," he whispered. "And we're not going to let anything happen to you."

Hopefully, this would all be over in five minutes, and Jordan could concentrate on rebuilding her life.

But less than a minute after walking inside the warehouse, Jordan spoke, and it wasn't to her father. "Allan, what are you doing here? Where's Michael?"

The curses from the other three men on the communication link were just as vile as his own. Michael wasn't there.

"If you'd got it right the first time, bitch, we wouldn't be in this situation." Jordan cried out, then there was some sort of muffled noise.

Gabe knew right away what had happened. Allan had punched her.

"I'm going in."

"If you do that, we lose our only chance at getting Michael," Gavin said quickly over the comm unit.

Kendrick grabbed his arm. "Let it play for a minute, Gabe."

It was Jordan's words that convinced him. "I'm okay. I'm okay."

Gabe knew she was talking to him. Knew she wanted him to stand down. But fury burned like acid in his gut.

"You won't be okay if you fuck up again," Allan responded, thinking she was talking to him.

"When is Michael going to get here?" Jordan's voice was shaky, but she was still going forward with this. Gabe had to let her.

"Good girl," Finn whispered.

Jordan had so many more people who cared about her than she thought.

"Michael isn't coming," Allan spat. "You and I are going to go to the bank. If everything is as you say it is, we'll meet with Michael afterward. If not, well, let's just say you and I are going to have a little bit of fun before I kill you."

Goddammit.

"Does she have what she needs to actually get in and out of the vaults, or did you give her fake information?" Kendrick asked.

"It's real. She should be able to get in and out with no problem." And thank God.

"Do we let this play?" Finn asked. "Track them afterward? Allan all but promised they were going to Michael."

"If not, we better move right now." Kendrick brought the binoculars back up to his eyes. "Because they are on their way out to Jordan's truck."

Everything inside Gabe balked at putting Jordan in this

danger, but she would remain in danger as long as Michael was out there. "Let it play."

Jordan was relatively silent on the ride into Oak Creek. Allan, not so much. He talked about how the two of them would be a good team. How he'd always known she'd wanted him even though she'd played hard to get.

Gabe wanted to kick his own ass for ever suggesting Jordan wanted what this guy offered.

Then break Godlewski's jaw so he never made the mistake of talking to her again.

Gabe and the Linear guys kept ample distance from the truck as they drove back toward Oak Creek to keep Allan from spotting a tail. Plus, they had the tracker; proximity wasn't necessary.

Finn called in and had Violet and Aiden waiting at the bank in case they needed to move fast to get Jordan out. Gabe didn't think it was going to be necessary, but he was glad to have them there.

Gavin and Finn drove into town and parked near the bank, but Gabe and Kendrick stayed on the outskirts. If Godlewski saw Gabe anywhere nearby, this would all be over.

Kendrick took off his headset so no one else could hear him and turned to Gabe. "Once she goes in that bank and actually accesses safe deposit boxes under your security care, that makes you an accessory. If this goes sideways, if whatever they take is not recovered, you're going to be tried as an accomplice. You better be sure you trust this woman."

"I do."

It was too late anyways because Jordan and Godlewski were walking into the bank. Godlewski provided the teller with the electronic master key code Gabe had given

Jordan, and a few minutes later they were escorted into the vault.

Jordan's transmitter was silent for long minutes.

"Anybody else getting anything?" Finn finally asked.

"Her transmitter probably doesn't work inside the vault," Gabe replied.

Kendrick looked at him with one Blasian eyebrow raised. Gabe had to admit, there were a lot of factors beyond his control—a lot of ways this could go bad quickly.

Every minute that they couldn't hear what was going on became more tense.

A few minutes later Violet's muffled voice came on the line. "Okay, they're coming back through the lobby. They're about to exit. Wait, shit." She stopped speaking abruptly.

"Violet had to change positions so Godlewski wouldn't notice her." It was Aiden's voice on the line this time. "Jordan made him go back to the cashier. Handed the cashier something. Said something, but we couldn't hear. Now they're exiting."

"Okay, they should be heading to wherever Michael is hiding," Gabe said. "Everybody stay back. We'll follow them on the tracker."

It was almost over. All they had to do was follow her to Michael.

"Fuck," Finn said. "I'm not getting any reading on the tracker. You getting a reading, Blaze?"

Gabe looked over at Kendrick, who had the laptop resting on his legs. "No, nothing."

"No reading at all?" Gabe asked. "If it's been destroyed, it should read as off-line."

"According to this, it's still online, we're just not getting any signal."

"Everybody reboot. Immediately. If there's not something wrong with the transmitter, then it's our reception."

Kendrick looked over at him. "Both computers out at one time? Unlikely."

Fuck. Gabe knew that.

"Neither the transmitter nor the tracking device has worked since they came out of the vault," Gavin reported.

Kendrick pinned Gabe with a stare. "We might have just played exactly into Jordan's hands. You heard her earlier today, that shit she said to her dad about not having anything left here, about how the people in Oak Creek have treated her. If there is anyone in the world who had a reason to want revenge on a town, it's Jordan Reiss. How long was she just supposed to take it, Gabe? And then her house burned down, the last remaining thing that had tied her here? I sure as hell wouldn't blame her for taking everything she could get and running."

Gabe scrubbed a hand down his face.

Before he could respond Aiden clicked on the line. "Guys, we've got a problem. Jordan's transmitter and tracking device are both sitting here inside the vault. Looks like she ditched them."

And now they had no way to follow her.

Chapter 32

Jordan knew she was in trouble the moment she stepped inside the vault with Allan and her transmitters started emitting feedback. The high-pitched squeal couldn't be ignored and there was no way for her to shut it off on her end. Hopefully, Gabriel would hear what was happening and shut it off from his end.

"What the hell is that sound?" Allan asked, searching around. "Security's going to be in here if we don't get it shut off. Do something!"

She looked around like she didn't know where the sound was coming from, trying to buy Gabe some time, but the feedback squeal just continued.

As she knew he eventually would, Allan figured out the sound was coming from her.

"What the fuck?" Allan reached over and grabbed her by the hair, jerking her head back. "That noise is coming from you."

He pulled her shirt open and quickly found the transmitter and tracker taped to her chest. His fist crashed into her stomach and all the air seemed to be sucked from the room. Jordan doubled over in agony, trying for long moments to suck in enough oxygen to survive.

"What are you doing, bitch? Because if the cops are on their way in here, I can promise you you're not making it out of this room alive."

Allan yanked both pieces of technology from where they were taped to her torso and ripped at the cord. The noise stopped.

He grabbed her by her hair and pulled out a knife, pressing it to the side of her throat enough to pierce her skin. "Are you working with the cops?"

Jordan's brain worked at a frantic pace. Was this still salvageable?

She pushed at his chest. Strength was the only thing someone like Allan would understand. "No, dumbass, I'm not working with the cops. I was making my own recording in case you and Daddy Dearest decide to double-cross me. Now are we going to do this or what?"

He let her go with a little laugh. "All right, I guess I can't blame you for trying to make sure you had some insurance."

She pushed at his chest again and this time he let go of her hair. "Don't hit me again or I'll leave your ass here, and you'll get nothing."

Things were already spiraling out of control. The plan had never involved bringing anyone all the way to the vault. If the info and codes Gabe had given her this morning weren't real, she was in trouble.

Allan put his knife away and pushed her forward. "Fine. Let's get this done and get out of here."

She took the electronic key, the master key Gabe had given her, and approached the first box. She almost cried in relief when it opened with a resounding click.

Thank you, Gabe, for trusting me. You just saved my life.

"Okay, this is more like it." Allan rubbed his hands together with glee. "Which boxes have the most good stuff?"

She had no idea. That had all been a bluff to entice Michael.

"I don't know. The boxes aren't in the order they're supposed to be." That didn't even make sense, but she went with it, trying to play off of what she knew about Allan. He hated this town.

"Damn town can't even get stuff in numerical order," she continued. "You start opening boxes and going through them while I look through the system for more information."

"Fine," he spat, taking the master key from her. "But we've got to hurry. Eventually they'll get suspicious about us being here too long."

He turned back to the boxes and she tried to figure out what she could do.

"Diamonds!" She turned to see Allan pouring a few diamonds out of a velvet jewelry bag into his hands. "Aww, and a death certificate for Mr. DiMuzio's mother. I guess we're stealing the family jewels. I never liked them anyway. Adam was okay for a while until he decided he was too good to mess with you anymore."

She could feel the bile pooling in her stomach. She was stealing from the DiMuzio family *again*.

If this went wrong, and there were so many ways this could go wrong, Mr. DiMuzio would never see his wife's diamonds again. Was Jordan doing the right thing? Should she just scream for security now and hope they got there before Allan stabbed her with his knife?

But if she did that, they'd lose the chance to capture Michael. And until he was behind bars, none of her friends would be safe.

Allan stuffed the diamonds into his pockets and opened another box. "Come on." He shoved her toward the terminal in the corner. "Do your computer magic and figure out which boxes have the most valuable stuff in them. We don't have time to open them one by one."

She turned back to the computer.

Think, Jordan.

She had to find a way to notify Gabe and allow him to track her now that the tracker was gone.

The electronic key. It could be tracked with the security system she and Gabe had been building the past few weeks. She would have to somehow get him the frequency code, which would be hard enough. She would also need some sort of transmitter, and there was only one available.

She held out her hand. "Give me your phone."

"Da fuck?"

Jordan barely refrained from rolling her eyes. "This ass-backward town has everything set up crazy. Just give me your phone. I'm not going to call anybody."

She breathed a silent sigh of relief when he reached in his pocket and handed her the phone.

"Key card, too. For just a second."

He handed that to her as he searched through one of the larger deposit boxes he'd just opened.

Jordan used the corner computer terminal to remotely access her cybersecurity program. There was no time for anything fancy; she used the key card access to connect Allan's cell phone signal to the program. It was bread-crumbs at best. All she could do was hope Gabe would pick up the trail.

But for any of it to work, he would need the code. She typed it in, praying he'd be able to figure it out and access the trace.

She handed the key card and phone back to Allan, who

was stuffing his pockets with anything of value. He grinned.

"You and your daddy really know how to stick it to this town. To be honest, I think the good people of Oak Creek were finally starting to like you again, and now you do this. I'll admit, I'm impressed. You fooled everybody."

Is that what Gabe would think? That she got this information from him and then used it against him? Against the town? Less than twenty-four hours ago, he had accused her of being in cahoots with Michael. Would the removed transmitter and stolen items just confirm what he'd been so sure of yesterday?

Would Gabe even look for the truth?

"Is that computer giving you any information or what?"

"No. We're on our own. We've got to get out of here. This is taking too long. I know it's not the big score we hoped for, but it's a lot."

"A couple more boxes."

He opened one of them and pointed at her to do the same. She did, grabbing a stack of cash and a Rolex inside the box. She felt sick as she stuffed both into the small bag Allan had brought.

He went to another couple of boxes before she finally convinced him they really needed to go. Once out of the vault, Allan made a beeline for the front door, but she grabbed his hand and dragged him toward the teller. She had to get the message to Gabe.

"What are you doing?" He whispered.

"Sending one last message to this town before I leave." She marched up to the teller. "Someone will be coming in here asking about me. You be sure to tell him he can have what we built together, I don't want it. And that his damn name is Gabriel, not Gabe."

So cryptic. Would he understand? Would he even be searching for a message from her?

"Yeah, and fuck this town," Allan added.

"Yeah, fuck this town," Jordan said weakly.

He dragged her away, and they made it to her truck, Allan laughing as she pulled out with no cops anywhere around. "That was almost too easy. Now let's go meet Michael, see if what we got was enough."

"Enough for what?"

"I'm afraid your daddy doesn't plan to keep you around if you can't pull your own weight. I hope for your sake he thinks this score is enough."

She sped away from the town that would think she'd betrayed it and prayed her guardian angel would believe her.

Chapter 33

"No, not again." Gabe pulled his car up in front of the bank, parking illegally, and bounded toward the door.

"No, what?" Kendrick asked, jogging to catch up with him.

Gabe walked inside. "No, I will not believe Jordan betrayed us. She didn't. I don't care what it looks like, I don't care what it sounds like, I don't care if she points a gun in my face when we find her. I damn well will not believe she betrayed this town. Betrayed us."

"Me either." Violet slipped her hand around Gabe's arm from behind him.

"I know things look bad," Aiden said. "But I'm giving her the benefit of the doubt."

Kendrick shrugged. "Fine. We work on an assumption of innocence."

Gabe knew Kendrick wouldn't be working on that assumption, but that was acceptable, smart even. But Gabe didn't care because Jordan *was* innocent, and by God, he would not be apologizing to her again tomorrow for not believing in her today. He'd done that too many fucking times. He would not let her down that way ever again.

Gabe looked around. "We need to do damage control. We may know Jordan isn't guilty, but nobody else is going to believe that when the evidence suggests otherwise."

"What I said about you going down as an accomplice still applies," Kendrick muttered.

"What?" Violet asked, her green eyes big.

At one time, Gabe might've tried to skirt the truth with his younger sister so she wouldn't worry. But Violet had more than proven she could handle what life threw at her. Gabe respected that.

"I gave Jordan the real master key access to the vault. I agreed to the decision not to bring in law enforcement. So yeah, that pretty much makes me an accomplice."

"But—"

He pulled his sister in for a quick hug. "But we're going to stop it long before it comes to that. Let's get to work."

They walked farther into the bank. It was still business as usual. Evidently, no one but Aiden had been in the vault yet.

"I went in as a customer, since I have a box in there." Aiden joined them in the corner of the lobby, outside of earshot from everyone else. "I didn't say anything, but it's going to be obvious to anyone who walks in there that there's been a robbery."

"Anything really bad?" Gabe asked.

Aiden shrugged. "A tiny drop of blood and the tracker and transmitter. I left both until I knew how we wanted to play this."

Gabe didn't like the thought of even a tiny drop of Jordan's blood being shed. She'd been through enough.

"Did you see anything that would suggest she was trying to get a message to us?"

Aiden shook his head. "The only thing suspicious we saw was when Jordan dragged Godlewski back across the lobby so she could talk to the teller as they were about to leave."

What were you doing, Rainfall?

"I need to talk to the teller then." He turned in that direction.

Gavin came on the communication headset. "Just FYI, the bank manager is on his way in. Somebody called him and let him know there was a 'swarm of Linear Tactical people' hovering in the lobby. You've probably got ten minutes before the shit hits the fan."

Gabe didn't waste time. He walked directly to the teller, Kendrick next to him.

"I understand someone said something suspicious to you?" he asked the teller, a professional, well-coiffed woman in her fifties.

She nodded stiffly. "Jordan Reiss and some guy I've seen around town, but I don't remember his name."

"What did she say?"

"Well," the woman huffed, "she said F this town. Except she used the real word."

He could feel Kendrick looking at him but didn't care. He didn't care what anyone said. They *would not* convince him Jordan had betrayed them, no matter what the so-called evidence said.

"That's it? That's all she said, 'fuck this town'?"

"She said some other stuff too, but that was the most important thing."

Gabe struggled to hold on to his patience. They didn't have time for this. "I need you to tell me everything she said. Exactly."

"Fine. She said someone would come asking about her.

I assume that's you. That you could have what you'd built together. And that your name is Gabe."

What the hell was that supposed to mean? "And then she said, 'fuck this town'?"

The woman tapped her nails on the counter. "Actually, the man with her said it first and she echoed the statement. Now if you'll excuse me, I have work to do."

Gabe stepped away from the counter and looked over at Kendrick. "I don't understand. There's no reason to go back to the teller just to slip in my name and tell the town to fuck itself. They would've wanted to get out as quickly as possible. This just drew attention to them."

Kendrick shook his head. "Gabe, we need to get you out of here. The manager's on his way, and it's going to become immediately evident that the bank has been robbed."

"No. I want to help Jordan." But fuck if he knew how to do that.

Kendrick gripped his arm and started pulling him toward the door. "I get that. And hell, Gabe, I work for you, so I'll help her too. But we've got to get you out of here, or you're not going to be doing anything but sitting in a holding cell until all this gets straightened out. You want to help Jordan? Then you need to leave *now*."

Kendrick was right. And the two of them made their way rapidly to the door.

Kendrick spoke into to his comm unit. "I got Gabe out of the bank."

"Smart," Gavin replied. "The sheriff's going to be there any minute."

Gabe pressed the talk button so he could be heard. "I'm going back to Finn's house. Jordan said more to the teller than what that woman remembers, I'm sure of it. I'm going to access the security footage before they eliminate my access to it."

"Zac and Finn are on their way to the bank to do as much damage control as possible," Gavin said. "But it's not going to be pretty when they figure out it's Jordan. I'm afraid most everyone in this town is going to want to shoot first and ask questions later, so to speak."

"That's why I'm going to find her first. Anyone who wants to shoot is going to have to go through me."

* * *

GABE WATCHED THE VIDEO FOOTAGE OF JORDAN'S conversation with the teller for the tenth time.

As soon as he'd gotten the video, he'd made a copy, and not a moment too soon. The bank had shut him out of his access just a couple minutes later.

Gabe had no doubt Jordan was trying to get a message to him. He just had to figure out what it was.

You tell him he can have what we built together.

She had to be talking about the security software. But what about it?

He watched the footage again, this time paying more attention to what Jordan was doing, rather than what she was saying.

Then he saw it. Her finger was tracing a shape on the counter as she spoke.

"Kendrick, get over here. Look at what Jordan is doing."

Kendrick hung up the phone on whoever he was talking to—presumably Gabe's lawyers to give them a heads-up for when they had to come bail him out later—and walked over. Gabe played it for him once and then again.

"She's definitely spelling something. The last letter is a y but I can't figure out the others," Kendrick said.

Y. And Gabe had already figured out the first letter was a *K*. "Key. She's spelling out the word *key*."

Kendrick watched it again. "I think you're right. But what does that mean?"

Of course.

Gabe shook his head as he stared at the screen. "Holy shit. That woman is so fucking brilliant. The security software she and I came up with together. She used the master key card I gave her for the vault. It can be tracked if linked to a cell phone."

He logged on to the system they'd created. Sure enough, a new security item had been tagged in less than an hour ago. "There it is."

"But it says you need a five-digit password to access it. I know Jordan didn't say any numbers in that video."

Gabe smiled. "Oh, she did. My brave, brilliant girl."

"What?"

Gabe typed in the numbers 26435.

The tracking device came on and showed them exactly where she was located.

Kendrick did a double take. "How did you know? Was it her name or birthday or something?"

"She told the teller to give me a message that my name is *Gabriel*, not Gabe."

"But Gabriel is too many digits."

"No, the code had to be five digits. *Angel*. The numbers correspond to the letters on a PIN pad. She always called me Gabriel because she said I was her guardian angel."

And her guardian angel wasn't going to let her down this time.

"Get the others. It's time to go."

Chapter 34

Every minute Gabe didn't show up, Jordan despaired he was never going to.

What if he hadn't figured out her clue? Or worse, what if he'd taken everything at face value and assumed she'd joined forces with Michael?

If so, she was in more trouble than she could get herself out of.

Michael was here. He and Allan were going over everything they'd managed to steal from the safe deposit boxes.

"I have to admit I'm pretty disappointed," Michael said. "First you send me to an account that was being watched. And now you bring me much less than the amount you anticipated."

"We had some problems in the vault. The key worked, I just couldn't tell what items were in which box."

Jordan was sitting on a hard chair against the back wall of a small, isolated house somewhere on the outskirts of Reddington City. Between her and the door was Michael, Allan, and some really scary guy with a gun whose size made Michael and Allan both look like children. Michael's hired muscle.

Allan's phone—her savior if Gabe figured it out and believed her—sat on the table next to everything they'd stolen from the vaults.

"Roughly a hundred fifty thousand dollars' worth of merchandise here," Michael said with a tsk. "That's not enough. That's not nearly enough."

"We had to take what we could. There wasn't enough time to go through every box," Allan explained.

Michael gave him a smile as if he was explaining something to a simpleton child. "I understand. It was a smash and grab. Honestly, Allan, I don't expect much more from you." Michael turned to Jordan. "You, I was hoping for a little bit more from."

"What are we going to do?" Allan asked. "How are we going to split this up? I mean, it won't take long for them to figure out this shit is missing. And then the cops will be after us."

"That's true, Allan." Michael nodded enthusiastically. "That's why we're going to need some sort of scapegoat. And unfortunately, it's your face, and Jordan's, that are on the security footage."

"Whoa, man." Allan started pacing back and forth. "I'm not taking the heat for this. I'm not going back to prison while you guys get some sort of family reunion."

Allan reached for his knife. Good. Maybe she could escape while they were fighting between themselves.

Michael held his hands out in front of him on the table in a gesture of peace. "Of course not, that would be totally unfair. Sit down, Allan, and let's talk about our options."

Allan sat across from Michael, hand still gripping his knife. "Fine. As long as I'm not going back to jail."

As soon as he sat, Michael stood and smiled at him

again. "No, that wouldn't work because you would immediately tell them about me, and nobody knows I'm involved."

"Damn right I would tell them about you."

"That's what I thought." Michael took a step away and nodded at his silent behemoth partner.

The hired muscle pulled out a gun and shot Allan between the eyes. He was dead before his body hit the floor.

Jordan couldn't help the scream that escaped her at the unexpected, and completely unnecessary, violence. She jumped out of her chair, edging herself against the wall, unable to tear her eyes away from Allan's body lying on the ground. Michael stepped over to her a few moments later, wrapped his arm around her shoulders, and pushed something into her hand, rubbing it against her palm. She finally tore her eyes away from Allan and looked down to see what Michael had given her.

It was the gun that had just been used to shoot Allan. She immediately dropped it, staring as it fell to the floor.

"Be careful," her father said. "That's a live weapon."

"What are you doing?" The words came out brittle, but that was exactly how she felt.

"One thing being on the run has taught me over the past few years is how to make the hard choices." Michael looked over at Allan. "And let's be honest, killing him was more of a service to society than anything else. Just getting rid of a violent criminal. And now no one will ever know I was involved. It was only you and Allan on the security video. They'll find his body here and assume you shot him and took off with what you stole."

Over her dead body. "I won't do it. I'll turn you in the first chance I get. I'll make sure everyone knows you had Allan killed."

Michael laughed, the good-natured, enthusiastic laugh she remembered from her childhood. The one that had helped convince the people of Oak Creek to trust him with their hard-earned money.

It had all been a lie, she realized now. Everything she knew about her father had been a lie.

"Oh, you won't turn me in. You'll be dead also, just not here in this room. If both you and Godlewski die here, then obviously there must be another party involved. You'll be buried where no one will find you. Not that many people will be looking."

Michael moved over to the table and began gathering the bounty from the bank. "You know, I almost feel bad robbing this town blind twice. Maybe now they'll really learn their lesson."

"So that's it? You're just going to kill me, your own daughter? You're more upset about robbing Oak Creek than murdering your own flesh and blood?"

"You know what, kid, I wasn't going to say anything, but maybe you're better off knowing the truth. Your mom was already pregnant with you when she met me—some soldier guy she met when she decided to have a free-for-all slut fest in Los Angeles. She didn't even know who he was or how to get in touch with him. She married me because evidently the women in your family don't make such good choices when it comes to men."

Jordan just stared at him. How many times had her mother said almost that exact same thing? The land was constant. People—*men*—would come and go, but the land would always give them what they needed.

Michael shrugged. "I was already on the run when I married your mom. Reiss isn't even my real name. I never liked that town, but nobody ever came to look for me there —go figure, since it's in the middle of fucking *nowhere*—so I stayed. Then I got into the whole family-and-kid thing. I even planned on going honest, with my fake Social Security number and working at the factory. Hell, I even stuck around once your mom died. But when my past caught up to me, I had to bail. Taking those losers' money to keep from going to jail wasn't as hard as I thought."

Something snapped inside her. "Those *losers* were our friends. You took money most of them had worked years to save. Some of them never recovered from it."

Michael just laughed. "Listen to you, just like your mother. She always loved that town so damn much. That land. That house. I bet it nearly killed you when it burned down."

Jordan refused to even think about that right now. And she damn well refused to discuss it with him.

Michael shrugged. "Sorry to throw all that stuff on you right before you die. It's got to be upsetting to find out your dad isn't really your dad."

She laughed at that statement. She didn't even attempt to stop the laughter that barreled out from her insides. She laughed until she could barely breathe.

"What the hell is so funny?"

She finally pulled herself together enough to answer. "I'm good at cybersecurity. Like, *really* good. Do you know how many nights I've lain awake afraid that was a skill that had been passed down to me from you?" She took a step closer to him. "That I might be so good at protecting people because stealing from people was in my genes, and I could see potential pitfalls? But it's not. There is *nothing* of you inside me, and that makes me the happiest person on the planet." Another step closer, toward him and the door. "Because I am not related to you at all."

"Yeah, well, you're about to be *dead* and not related to me."

This was her only chance. They couldn't shoot her inside the house if they wanted their plan to work, so she ran. The chances of getting away were probably nonexistent, but she was going to damn well try.

She bolted for the door, throwing chairs behind her as she went. Michael and his crony both cursed as she reached the door and threw it open.

She didn't slow down as she ran into the yard. She thought about hiding behind one of the many trees, but that would just give them time to catch up with her.

"Shoot her!" Michael yelled.

She pushed for more speed, but it wouldn't be enough. A raging force threw her to the side as two shots fired out. She hit the ground hard, all the air knocked out of her. Gunfire cracked again, but she didn't feel anything but a heavy pressure. She finally managed to turn her head to the side and realized the pressure was from someone lying on top of her. Huge arms surrounded her.

"I've got you, Rainfall," a deep, familiar voice murmured in her ear.

Someone began yelling. "Gabe! Gabe, man, are you all right? It looked like you took both hits." Zac ran up to them, Gavin a half step behind.

Gabe groaned as he rolled to his side but kept his arm around her, spooning her against him. "Kevlar took it."

She jerked around so she could see him. "You've been shot? Again?"

"Vest," he muttered. "But I've probably got a cracked rib. I'm okay," he told the men. "Get Michael."

Zac and Gavin left to go help the rest of the team. Jordan's hands flew to Gabe's back to check for signs of bleeding. She didn't find any, but her heart was still racing.

"I got your code." He winced as he reached for her hand at his back and pulled it between his own.

She relaxed a little. "I was afraid you were going to think I had tricked you again."

"Not even for one second. I refuse to believe that about you ever again."

Tears filled her eyes. "Gabe . . ."

"*Gabriel.* I know I don't deserve it, but I hope someday you'll call me Gabriel again."

She ran her fingers along his chiseled jaw. "You just saved my life. I think it's fair to call you my guardian angel." Fear coursed through her body once again at the thought of how close he'd just come to dying. "You couldn't have known the bullets would hit the vest. They could've hit you in the head. They could've gone through the vest. They could've—"

He reached a hand behind her nape and jerked her against his heart.

"I didn't care. I will take *every* bullet for you. Today and always."

Chapter 35

Jordan thought Oak Creek might throw a parade; they were so excited when Michael was arrested.

Michael Reiss, a.k.a. Simeon Matthew Thompson, was wanted in two states—beyond Wyoming—for theft, fraud, and piracy. Now the authorities could add murder to the list since Jordan had been there to witness it.

The people of Oak Creek wouldn't be getting back the money Michael stole, but he would be going to prison for a long, long time.

Jordan had expected to go back to town in handcuffs, but Sheriff Nelson had told her that he understood training exercises sometimes went wrong. And, hell, lots of people had already come forward to explain she'd been working under duress.

She wasn't surprised her friends had stuck up for her. But she was surprised the sheriff believed her.

The older man had just shrugged. "Everything is here and accounted for. You stopped three criminals who had stolen a great deal from Oak Creek residents. And at great risk to yourself. In my book—and in my official report—that makes you the hero of the story, not the villain."

Jordan could hardly process everything that had happened to her. She'd ridden back to town with the Linear team, Gabriel insisting on staying by her side. When Zac called Annie to let her know everything was fine, she'd demanded Gabriel come to the hospital to have his ribs checked out.

And although she knew it was cowardly, as soon as he was taken in from the waiting room, Jordan slipped out of the building.

She had to go home.

She sat in her truck, staring at the charred remains of her house for a long time before finally putting her head down on the steering wheel and crying.

She didn't waste one tear on the man she'd thought was her father, but she had plenty of tears for everything else.

She cried for the home she'd lost. She cried for the mother she missed every day. She cried for the biological father she would never know. She cried for the wife and child whose life she had taken.

And for the first time ever, she cried for herself.

Because although she wasn't without blame, she was no longer going to take *all* the blame. The people of Oak Creek could either accept her or not. She'd spent her entire adult life, even when she was in prison, trying to find a way to pay a debt that wasn't hers.

No more.

When her tears were finally gone, she got out of the truck and sat on the hood, staring out at the land.

It was time to start over. She would've preferred to do it here, because here was always going to be home, but that wasn't an option right now. She needed to rebuild in every possible way, but she didn't have the energy or the patience to fight the town while she did it.

She looked at the burned house again. Not to mention she didn't have the money.

But she would. She would finish out her parole working whatever job she needed to, then find a way to start her cybersecurity company. Hell, she would even use what happened with Michael as a selling point. And she would make it into a successful business.

This wasn't the path she'd planned to take to get there, but it was the one she would have to walk.

She heard a car pull up behind her but didn't turn around. She'd known Gabriel would come find her when he figured out she was gone.

A few moments later, he was leaning up against the hood of the truck with her.

"When I picture you in my mind, it's you sitting on that front porch rocker, staring out at the land."

If she'd had any more tears left inside her, she might've started crying again. That rocker was gone now.

But she didn't have any tears now, only resolve.

"My mom always told me that the land was constant. That you might make bad choices in life or in love, but the land would always take you back no matter what."

"Rainfall . . ."

She turned to him and smiled, touching his arm. "It's time for a new start for me."

And because she loved him, she told him everything. She told him what Michael had said about not being her father. Told him about what the $622,000 had been for and wasn't surprised to hear he'd already found out. Told him how she was going to develop the cybersecurity company using skills that were hers alone and not passed down by bad genes as she'd feared.

And she told him how she had never wanted to leave this place, but she couldn't stay here now, not anymore.

He listened. He held her hand and listened through it all. He didn't try to fix it, didn't provide platitudes that wouldn't change anything. He just stood next to her, silently offering his strength, and supported her.

And when she was done, he climbed—cracked ribs and all—up on the hood of the truck behind her. He leaned back against the windshield and pulled her back against him, wrapping his arms around her.

And they watched the sun set over her land one last time.

* * *

Jordan agreed to stay until Finn and Charlie's wedding.

She even agreed to be a bridesmaid.

She enjoyed every minute of the day, watching two people who had found each other again, despite all the forces against them, pledge their lives to one another.

Charlie's father, suffering from a degenerative brain disease, hadn't been able to walk her down the aisle, but her mother had, and the two of them had pushed her father in a wheelchair together.

Little Jess had sat in his lap, tossing her flower petals as they passed down the aisle before jumping down and running to stand next to Ethan, who stood with his father.

There wasn't a dry eye in the house.

After the ceremony, the party moved to Linear Tactical's massive training center warehouse. All the equipment had been moved out and most of Oak Creek had moved in to celebrate two of their favorite people joining their lives.

Nobody had harassed Jordan. No one had shunned her

on the dance floor. No one had made any snide comments. Every once in a while, she felt like people were talking about her, but it never seemed to be in a negative spirit, so she just ignored it.

This was all she had ever really wanted, not for them to be open and friendly with her, just to let her live in peace.

It was enough.

Especially since she knew she was leaving the next day.

For the past week, she'd seen Gabriel every day, even though he was in the middle of finalizing the sale of his business.

Every day, he'd driven in from Idaho Falls and taken her out to dinner. Then they talked or went back to Charlie and Finn's house, where Jordan was staying, and watched a movie, or played a game, or got roped into helping with something for the wedding.

And every night he left.

By the third day, when she asked what he was doing—particularly because there had been no sex involved in any of their outings—he'd just smiled and said he was courting her.

It was both the most wonderful and the most frustrating thing she'd ever experienced.

He knew she was moving to Reddington City tomorrow. The newlyweds needed their privacy, and Jordan was going to take her old job at the café again. She'd rented a room from Betty Mae, the owner, so she wouldn't have to drive so far every day.

Gabriel had explained that he could court her from Reddington City too.

He'd danced every dance with her at the reception. Except for the ones they'd missed because she'd dragged him into a utility closet at the other end of the warehouse, far away from all the wedding festivities, and told him his courting days would be over for good if he didn't give her what her body needed right then.

The fact that he'd had to stuff her ripped panties into his pants' pocket by the time they were done had just made it all the sweeter.

After the bride and groom had left and everything was winding down, a fit of sadness hit Jordan. She was only leaving Oak Creek for a short time, and only because she didn't have any choice, but she didn't want to go.

When she had been in prison, she'd promised herself that once she got back, she would never leave that house and land again. But she was.

Gabriel slipped an arm around her hip and pulled her back against him, kissing the top of her head. "Do I need to find another closet for us? There's no shortage around here."

"No." She managed a small smile. "Just big changes for me tomorrow."

He spun her around until they were face-to-face. "Why don't you go by and look at your land tomorrow before you leave. I think it would be good for you."

She hadn't been back since the night Michael had been arrested. She just hadn't been able to face seeing that again.

"Yeah. That's probably a good idea," she said.

But the next morning, truck loaded up with what few belongings she had left, she wasn't able to do it. She didn't want the picture of her charred house sitting silently on the land to be the last picture in her mind. She couldn't bear it. She drove out of town, trying not to look in the rearview mirror.

Which was why she didn't see the police lights until they were right on her.

She pulled over. This was not how she'd wanted to exit

Oak Creek. She rolled down her window as Sheriff Nelson walked up.

"I promise I haven't stolen anything, Sheriff."

The man chuckled, removing his hat and rubbing his dark, bald head. She'd lost count of how many times she'd seen him do that over the years. She'd known this man since she was a baby.

"I know you didn't, Jordan. But I was wondering if you would do something for me. You don't have to, and I can't make you. And it's got nothing to do with law enforcement."

"Sure, Sheriff. What do you need?"

"I need you to follow me in your truck. Will you do that? Even if you don't like where we're going? There's something you need to see before you leave town."

She laughed nervously. "You're not taking me to the holding cell, are you?" she asked, only half joking.

He winked at her. "Nope. No more cells for you."

"From your lips to God's ears. Lead on, Sheriff."

She followed him as they drove through Oak Creek to the other side of town. A few minutes after that, it became clear exactly where the sheriff was leading.

To her house.

Damn it, Gabriel had probably put him up to this, although she didn't know how he knew she hadn't gone by to see the house. She sighed. He was probably right. Seeing it one more time before she left was probably a good idea.

By the time she got to the end of her driveway, which was difficult because of all the cars parked there, all she could do was stare, flabbergasted.

All the charred remains of her house were gone, and in their place an almost completely brand-new house stood. People—not just construction workers, but people she knew from Oak Creek—were working *everywhere*. They were painting the outside, carrying hardwood flooring inside, plumbing, roofing, installing windows.

The Linear guys were doing some of the work, but it wasn't just them. It was almost the entire town.

Sheriff Nelson appeared at her truck's door and opened it. Her eyes flew to his.

"I-I don't understand. Gabriel?"

"Collingwood certainly had a big part in all this, considering he was most familiar with the original plans of the house. But everyone came together this past week to get as much of it done as possible."

"But why?"

"Because you're one of us, Jordan. What happened last week with Michael made everyone realize they'd been blaming the wrong person for way too long."

She got out of the truck and stared at everyone working so hard on a home for her. "But they didn't have to do this. I never blamed them for hating me."

"They didn't *have* to do it, but they *wanted* to. I think this is their way of telling you they hope you'll stay. You're a part of Oak Creek, and we take care of our own."

Hours later, everyone was gone except Jordan and Gabriel.

As soon as she'd been able to get her emotions under control, she'd grabbed a hammer and gone inside to help in whatever way she could. And had been met with smiles everywhere.

When Mr. DiMuzio had shown up at lunch with pizzas for everyone, she'd been in tears once again.

"I can't believe you did this," she said to Gabriel as they sat on the steps of her new porch, looking out at her land.

She had her home back. Never in her wildest dreams had she thought it would happen like this.

"I didn't have to twist anybody's arm. They wanted to do this for you." He leaned over and kissed her temple. "There's one more thing you need to go over."

He jogged to his car, got some papers out of the back seat, and came back to her.

"First, this is the deed to the house. Everything is legal and, hopefully, structurally sound."

She couldn't quit smiling. "It looks pretty damn solid to me."

Gabe shifted uncomfortably in front of her, and she looked up at his face, shocked to find him looking so anxious. "And then I have two more sets of papers. Both are agreements from capital investors who believe in your abilities in cybersecurity. There are different options, but either investor will back you in starting your own company."

Her jaw dropped. "Are you serious?"

"Very much so. One is Ian DeRose, the same man who bought Collingwood Technology. I showed him some of what you can do, and he is definitely interested in backing you. You would have to work out details, but it would be your company."

"I can't even believe this."

He shifted again. "But I hope you'll consider the other option before making your decision. It's a bit more unorthodox."

She was still trying to wrap her head around the fact that she had options. "Okay."

"The second option is a partnership."

"With Ian DeRose?"

"No, with Gabriel Collingwood. Collingwood is no idiot and recognizes your abilities and talents. He is interested—*very* interested—in a merger with you. Building a business that the two of you would run together."

A giddy heat swept through her. "I know I don't have a lot of business savvy, but that offer doesn't sound very unorthodox to me."

"Well, the unorthodox part comes in because Collingwood Technology would still be the name of the company. It was part of my agreement when I sold the business to Ian DeRose. He's got to come up with a new name. Mine comes with me."

She smiled up at him. "Keeping the name of a company that has a stellar reputation? Excellent suggestion. But still, not very unorthodox."

"No, the somewhat unorthodox business transaction can be found in this contract." He handed a stack of papers to her.

"Do I have to read all of these now?"

"No, just skip to the last page. I think it'll be evident exactly what I'm asking you."

She turned to place the papers on the porch, frowning when they made an odd thumping noise against the wood.

There was something heavy attached to the last sheet.

She flipped them open and found a ring taped to the page.

Eyes huge, she spun back around to face Gabriel and found him down on one knee.

"Be the other half of Collingwood Technology. You're already my other half, the half I can't live without. I know you need time, and we can take as much time as you need, but I just want you to know that I am all in."

She slid down one step closer to him, ring in hand.

"I know you feel lost right now, like you don't have a name or a family. But I want to be that for you. Let me be your family. Take *my* name. Be my partner in every way. I want to sit on a rocker on this front porch when we're both old, still looking out at this land. I want to weather every season, every storm, everything life has to throw at us, with you."

"Gabriel." Her guardian angel. She ran her fingers through his thick hair. "Yes. Yes to all of it."

He stood, wrapping his arms around her and crushing her to him. He slipped the ring on her finger. She wasn't surprised when it was a perfect fit.

Then, just like he had on the first day they met, he kissed her on the porch.

A kiss full of promise.

A kiss that told her she would never be alone ever again.

A kiss from an angel.

Acknowledgments

Jordan was never supposed to be a character in the Linear Tactical books, but she showed up in book 1 and pretty much demanded her story be told.

So a special thanks to my reader and editing team who told me to ***listen to her*** and write her story. It ended up being one of my favorite.

There are many people that deserve my gratitude for making this book:

As always, my husband and kids for putting up with my craziness. Old hat to them by now.

To my Bat Signal tribe: Ladies, your friendship and encouragement means everything to me.

To my editors and alpha readers: Elizabeth Nover, Jennifer at Mistress Editing, Marci Mathers, Elizabeth Neal, Stephanie Scott, and Aly Birkl. Once again, thank you for your patience, consistency and hard work. I depend on you so much and you never let me down.

And finally, to my readers, especially the Crouch Crew: THANK YOU. You make me feel special and treasured and it's such a wonderful feeling. I'm going to keep writing books that you love—because I love you guys!

~ Janie

Also by Janie Crouch

LINEAR TACTICAL SERIES

Cyclone

Eagle

Shamrock

Angel

Ghost

Shadow

Echo

INSTINCT SERIES

Primal Instinct

Critical Instinct

Survival Instinct

THE RISK SERIES

Calculated Risk

Security Risk

Constant Risk

Risk Everything

OMEGA SECTOR: CRITICAL RESPONSE

Special Forces Savior

Fully Committed

Armored Attraction

Man of Action

Overwhelming Force

Battle Tested

OMEGA SECTOR: UNDER SIEGE

Daddy Defender

Protector's Instinct

Cease Fire

Major Crimes

Armed Response

In the Lawman's Protection

OMEGA SECTOR SERIES

Infiltration

Countermeasures

Untraceable

Leverage

About the Author

"Passion that leaps right off the page." - Romantic Times Book Reviews

USA TODAY bestselling author Janie Crouch writes what she loves to read: passionate romantic suspense. She is a winner and/or finalist of multiple romance literary awards including the Golden Quill Award for Best Romantic Suspense, the National Reader's Choice Award, and the coveted RITA© Award by the Romance Writers of America.

Janie recently relocated with her husband and their four teenagers to Germany (due to her husband's job as support for the U.S. Military), after living in Virginia for nearly 20 years. When she's not listening to the voices in her head—and even when she is—she enjoys engaging in all sorts of crazy adventures (200-mile relay races; Ironman Triathlons, treks to Mt. Everest Base Camp) traveling, and movies of all kinds.

Her favorite quote: "Life is a daring adventure or nothing." ~ Helen Keller.